FARTHING ABBEY

BY THE SAME AUTHOR

Yemen Rediscovered (*Longman*)
Bahrain: Gulf Heritage in Transition (*Longman*)
Syria in View (*Longman*)
Scotland through the Ages (*Michael Joseph*)
London Heritage (*Michael Joseph*)
Traveller's Companion to the West Country (*Michael Joseph*)
Journeys into Medieval England (*Michael Joseph*)
Ireland through the Ages (*Michael Joseph*)
Architectural Heritage of Britain & Ireland (*Michael Joseph*)
Victorian Britain (*Weidenfeld & Nicolson*)
New British Architecture in Germany (*Prestel*)
FlipDesigns (*Prestel*)
FlipSigns (*Prestel*)
Mrs Mulroony's Fly-Away French Bloomers (*Lulu*)
Off Course (*Lulu*)
Conundrum's Book (*Lulu*)
Dream of a Summer Night (*Lulu*)

FARTHING ABBEY

Michael Jenner

ISBN 978-0-9558480-1-8

For my ancestors.

'The fort remains after each in his turn,
And the kings asleep in the ground.'
(From an old Irish epic.)

A HOUSE AWAITS
SEPARATE LIVES
CRITICAL VIEWS
WORLDS COLLIDE
WELCOME HOME
SECRET STAIRCASE
THE ANCESTRAL BED
ATTIC SPLENDOUR
UNCANNY RESEMBLANCES
EXOTIC DELIGHTS
TEMPLE OF VENUS
CHINESE BOUDOIR
LANDSCAPES OF THE MIND
SUMPTUOUS REPAST
CLOISTER GARTH
IN VINO VERITAS
MANLY SPORT
THE ORANGERY
LADY IN THE LAKE
ILL MET BY MOONLIGHT
WITCHING HOUR
ARTIST AT WORK
BRIEF ENCOUNTERS
PORTRAIT OF A LADY
TOGETHER AT LAST
MOMENT OF TRUTH
ONE FOR THE ROAD

A HOUSE AWAITS

The hot summer sun spills across the flagstone roof of Farthing Abbey, enflaming its crooked crown of chimneystacks, twirled and twisted like barley sugar, bent as the masts of galleons at sea. The burning light plays teasingly along the gapped teeth of the battlements and the grotesque faces of the eroded gargoyles. Their sightless eyes of weathered limestone stare out unblinking at the fiery globe.

The windows of this crumbling façade, where they can be glimpsed beneath the smothering ivy, display every variant of Gothic from an austere lancet at one end to an ornate ogee at the other. An oriel window protrudes off centre, a prominent nose defiantly refusing to sit in the middle of its face. Thus the untamed medieval core of Farthing Abbey throws down a gauntlet to the refined classical symmetry of the Palladian Villa added some centuries later.

The sun can only enter the main ground floor room in dappled spots that shimmer faintly on a long, bare table of scrubbed wood. The light does not dispel the subaqueous atmosphere of a weed-choked pond. It is just bright enough to make out a number of portraits. Crudely framed and of dubious artistry, a gallery of rustic characters gaze blankly forth.

A ruddy-faced butler of Pickwickian proportions holds a bottle of port in one hand, corkscrew in the other. A matronly housekeeper flanked by piles of starched linen, sits with an open ledger on her lap. A groom in scarlet waistcoat and black topper grasps the bridle of a stalwart carriage horse, while a gamekeeper leans on a fowling piece, proud as a musketeer, a basket of dead rabbits at his feet.

One picture stands out sharply from the rest as the work of a superior hand. This is no oil painting on the wall but a yellowing sheet of paper left casually on the table. The modest pen-and-ink drawing is a charmingly executed sketch of a plainly dressed but radiantly beautiful young woman. She sits on the grass in front of a round temple. A sample of embroidery lies by her side on a woollen rug. She is clearly a cut above the others, perhaps a governess or lady's companion. It all depends whether the needlework represents a hobby or a chore.

Absence and emptiness now pervade the Servants' Hall. The silence is eerily amplified by the many years elapsed since all those characters were painted. There is nothing to suggest any occupation more recent than the Edwardian era, roughly the vintage of the butler's frock coat draped over a high-backed chair at the head of the table. This long black garment hovers patiently like an undertaker's usher.

The quiet is now broken by a grandfather clock striking the hour. The minute hand trembles and pauses before moving on a tiny fraction towards the next numeral on the dial. It feels as if time itself is taking its time, dragging its heels. What is the point of this headlong rush towards the future, the steady tick-tock is asking, when we will all get there just the same, no matter how fast or how slow we travel?

Midway through the chimes, an old man awakes from his slumbers. The afternoon sun falls on a tangle of snow-white hair crudely plastered back in a ragged coiffure clearly in need of a trim by a hand more expert than his own using blunt kitchen scissors. For a while the butler gazes at the almost empty cup on its cracked saucer in front of him on the table. Then he glances up at the clock and retrieves a silver watch from a waistcoat pocket to confirm it is just after 5 pm.

Withers - to give the old man his name - now tries yet again to make sense of the imminent upheaval. The last fifty years, under Sir Horace Lloyd-Beauchamp, had seemed eternal. Little disturbed the tranquil isolation of Farthing Abbey. Only faint echoes of the outside world seeped through the high walls around the estate. With the passage of time, all other domestic staff had retired or found employment elsewhere, finally leaving Withers in sole occupation of the Servants' Hall but for the weekly visits of Mrs Lard from the village. This taciturn lady saw to the ever more frugal shopping list of her reclusive gentleman and of the equally reclusive gentleman's gentleman.

Sir Horace's withdrawal from the real world began soon after he sold a chunk of the ancestral estate for council housing in the 1950s when quick cash had been sorely needed to restore his battered finances. But the shame of parting with those precious acres, in the possession of the Lloyd-Beauchamp family since the Dissolution of the Monasteries, weighed heavily on the squire's sense of tradition. He vowed never again to have any truck with modern material matters.

Sir Horace deposited the proceeds from the land sale in a bank account, from which Withers drew just enough to settle the household bills. As the nest egg dwindled in value, and interest failed to keep up with inflation, so it fell to Withers to relay the unwelcome news to his master. But Sir Horace seemed not at all displeased to be worth less and less. In fact, the steady drop in income encouraged in him a natural taste for a spartan life of minimal expenditure with no social contact. The elderly squire was responding to an old instinct to pull up the drawbridge in times of trouble.

For his part, Withers never questioned the sanity of his master's wishes. He accepted without demur that Sir Horace must have his own good reasons for living like a hermit and a pauper. The butler even took it stoically when ordered to serve Sir Horace his twice-daily meals no longer on the great oak table in the Privy Parlour but on a cheap plastic tray delivered through an L-shaped hatch cut into the wall of the Squire's Bedchamber. Farthing Abbey had once been home to a community of Carthusian monks who followed a regime of the strictest solitude. Now, some unseen force seemed to impose an identical lifestyle on the last two remaining residents.

And then, there was one. At first, the death of Sir Horace went unnoticed by Withers. Only after several days, with the meals remaining untouched on the tray, did the butler dare enter his master's inner sanctum. Rank odours of death wafted forth as he opened the oak door. Sir Horace lay on the floor in a pitiable state, an emaciated corpse wrapped in a ragged nightshift for a shroud. A plaintive expression suggested death found him beseeching his maker for mercy or forgiveness.

Weeks passed uneventfully after the thinly attended funeral of Sir Horace. For a while Withers believed life might yet resume its old pattern. But as the sole surviving occupant, he gradually became aware that Farthing Abbey had ideas of its own. Now abandoned to its solitary fate, the house fell into a dark brooding, as if chewing over memories of countless human lives consumed within its walls. He could sense accounts being drawn up with careful note of payments due and sums owing. Withers, himself a meticulous keeper of books, accepted this as the right and proper thing. He would not wish to turn back the clock when the day of reckoning finally came.

Meanwhile, he could feel the simmering impatience of a great destiny barely able to hold itself in check. Sensitive to every mood in the ancient house, he noticed small but unsettling phenomena. Chill drafts blew impishly in unexpected places. Doors would suddenly be hard to open. Well-oiled hinges squeaked in protest after decades of silent service. Beams, panels and floorboards creaked like planks of a ship riding out a storm. It felt like the cargo below deck was shifting. Or was it some vile monster straining at the leash?

As the house became ever more absorbed in itself, the familiar became suspiciously alien almost as if he were seeing things properly for the first time. Objects Withers had known all his life assumed a disturbingly different aspect. The grand portraits of the Lloyd-Beauchamp squires in the Long Gallery and the Library seemed decidedly less sure of themselves. No longer lords and masters of all they surveyed, they now assumed the helpless air of hunting trophies bagged and mounted by Farthing Abbey itself. The old butler averted his gaze from them on his slow progress down dusty corridors and vaulted passages where the ancient masonry felt taut with foreboding like a spider's web flexing sticky threads to ensnare one last victim for an as yet invisible predator.

Then, out of the blue, a letter from a solicitor had arrived advising that the new owner, a Mr Gervase Lloyd-Beauchamp, was entering into his lawful inheritance. In the same post was a letter from the gentleman himself to the effect that he would be visiting the following weekend and bringing with him a handful of invited guests.

Far from feeling relieved he will not be holding the fort on his own for much longer, Withers finds himself wondering whether this intrusion is a good omen. Might it not be better for the house to be left to its memories? There has been such an implacable atmosphere of late, almost as if Farthing Abbey had lived too long, seen too much, and now entertained an overwhelming wish to die. A house with a death wish?

Is such a thing possible? Withers doesn't care to think in these terms. But he knows all too well that things are coming full circle. Time is finally running out.

The new owners and their guests are expected tomorrow. There can be no turning back. Whatever will be will be. He rubs his eyes and reads the letter through once again line by line. Then he casts a tender glance at the pen-and-ink sketch of the fair young lady. He folds it carefully and places it between the pages of the fat tome that once served as his pantry book.

Finally, he bows his head, acknowledging the inevitability of this unknown future which feels tangibly present, like something hard and physical that has already happened. He rises painfully from his rickety wooden chair and walks over to the sink where he rinses out the teapot. While engaged in this simple task he is able, albeit briefly, to free his mind from the dead weight of anxiety and fear of what lies ahead.

SEPARATE LIVES

The late afternoon sun burns strongly through the window of a fashionable apartment in London's Docklands. Its intense heat threatens to bring to the boil a private scene bursting with some domestic tension of the marital sort.

'Confound it, woman! How long do you think you can play the virgin queen with me? I may not have been the ideal husband. I'll be the first to admit that. But a man still has a right to avail himself of his lawfully wedded wife. And it's more than a right. It's a duty.'

He has rehearsed the lines many times.

'And a sacred flaming duty, goddammit!'

But instead of giving voice to his intense frustrations, Gervase Lloyd-Beauchamp only thinks the words while he attempts a jovial smile that sits grotesquely on his face like a lopsided carnival mask.

'So, great-uncle Horace finally popped his clogs, eh? Well, what do you say to that, Ophelia?'

'Yes, dear.'

'And I was beginning to think he would never peg out. Ghastly prospect, eh? Just imagine that.'

'Yes, dear.'

'At least the old boy had the decency after all not to bequeath the ancestral domain to the National Trust or one of those awful charities for the deserving poor of the parish. God perish the thought.'

'Yes, dear.'

'You know, there was a time I thought the old bugger had gone totally ga-ga and would leave it all to that loopy old butler of his. Doesn't bear thinking about, does it?'

'Yes, dear.'

'What do you mean 'yes dear'? You mean 'no dear'. No, it doesn't bloody well bear thinking about.'

'No, dear.'

'That's right. You're damn right it doesn't. Still, it's a bit fishy he didn't make a will. But I suppose he must have decided in the end that blood is thicker than water. A family estate stays in the family. Come hell or the Inland Revenue. Doesn't mean you have to like your heirs. Or your ancestors for that matter. Birthright is birthright. Individuals don't count. What's important is the pure bloodline of Lloyd-Beauchamps stretching back into the mists of time.'

Gervase hesitates.

'And forward too far into the future, of course. It's a living chain reaching out from father to son. Or failing that, from great-uncle to great-nephew. Same principle. Break one single link and the whole bloody thing falls apart. Continuity and tradition. That's the name of the game. You do understand that, Ophelia, don't you?'

'Yes, dear.'

Gervase makes it sound as if the Lloyd-Beauchamp males had mastered the art of procreation without the involvement of females. Ophelia fervently wishes they had. But she leaves the thought unspoken.

'A crying shame I don't get the baronetcy too. Sir Gervase Lloyd-Beauchamp Bt. Well sod that, I say. It's handing on the property that matters. And when I've done my bit, it'll be the turn of the next chap to go in to bat. Just like cricket.'

'Yes, dear.'

A long pause ensues. Gervase Lloyd-Beauchamp doesn't like to remind himself of his own demise. What casts a darker shadow is a more immediate concern. The way things are going, would there be anyone to go in to bat after him? As yet no fruit has sprung from his loins. Not that he and Ophelia haven't done their stuff. At least in the beginning they had. But the ancestral lance hasn't seen action for longer than he dares to recall, and he knows he can't afford to let much more time slip away without providing himself with an heir, preferably a strapping son in his own image.

Gervase now looks at himself approvingly in the mirror as he straightens his tie. His ruddy complexion the hue of rare roast beef combines with his salt and pepper hair, mustard yellow waistcoat and cabbage green tweed jacket to create the vague impression of a Sunday lunch. Out of all this his eyes shine with a watery blue, watchful and remote, both hiding and seeking at the same time. Through them Gervase now studies the reflection of his wife over his shoulder.

Ophelia has feminine mystique as well as physical beauty. There is something waif-like about her misty-eyed expression. Her red hair and alabaster skin have an ethereal, timeless quality. She doesn't look her thirty-two years. At forty-five, however, Gervase appears well embarked on middle age. To see them next to one another, you might have thought uncle and niece rather than husband and wife. The age difference, which once made Gervase feel manly and masterful, has now become a threat. His life options are narrowing, while hers are still wide open. She makes him feel old.

Gervase's mature authority had been his prime, perhaps his only attraction to the innocent young Ophelia. Had she seen in him a father figure to replace the one who died when she was too young to remember him clearly? Whatever the reason, at the age of twenty-one she had, for want of a better idea what to do with herself, consented to his persistent suit to make her Mrs Lloyd-Beauchamp. Affection, she had assured herself, would follow in the fullness of time.

Only after their marriage vows were exchanged had the bride submitted to the physical obligations of the relationship. This was her first full experience of lovemaking. But this was hardly the right way to describe what generally began with a rough assault and soon ended with a brutish grunt. Although Gervase had his way with his young wife whenever he pleased, he was invariably left with the sensation of a hollow victory achieved over an elusive foe and the sense of an unresolved struggle to be resumed on another occasion.

Ophelia bore the brunt of his angry sexual passion at first with fortitude, while hoping for a more tender side of his character to emerge. But Gervase remained rough and remote. As time passed Ophelia gradually learned to accept her lot. She convinced herself this was all entirely normal and no cause for unhappiness. And so she put on an outward sham of normal wedlock. But behind the artificial facade she retreated steadily inside herself, admitting little and feeling even less. By imperceptible degrees, she even came to believe that the image facing her in the mirror was that of a contented woman.

Gervase now turns to face his wife front on as he finally declares himself content with the tidy knot in his old regimental tie. Ophelia is seated by the window of their warehouse apartment in Bermondsey gazing out at the bleak urban scene transformed by the hot sun of early June. It casts a golden glow over the gleaming tower of Canary Wharf. Once a brave symbol of hope, it now stands like a tombstone for his failed ambitions and shattered dreams.

Settling here on their return to London after ten years in Hong Kong had been Gervase's idea. He knew that his sort belonged in the stuccoed gentility of Belgravia or Kensington. But he couldn't afford the right sort of place. Docklands had seemed a handy solution, convenient for the City and his job in one of the smaller merchant banks. It carried none of the social stigma attached to the no man's land of London's sprawling metropolis east of the Grays Inn Road.

It had turned out to be a ghastly mistake. Gervase hadn't fully understood the fact that his classier neighbours had their true homes elsewhere in listed mansions and bijou farmhouses in the verdant shires. He soon came to dread being asked where he really lived. There was, of course, the occasional weekend in the country, but not nearly often enough for him to sustain his idea of himself as a man of yeoman stock, the very backbone of rural England.

Instead of his pulse quickening at the end of the week, Gervase invariably fell prey to a deep gloom. On Friday evenings, while others were racing home along the motorways out of London, he would drift back morosely to their flat. Browsing through a pile of old numbers of *Country Life* and *The Field* only sharpened his depression. No matter how much single malt or vintage port he put away, this did little to raise his spirits. He would brood over missed opportunities and think back with regret to the good times he had enjoyed during their stay in Hong Kong.

Soon after their arrival in what was then the Crown Colony a local business contact recognised in Gervase Lloyd-Beauchamp a man ready to penetrate all the erotic mysteries of the Orient. He gave him a Kowloon address with a knowing nod.

'They'll give you whatever you want. Anything. As long as you pay the price.'

Gervase needed no more encouragement than that. Once that connection had been made, Ophelia noted a marked cooling of her husband's demands on her unwilling flesh. Eventually, he ceased bothering her altogether. One day, to her intense relief, Gervase even agreed to her timid request that they should sleep in separate beds. On account of the oppressive heat, she had said. Mercifully released from her physical bondage, Ophelia was not anxious to know the reasons why. Instead, she filled her life with an obsessive pursuit of art and design. She read books, attended lectures and collected *objets d'art* and occasional bits of *Chinoiserie* on countless forays through the shops and markets of the Far East.

On their return to London she found further distraction decorating their new Docklands apartment. Gervase stood well back and gave her free rein, sensing this was the last tenuous bond that held them together. He permitted her to spend money they could ill afford on any fanciful scheme the glossy magazines cared to suggest. They both knew the moment she stopped, it really would be curtains and no mistake.

The solicitor's letter, advising Gervase he had inherited his great-uncle's estate of Farthing Abbey in Oxfordshire couldn't have come at a more opportune moment. A centuries old country house would give them something to work on together as man and wife. In his new capacity as lord of the manor and country squire Gervase could at last indulge his taste for the simple outdoor pleasures of rod and gun, while Ophelia would be absorbed by the endless task of refurbishing the place. It wasn't a bad prospect for either of them.

'Farthing Abbey. Who would have thought it possible after all this time? Great uncle Horace and I didn't exactly hit it off, you know. Never once asked me over, can you imagine? Seems he took an immediate dislike to me. Can't for the life of me think why.'

Ophelia has heard it all so many times before during the last few days. She knows Gervase will now go on to say what an exciting prospect and such a great challenge. He won't exactly specify a new start, because that would be to admit one is needed. But he will drop enough hints to make her realise that separate beds and a denial of conjugal rights, with their implications for the continuation of the Lloyd-Beauchamp family tree, cannot be allowed to continue indefinitely.

'The Lloyd-Beauchamps are an ancient line, you know. We go back to the Norman Conquest. But now we must embrace the future. The two of us are merely a conduit for history to flow through.'

Ophelia does not respond to the call of playing the conduit. After a long period of abstention, she has rediscovered the calmer joys of celibacy and in the process attained a delicate, disembodied state of untouchability, virtually a second virginity. It is indeed as if her maidenhead has been miraculously restored and she has reclaimed her girlhood purity. She now clings to this blessed state of wellbeing with increasing desperation amidst alarming signs of her husband's renewed ardour.

As for Gervase, her persistent rejection has left him somehow unmanned. He sometimes toys with the idea of using physical force, as at the beginning of their marriage, but he holds back, curiously fearful of the aura of impregnability which now surrounds her.

'A conduit for history. Yes, that's what we are.'

In order to deflect this line of conversation, Ophelia enquires whether all arrangements are in hand for the weekend.

'Yes, indeed. PR lady called Suzi something or other has lined up the guests. There's an architectural writer. Some crusty old hack, I gather. Seems we'll need a guidebook as well as a good write-up in his magazine. He's bringing a photographer to do the snaps of the house. Then a chap from the tourist board. To advise on marketing, visitor facilities and so on. And who else? Some lady writer researching a new story. Can't see much point in that. But Suzi says if we can persuade her to make Farthing Abbey the location for her next best-selling romantic novel, that could lead to a TV series as a spin-off. Then we'll be home and dry. The place will practically promote itself.'

'But how are we going to cater for them all?'

'I've told you not to worry about that, my dear. Everything under control. The PR lady can't be there in person but she's fixed things with an outfit called *Invisible Hosts*. They spirit up a four-course meal to be served by the old butler who seems to come with the house. Guests will think we have our very own gourmet chef toiling away below stairs.'

Ophelia nods silently. So her role would be to play out the charade of the gracious lady of the house. She reckons she can handle that. She has become rather good at acting her part, at least in public.

'All sounds rather fun, what? Jolly well better be. It's going to cost a fortune. But we're going to have to sell the old pile like hell to the punters just to cover the death duties.'

Gervase isn't at all daunted by the difficulties. Already he feels ten years younger anticipating pleasures ahead. No longer is he marking time. At last he has caught up with his destiny. To be master of Farthing Abbey is all that matters now. The inheritance of the Lloyd-Beauchamps is in his hands. He has a focus for his life. Everything – even the second taming of his wife – will sort itself out around the hard fact of that enduring structure and its venerable masonry.

'You know what, Ophelia? I have a feeling that Farthing Abbey is going to change our lives.'

'Yes, dear.'

A clunk of crystal tumbler on silver coaster rounds off this exchange. A heavy silence falls on Gervase and Ophelia. At this moment, the sinking sun explodes from behind a dark cloud. Suddenly, the western sky is a blazing furnace of red and orange. Speechless, they gaze out toward it, their separate lives momentarily fused together in the all consuming fire.

With the sun shining into his front parlour on this fine Saturday morning at the beginning of June, Peregrine Gargoyle is a picture of self-contentment. He sits in a high-backed, late-Victorian armchair which offers comfort and shelter as perfect as a shell to a crustacean. He almost purrs between sips of Single Estate Darjeeling laced with the tiniest dash of milk, which he imbibes from a bone china cup of neo-Grecian design while nibbling delicately at a thin slice of brown toast coated with a faint smear of bitter marmalade.

'O ye mullions and transoms of old England! I wonder what this Farthing Abbey has to offer.'

Hundreds of books fill the fitted shelves that line the walls on all sides. More are stacked up in neat piles on the desk. This formidable library on every conceivable aspect of architecture has been donated over the years by sundry publishers despatching review copies to the magazine *Houses and Castles* in the hope of a favourable mention on Gargoyle's jealously guarded book page which he rules over with a rod of iron.

Peregrine Gargoyle is also an author in his own right. He has penned a meticulously researched treatise on *The Form and Decoration of the Late Saxon and Early Norman Arch in the East Midlands*. It was, in every sense, the last word on the subject. But for some inexplicable reason the opus failed to find a taker. As a last resort, he had it printed privately and bound as a pair of handsome green leather volumes which he placed on his mantelpiece. Eventually, he decided his unpublished jewels were best kept in the bottom drawer of his desk. This act of concealment allowed him to suppress the painful memory of thwarted ambitions.

It was not long before his true vocation revealed itself. From the moment he landed his present job as chief reviewer and feature writer at *Houses and Castles*, other men's books became grist to his critical mill. And what splendid sport that offered. At first, he bared his claws quite shamelessly as he tore into works he deemed far less worthy of publication than his own rejected efforts. But this pleasure soon wore thin. Experience taught him the use of a deadlier weapon. He would observe, for example, 'this knowledgeable author writes well enough, but do we need another exposé on Decorated Gothic when the glories of Early English have been ignored for so long?'

Aspiring authors were thus left to mull over the sad irony that they had done nothing really amiss except to write passably well on the wrong subject. In this way, the years have passed serenely, while the dreaded initials of P.G. - for he has never used that of his middle name Ignatius - have been appended to numerous notices in *Houses and Castles*.

As a young man, Gargoyle had felt it was a cruel trick of fate he had not inherited one of the stately homes of England, or at least some modest mansion which he would have been proud to cherish. But that was not to be. His small abode on the fringes of Clerkenwell, one of a terrace of five sheltering under a communal stucco pediment, had been left to him by a maiden aunt, almost by way of a consolation prize.

Gargoyle quickly learned to content himself with vicarious ownership, visiting countless country houses in the course of his work. He spread his affections far and wide. An average week might see him dallying with a nice piece of Palladianism in Wiltshire, pursuing a Baroque affair in Buckinghamshire, indulging a flirt with a frivolous bit of Rococo in Kent or even entertaining a brief Orientalist fantasy in Sussex.

He has grown to relish his power as architectural pundit. No longer is he the beggar at the feast, but a person from whom such houses draw their very sustenance. He knows he can pander to the gentry by a small word of praise for their Jacobean plasterwork or cut them down to size by comparing their Elizabethan long gallery unfavourably to that of a neighbour. If he were now to be offered a Chatsworth or a Blenheim, Gargoyle would be sorely tempted. But ultimately he would decline. For he has tasted the keener thrill of being lord judge and supreme arbiter of everyone else's cherished possessions.

Peregrine Gargoyle has weathered life's storms for something over half a century, during which his thin, ascetic face has acquired a timeless Cistercian quality. This endows him with the gravitas to which he had aspired already in his youth, although he wonders why his bushy eyebrows haven't had the good taste to convert from black to grey in harmony with his flowing silver locks which he wears a trifle longer than convention generally allows for a man of his age.

On the three-legged pedestal table beside him lies an open letter. Gargoyle now peruses it yet again through his gold-rimmed, half-moon spectacles with a thoroughness which suggests he is looking for a clue which has thus far eluded him. It is the invitation to Farthing Abbey which he received the previous week from the newly founded and pretentiously named *Suzi de Blanc Smith Creative Consultancy* in Knightsbridge.

Gargoyle pinches his nose in displeasure. Suzi de Blanc Smith! He is relieved Susan Whitesmith, his ex-colleague on the magazine, will not be there in person. Even when she was posing as a writer, he always thought she was more of a shallow PR type. Now her so-called *Creative Consultancy* has proved him right.

Still examining the letter, Gargoyle falls again to wondering whether Farthing Abbey can really be worthy of the full treatment in *Houses and Castles*. He has never heard of such a place. Nor is there any reference to it in Pevsner's *Oxfordshire*. That is suspicious to say the least. But the letter also mentions the guidebook which the new owner of Farthing Abbey, a certain Mr Gervase Lloyd-Beauchamp, intends to commission from him. So, in the end, Gargoyle has swallowed the tempting bait and accepted the invitation, requesting the magazine to book a photographer. It is now too late for second thoughts. The appointed day has arrived.

Gargoyle rises to his feet with an elegant flourish and exits with measured tread. His small leather suitcase stands in readiness in the hall. He picks it up and steps outside. Having securely locked the front door, he pauses briefly to admire its Ionic pilasters crowned by a comely fanlight. He knows it is but a humble affair, but at least it does serve to recall that Augustan age when classical values had been the inspiration of refined society. Thus uplifted, Peregrine Gargoyle walks off down the road, overlooking the garbage and graffiti which disfigure this once dignified enclave of late-Georgian urbanism.

He does not have long to wait for a bus. Soon he is making excellent progress towards Bayswater. He scrutinises a piece of paper on which he has noted the address of photographer Adrian Lenshood, who will drive him to Farthing Abbey. Now that he is en route, Gargoyle has to confess that he is a trifle intrigued by this assignation with a country house, which has conspired hitherto to escape his attention.

At that moment, Adrian Lenshood is still fast asleep in the basement flat of an imposing Victorian house in a leafy road off Holland Park Avenue. The dozing photographer floats in a state of blissful withdrawal. He prefers the day to begin grey and overcast, soft and gentle, with the minimum visual shock to the senses. But on this fine morning, an aggressive shaft of the brightest daylight has forced its way through the gap between the curtains like a violent intrusion on his dark privacy. But what eventually wakes the sensitive sleeper is the sound of his doorbell. Its strident ringing reverberates with an angry insistence that goes right through his head.

'Who the devil can that be?'

Adrian Lenshood opens the corner of an eye. The time, according to his bedside clock, is just a few minutes after 11 am. He stands up and hesitantly draws back the curtains. The sunshine hits him like a slap in the face. He recoils with pain.

Hastily wrapping a Japanese robe round his naked body, he stumbles towards the front door. Through a frosted glass panel he can make out a rather agitated profile. This he now recognises as Peregrine Gargoyle whose feature story on some old pile or other he has been asked to illustrate with his own expertly composed photographs. Reluctantly, he opens the door.

'Oh, it's you, Gargoyle. Rather early, aren't you? I had it down for a 12 o'clock start.'

'That's as may be, Lenshood. But it's always as well to allow adequate time for the unexpected. Heaven knows how long you might have slept in if I hadn't called at the right moment.'

'It'll take me a few minutes to get ready. I suppose you had better come in and wait while I grab a shower.'

Peregrine Gargoyle reluctantly follows Adrian Lenshood through the gloomy passage of the basement flat. A solitary and a celibate by nature, it feels almost illicit, for him to be entering another's personal sphere, especially someone *en déshabillé*. Gargoyle shudders, as if steeling himself to confront something unpleasant.

'You really should get yourself a proper house, Lenshood. Most unhealthy living underground like this.'

Adrian Lenshood does not reply. He remembers his last encounter with Peregrine Gargoyle at the offices of *Houses and Castles*. Having spread out the results of a shoot on the light box, he had been kept waiting for ages while Gargoyle peered and sniffed at the images painfully extracted from a very dull country mansion under even duller light conditions. With every little sigh of disappointment, Gargoyle insinuated in his devious way that the photographer was to blame both for the shortcomings of the house and for the bad weather.

So Adrian Lenshood feels no joy at the prospect of an entire weekend working alongside Peregrine Gargoyle. As for Farthing Abbey, it will be no different from any of the other stately piles he has photographed over the years. In his mind they have all coalesced into one amorphous mass of heritage in aspic. The day is long gone when he had looked forward to his photographic assignments with eager enthusiasm.

'Won't take me long to get ready. Make yourself at home.'

Left alone, Gargoyle looks about him with a snort of derision at the odd assortment of black and white photographs and cheap colour reproductions of modern paintings by the likes of Matisse and Picasso. Gargoyle's own taste in art stops well before the end of the 19th century. Despairing of the lack of discernment in Lenshood's pictures, he casts about for any clues as to his domestic arrangements. But it is impossible to tell whether the photographer is living on his own.

Gargoyle feels a sudden tinge of excitement to be prying however harmlessly into another's private stuff. He has kept his distance from the general run of base humankind for so long that being in someone else's space like this puts all manner of dangerous ideas into his head. He can't recall ever having been intimate with anyone. Indeed, apart from a brief infatuation with a younger boy at boarding school, Gargoyle has steadfastly eschewed the ways of the flesh for a nobler calling. Even that one passing moment of weakness lies so far behind him that its memory is well and truly buried beneath the massive weight of all the art and architecture that has absorbed his energies ever since.

For want of anything else to do, Peregrine Gargoyle sits down on what he takes to be a chair, only to sink deep into something endlessly yielding. It swallows him whole. His attempts to extricate himself by wiggling arms and legs only succeed in getting him more firmly ensconced. He kicks and struggles like a beetle laid out on its back. At least that is how he looks to Adrian Lenshood who now puts his head through the open door en route from bathroom to kitchen.

'That's it, Gargoyle, make yourself comfortable. Nothing like a beanbag is there? The coffee should be ready soon. Be right with you.'

With an ungainly roll, Gargoyle comes tumbling out onto the floor and scrambles awkwardly to his feet.

Angry thoughts run through his mind. Damn nuisance these photographers, mere artisans posing as artists. Fondly, he recalls the good old days when pictures had been no more than decoration to a worthy piece of serious writing. Now, it is all to do with spreads and layouts. His precious texts are squeezed around the illustrations like so much toothpaste from a tube.

Adrian Lenshood, having hastily put on jeans and a shirt, reappears from the kitchen. He proffers a mug of coffee towards his guest, who feels another distinct twitch of malaise at the casual domesticity of the scene. They might be a co-habiting couple having breakfast. To his alarm Gargoyle observes that his outstretched hand is shaking.

'Don't fuss, Lenshood Just put it down here, somewhere, anywhere.'

'Right, OK. I'll be ready in a couple of minutes. Must just check my gear.'

It is almost noon by the time writer and photographer emerge from the basement flat and climb the steps up to street level. Adrian Lenshood places tripod and baggage on the back seat of an ageing Saab. Under the uncomfortably close scrutiny of Peregrine Gargoyle, who has now regained his customary composure, he starts the engine.

'I say, Lenshood, what is that strange little growth on your chin? If you are cultivating a beard, then for heaven's sake, do it properly. Be inspired by the great bushes of facial hair as worn by Ruskin,

Morris and their ilk. That paltry effort of yours looks decidedly minimalist.'

Adrian Lenshood knows better than to respond. In any case, the restless critical faculties of Peregrine Gargoyle are soon lambasting the shameless vandalism of the modern age as made manifest by the brutal gash carved by the Westway slicing through the Victorian splendours of Westbourne Park and Ladbroke Grove. After that, the two men hardly speak as they head out of suburban London towards Farthing Abbey.

WORLDS COLLIDE

George Burp sniffs the stale air trapped inside his speeding car. The pong of ancient fish and chips mingles with the lingering whiff of kebabs, curries and burgers consumed in one lay-by or another. Cheap cigarillos add their pungent perfume to the delicate mix which has begun to register the frequent presence of the dyspeptic old Labrador Burp has to exercise now that his father is no longer able to walk the family pet.

The resulting concoction is a thick atmosphere as sweet to George Burp's nostrils as that of a foetid swamp to a toad. It constitutes a personal biosphere that sustains and reassures him. Only one thing is missing. But he can now feel a rumble deep in his vitals, to which he silently gives vent, while noting from a road sign that he is crossing the county line from Wiltshire into Oxfordshire.

'I wonder who put the fart in Farthing Abbey.'

For George Burp the act of passing wind has acquired a special significance. The breakdown of his teetering marriage had been hastened to its desired end by a prolonged barrage of flatulence that left poor Mrs Burp on the ropes, quite literally gasping for air.

He still can't figure out how she had inveigled herself into his life. But the wisdom of hindsight tells him there must have been a point to getting himself hitched just the once, if only to be inoculated against a particularly dangerous virus. For since then, whenever the idea of matrimony has appeared however distantly on the horizon, he simply remembers his entanglement with Mrs Burp and is instantly prevented from repeating the folly.

On this fine summer day, such dark memories are far from his mind. George Burp sits happily at the wheel of his Ford Mondeo and watches his mileage slowly accumulate. He derives endless pleasure totting up the allowance he collects as he drives about the country in the course of his job with the *Shires of Middle England Tourist Board*.

He has spent the previous evening playing skittles at *The Cat and Fiddle* near Cricklade with some old cronies from the *North Wiltshire Angling Club*. Five pints of *Old Brewery Special* prevented him from driving home. His head is still fuzzy. He now glances at the dashboard clock. It is just after 12.30 pm as he parks the car outside his semi-detached house on the outskirts of Witney and lets himself in.

He takes one glance at the domestic chaos awaiting him and decides he will stop for lunch somewhere en route to Farthing Abbey. A shave, a shower and a quick change of clothes must do for the time being. Soon he is back on the road. George Burp now begins to contemplate what lies ahead with a tinge of apprehension. Although no stranger to the stately homes of England, he hasn't been invited to one as a house guest before. To his dismay, he feels a phantom muscle twitch as if in response to centuries of forelock touching by generations of oppressed Burps.

Farthing Abbey is a new one on him, but he is vaguely familiar with the nearby town of Castle Farthing and has sunk a jar or two in the local hostelry, an establishment called, as far as he can remember, something reassuringly predictable like *The Castle Inn*.

It is almost 2 pm when he arrives at the pub. He notes it has been renamed *Ye Jolly Yeomen of Days of Yore*. With misgiving, he steps inside. Where previously there had been a few horse brasses and copper kettles, the decor now resembles a local history museum crammed with assorted bric-a-brac from old farm implements to Victorian dolls, stuffed birds and coronation mugs.

The menu, entitled *A Taste of Merrie Olde England*, is printed in mock Gothic script on a rolled parchment. The cosy snug where the locals used to play dominoes is now *The Dungeon Bar*. The toilets are signed *Wenches* and *Knaves*. The barmaid wears an Elizabethan dress, cut very low to reveal a generous pair of breasts which wobble endearingly while he watches his pint of bitter dribble reluctantly from a plastic nozzle.

Burp orders himself a *Yeoman's Platter*. This turns out to be a slab of York pie garnished with a limp lettuce leaf, crumpled spring onion and half a tomato. The egg yoke stares at him out of the processed pork meat like a jaundiced, baleful eye. Burp sits there brooding. He eats his lunch in a mood far from jolly and leaves without ordering the second pint he would usually have drunk as a matter of course.

He still has time on his hands, so he sets off for a stroll through the alleyways of Castle Farthing. The castle itself is a Norman mound or *motte*, of which nothing remains but the earthwork itself, contained within metal railings. These have been prised apart in places, allowing the bored youth of Castle Farthing to enjoy the facilities, once the exclusive preserve of their forefathers' feudal overlords.

The site is also visited infrequently by members of the *Castle Farthing Local History Society* who obtain the key held by the owner of the curio shop *Bygone Thynges*. This gentleman also organises the periodic removal of the beer cans, cigarette packets, used condoms and syringes that tend to accumulate on the summit of the *motte*, much to the dismay of the more sensitive amateur antiquarians.

Burp enters a shop to pick up a reserve supply of his favourite cigarillos. He feels he might need them. His subsequent enquiry about the precise location of Farthing Abbey brings an unhelpful response.

'Farthing Abbey, you say?'

Then, after a thoughtful pause.

'You mean the old house in the park.'

Burp isn't sure whether this second comment is a question or a statement of fact.

'No one's been there for years and years except for Mrs Lard.'

'Mrs Lard?'

'The butcher's wife.'

There follows another lengthy pause.

'And she says it's a right old dump.'

This comment is solemnly volunteered by a portly woman who has silently entered the shop.

'Mrs Lard says there's bound to be changes at Farthing Abbey now the old squire is dead and buried. The solicitors have been looking for the rightful heir.'

The newcomer appraises Burp with a glance.

'Don't suppose you happen to know who that might be?'

Burp says nothing. He reaches out to take his cigarillos and change.

'Thought not.'

'Which direction did you say I should take to get to Farthing Abbey?'

'I didn't.'

The customer comes to his rescue.

'Main entrance is a couple of miles out of town, on the Chipping Norton road. A fair stretch after the Shell garage, but just before *The Happy Eater*. I suppose you are expected?'

'Oh yes. I'm expected all right. Worse luck.'

This comment is in a low mutter for his own benefit as he leaves the shop. Two inquisitive gazes are locked onto his departing back like twin laser beams.

Suddenly, George Burp stops in his tracks. He remembers something important he had promised to do. He had received a call the previous day from a PR lady called Suzi de something fancy asking him to collect another of the guests off the 14.57 at Castle Farthing Junction. A lady novelist or suchlike, he vaguely recalls. He glances at his watch. He is a full twenty minutes behind schedule.

Even as George Burp points his rusting Ford Mondeo towards Castle Farthing Junction, a literary lady by the name of Araminta Fettiplace is pacing the deserted platform, fuming at the lamentable manners, incredible sloppiness and unpardonable incompetence of the nincompoop who should have there to assure her onward conveyance. A screech of tyres informs her that her driver has finally arrived. George Burp advances towards her, mumbling a few unintelligible remarks by way of a lame apology for his delay.

'The 14.57 usually gets in half an hour late on a Saturday. On account of the engineering works. I suppose they must have finished. Still, no harm done. Burp's the name, by the way. George Burp.'

'Fettiplace. Araminta Fettiplace.'

Her haughty tone reduces him firmly to the rank of a chauffeur. He snatches up her weekend bag sporting a William Morris floral design. He leads her to the car and holds open the door for her. Araminta Fettiplace casts a look of horror at the rear seat strewn with all manner of revolting stuff from discarded clothing, dog hair and dirty food containers to empty maggot tins. She sniffs the air with suspicion as she lowers herself as lightly as possible onto the front seat.

'What an amazingly putrid smell. You are not transporting a corpse by any chance, Mr Burp, are you?'

'Must be my father's dog. He's been a bit unwell of late. Upset tummy mostly. I'll open a window.'

'Open all the windows for heaven's sake and the roof as well. Then hopefully I might survive the journey. This awful stench doesn't do anything for one's artistic sensitivity, you know. How can the poetic imagination roam free amidst all this squalor?'

The full aroma hits her once more.

'Mr Burp, I really think you should see a vet.'

'Me? A vet?'

'For your father's dog, I mean. To judge by its body odour it must be at death's door.'

Burp smiles sweetly as he recalls how he dealt with the former Mrs Burp, while releasing yet another silent one for good measure.

'So sorry for any inconvenience, Mrs Fatplace.'

'It's Fettiplace, if you don't mind, Mr Burp. And kindly call me Ms not Mrs.'

This is barely audible. Araminta Fettiplace has stuck her head out of the window. But George Burp has registered the remark. He strokes his chin as he wonders how to respond to this unexpected revelation. She fancies him. No doubt about that. Must be his animal magnetism. Will it be worth the effort though? He'll have to give it serious thought. While he ponders the matter, the rest of the short journey passes, to the relief of both parties, in silence.

WELCOME HOME

Withers is already standing valiantly at his post by the main entrance of Farthing Abbey as Gervase Lloyd-Beauchamp brings his Range Rover to a dignified halt, crunching the gravel drive. Things are surpassing expectations. The house looks like the genuine article. Even the butler emerges bang on cue to greet him at precisely the right moment.

Withers may present a solitary figure beneath the portico, but he carries himself like the head of a delegation, as if an entire phantom household of invisible maids and grooms are lined up behind him to pay their respects to the new master.

'Welcome home, sir. We hope you enjoyed a comfortable journey.'

Gervase can hardly believe his ears. The words have stunned him. He doesn't even question the curiously outmoded apparel of his putative butler. Welcome home. A homecoming is just how it feels to be entering Farthing Abbey. As if he has merely been absent for a while. He runs a proprietorial eye along the noble façade. He is seeing the place for the first time, but Farthing Abbey exudes a compelling familiarity. A gut feeling tells him this is his native earth, the hallowed ancestral turf where Lloyd-Beauchamps have been born and raised for centuries past.

'Home, you say. That's nicely put, er ...'

Gervase had not bothered to make a mental note of the butler's name when he read the solicitor's letter.

'You may call me Withers, sir.'

The old man says this with the faintest ghost of a bow and in a tone so detached as to suggest the name was something provisional he has merely pulled out of the air on the spur of the moment.

'Withers? Thank you, Withers. As you know I am Mr Gervase Lloyd-Beauchamp and this is my charming lady wife, Ophelia.'

'Madam.'

Ophelia's attention is on the rampant Virginia creeper smothering the house. For a fleeting moment she fancies she sees the green leaves flare up in their red autumn glory. She feels faint. A sudden chill runs up her spine in defiance of the heat. Something is not quite as it should be, but she cannot put her finger on anything out of the ordinary. On the surface, everything seems normal. Except for Withers, who is looking at her intently in a most disconcerting way.

'Madam?'

She notes something odd in the butler's manner to her. There is a query in his tone to suggest a degree of unease at her presence. Whereas Gervase is warmly welcomed home, perhaps she counts merely as a trifle the master has brought back like one of those marble statues gentlemen used to collect on their continental travels? But this is not the time to pursue the thought. Courtesy demands she gracefully extend to Withers what she hopes he will accept as a hand of friendship.

'Withers. So pleased to meet you.'

The butler does not take her hand, but contents himself with a formal bow of the head and another curious look at her before turning his attention once more to Gervase.

'How was Italy, sir? Everything to your entire satisfaction, I trust?'

'Italy? We've only come from London, man. I mean, Withers. Only set foot in Italy once, and never again. Far too many bag snatchers and bum pinchers.'

'Indeed, sir.'

It is hard to tell whether Withers now realises his mistake, or accepts that the squire changed his travel plans. For the butler continues without further ado.

'But who needs Italy, sir? Or even Greece, when you have wonders such as these to behold on your own magnificent estate?'

Gervase and Ophelia take a proper look at the west front of Farthing Abbey. It is a dignified structure with tall sash windows either side of the central door at first floor level reached by a sweeping double stone staircase adorned with a pair of heraldic lions at the base and various urns on the balustrade. It is a very fine residence, although there is something odd about the colossal Greek Doric columns clumsily attached to the façade. It looks as if an elegant Italian villa has been imprisoned within a massive Greek temple and which peeps out forlornly through the bars of its cage.

'I trust you are sufficiently pleased with the general effect of the Grecian improvements, sir. The work has been executed as well as if you had been here yourself to supervise it.'

Gervase is again wrong-footed by his butler's eerie assumption that he is returning after a long absence. Does Withers really believe that he, Gervase, had been around a couple of centuries ago and actually left instructions for the builders?

'Splendid. Yes. Quite splendid. Now do carry on, Withers.'

The word 'carry' has a galvanising effect on the aged butler.

'I will attend to your baggage, sir. Right away.'

At this point Withers seems to become suddenly aware that he has no young grooms and stable lads at his beck and call. No-one will come running when he crooks a forefinger. He is just an old man on his own. Solemnly, he makes his way to the rear of the Range Rover and bends down to grapple with the handle at the back of the car.

Gervase feigns not to notice his difficulties. Diverting his gaze, he leans back, legs splayed, contemplating the portico of the Palladian Villa. His own limbs feel as solid as the Grecian columns, as if already the fabric of Farthing Abbey is becoming a physical part of himself. Yes, he has to admit that he is entirely satisfied with the general effect.

Ophelia, meanwhile, observes the pathetic efforts of the butler to lift Gervase's heavy leather suitcase. This Withers is obliged to abandon, but he manages to remove Ophelia's much lighter weekend bag.

'Gervase, don't think you should give Withers a helping hand?'

But Gervase's seigneurial instincts are developing fast. It would be a *faux pas* of the greatest magnitude to be seen actually carrying his own suitcase. The whole master-servant relationship would be undermined and centuries of carefully crafted class barriers thoughtlessly torn down. So he ignores Ophelia's entreaty and waves a dismissive hand at the butler to indicate he should proceed forthwith into the house.

'Lead on Withers. You can see to the rest later.'

'Very good, sir.'

Gervase resumes his previous posture to recapture the delicious sensation of power surging through his loins as he absorbs every detail of Farthing Abbey. He watches with pride and puzzlement as the quasi funereal figure of Withers ascends the grand staircase with all the solemnity of a high priest approaching a temple shrine.

Ophelia, he is pleased to note, cuts a fine figure against the Grecian colonnade. She really looks the part as the squire's lady, the mistress of the house. Gervase is about to follow her indoors when the Ford Mondeo of George Burp delivering Araminta Fettiplace arrives. The lady's head is stuck out of the car window in the strangest manner. She seems to be gulping fresh air as if for some deep breathing exercise. No sooner does the car come to a halt than she springs out as if leaping ashore from a sinking ship. In her eagerness to make good her hasty exit, Araminta Fettiplace reveals a tantalising view of a shapely pair of thighs.

'Mr Gervase Lloyd-Beauchamp, I presume?'

Gervase nods stiffly.

'Araminta Fettiplace. Pleased to meet you.'

Gervase has but the vaguest notion who she is.

'Delighted I'm sure. Well, what do you think of the place?'

'Simply wonderful. Oozing with ambience, Mr Lloyd-Beauchamp. I'm sure some fascinating people have lived here. There could be not just one but several novels lurking here within these walls. I must admit I feel creatively inspired already.'

'That's the spirit, Araminta. You are just in time to witness a moment of history. The master of Farthing Abbey taking formal possession of the old family pile. Another Lloyd-Beauchamp poised to mount the grand ancestral stair and cross the threshold of destiny. All rather fun, what?'

Gervase is in the act of gallantly offering her his arm. But his symbolic gesture is ruined by George Burp who now pokes his head from the car window and hails them with what he thinks is a cheery greeting. Gervase treats him to a black look.

'Allow me to settle your fare, Araminta. I insist.'

With a low growl, George Burp advances a few steps across the gravel before regaining control of his temper. It isn't just the assumption that he is a cab driver. Even as they entered the grounds of Farthing Abbey, he has conceded to himself that his passenger is not such a bad looking prospect after all. But no sooner has he decided he is sufficiently attracted to Araminta Fettiplace than here is the lord of the manor already making a play for her. George Burp resolves not be outclassed in any way. So it is with an exaggerated display of civility that he fishes out a card from his breast pocket and offers it to Gervase.

'George Burp, Product Marketing Consultant from the *Shires of England Tourist Board*.'

Gervase does not even glance at the card. Just as well, for it is in reality a small envelope which once contained a couple of spare buttons for Burp's bargain sports jacket from C&A.

'Well Burp, you can make yourself useful. You don't mind carrying your own luggage, I'm sure. And there are one or two bits and pieces in the Range Rover while you're at it. There's a good chap.'

Burp turns away, seething with fury. He drags his feet as he goes to fetch his bag. He would damn well ignore the bloody Range Rover. These baronial buggers never change. That Lloyd-Beauchamp needs to be taught a lesson. It looks like it's going to be a long, hard slog of a weekend.

Gervase, meanwhile, attempts to resume his jovial banter with Araminta Fettiplace. But the magic mood has been broken and he opts against offering his arm. Instead, he ushers her to walk in front of him. This permits him the close sight of her well formed bottom swaying saucily before him as he walks close behind her up the stone staircase. He reckons he has got her number. Gervase is thus restored to previous good spirits as he prepares to enter the Palladian Villa and claim his inheritance.

Drawing breath, he steps inside. The Vestibule is decorated with an absolute riot of Rococo arabesques in dazzling white plaster. A bit over the top, he thinks, but Gervase reassures himself it is exactly the sort of thing grand houses always have. Once again, he remarks how well Ophelia looks in this setting. She seems made for it. He is seeing her in her true element for the first time. She comes floating down the stair, which emerges from the walls with no visible means of support, an ethereal being whose feet hardly touch the ground.

Gervase performs the introductions.

'Ophelia, Araminta. Araminta, Ophelia.'

The two women smile at one another.

'Well, Ophelia, what do you think?'

'Think of what, Gervase?'

'Is the new mistress of Farthing Abbey not pleased with her abode?'

'I've hardly had a chance to take a proper look.'

Gervase now addresses Araminta Fettiplace.

'Withers will do the honours.'

The butler goes off to fetch the lady's luggage. Outside, an irritable George Burp bends his ear.

'Nice little property, I suppose. But I get to see a lot of places like this. Needs a bit of work on it, if you ask me. Must cost a fortune to heat in winter.'

Withers pays no heed. He makes another futile attempt to lift his master's suitcase from the rear of the

Range Rover. This is too much for George Burp, mindful of the frailty of his own aged father. So he does the honourable thing and goes to his aid. He lugs the heavy leather suitcase up the stair to the front door, hastily dumps it just inside the Vestibule and takes off smartly before its owner can catch him in the act. Withers salvages some professional pride by carrying Araminta's delicate bag. Burp, having collected his own affairs, now enters the Palladian Villa and slowly climbs the staircase behind the butler.

Gervase remains alone in the Rococo Vestibule. His thoughts are taking wing like the swirling plasterwork. He is in a different world when Ophelia calls down to him from the upper landing.

'Oh look, Gervase, there's your suitcase right behind you. But I don't think Withers can manage the stairs with it.'

'I reckon old Withers must be just about ready for the knacker's yard. God knows what we're employing him for if I'm going to have to hump my own luggage about the place.'

Having first checked thoroughly there is no one about, Gervase picks up his suitcase with ill humour. He is struggling upstairs with it, when another figure enters the Rococo Vestibule.

'Good afternoon, my good man. Be so good as to kindly inform Mr Lloyd-Beauchamp of my presence. Peregrine Gargoyle Esq., if you please.'

Gervase turns on him a look of pure venom.

'My good man? I'll have you know I'm not your bloody ...'

Gervase doesn't need to finish his sentence for Gargoyle to realise the enormity of his awful gaffe.

'I say. I'm terribly sorry, if I've made a mistake, Mr ... er...?'

It is too late for apologies. Gervase tightens his grip on the suitcase and scuttles upstairs. Gargoyle just stands there, ashen-faced. His only consolation is that no one else is present to witness his embarrassment. But, even as he turns, he comes face to face with Adrian Lenshood, who seems suspiciously eager to pretend he has heard nothing at all.

'Strange sort of place, don't you think, Gargoyle?'

For once in his life, Peregrine Gargoyle is most uncharacteristically silent.

SECRET STAIRCASE

Red with rage, Gervase pauses on the top of the stairs and lets go of his cursed suitcase. He coughs impatiently to summon Withers but he gets no response. Gervase then puffs out his chest and struts to and fro along the landing like a ship's captain on the bridge.

His eyes narrow as he sees that arrogant fool Peregrine Gargoyle climbing the staircase followed by Adrian Lenshood. Gervase snorts at them both for good measure. Gargoyle wears a pained expression and shuffles awkwardly, as if to make himself as unobtrusive as possible. He mumbles an apologetic greeting. Further embarrassment is avoided by the appearance of Withers who accompanies writer and photographer to their rooms. At last, the butler returns to attend to his master.

'Now, sir, if you please, I will bring you to your quarters.'

Then he spots Gervase's suitcase.

'I see your baggage has followed you upstairs.'

'Good lord, so it has, Withers. Fancy that. One of the guests must have been trying to be helpful.'

'I am afraid to inform you, sir, that it will have to be taken down again.'

Master and butler eye the suitcase with separate misgivings, the one unable and the other unwilling to carry it. Gargoyle, lurking in the background, quickly perceives a chance to make amends for his blunder.

'Excuse me. If I may be of some assistance, Mr Lloyd-Beauchamp. It was probably young Lenshood, my photographic assistant. He's always carrying heavy bags. He means well but he simply can't leave anything where it should be. I'll go and fetch him.'

Gargoyle strides with poise and authority to the far side of the landing and raps on Adrian's door.

'Ah, Lenshood. Mr Lloyd-Beauchamp would be grateful for your assistance in removing that suitcase. It's far too heavy for Withers. Now come along, there's a good chap.'

Burp overhears this through his own half open door. He is glad there is someone other than himself to be bossed about. But he makes a mental note Gargoyle is to be watched as keenly as Lloyd-Beauchamp.

Burp inspects his quarters. The angled ceiling tells him he is right under the roof. The wallpaper is faded and peeling, the furniture sparse and threadbare. The heat of the day has penetrated the attic storey. The atmosphere is heavy and soporific. Burp looks about for a wash basin. All he can find is a china jug and bowl on a mahogany dresser. Peering inside, he sees a half-drowned fly thrashing about in some murky water. He removes the insect with the stem of his toothbrush, ferries it to the window and ejects it unceremoniously. The wet fly plummets to the ground.

In spite of himself, Burp can't help admiring the splendid vista over the Landscape Park of Farthing

Abbey. The Scenic Lake, shimmering silver under the blazing sun, snakes away between lush meadows planted with trees. A circular temple nestles on a grassy knoll. An ancient church pokes its graceful tower out of a patch of woodland. Further afield an avenue leads the eye on towards an obelisk on the brow of a hill pointing upward like a colossal finger raised in warning.

Burp surveys the terrace directly beneath him where a table has been laid out with cups and saucers. A slow moving woman of stern, impassive countenance and ponderous bulk is counting out sandwiches and stacking them on plates where they lie exposed to the sun. Already they curl at the edges. Burp can almost smell the rancid butter and feel the warm, slimy cucumber on his tongue.

Mrs Lard, the domestic help, as Burp now observes, is fishing a small black object out of the milk jug with a teaspoon. He has no doubt this is his waterlogged fly. He swiftly draws back from the window as the lady looks up to the heavens, fearful that other dying insects might be about to drop out of the clear blue sky. A fly in the milk is, Mrs Lard knows deep in her bones, not a good sign. Not at all a good sign.

Having wetted face and hands and wiped them on the tiny towel, Burp pulls a comb through the thick straw of his hair. He looks at his robust country face in the oval mirror and sees a reflection that can hardly be faulted for its rude good health and rugged endurance. He bears his fifty years pretty well, albeit in a wide-eyed yokel fashion. You could say what you liked about

George Burp, but you would have to admit there was no side to him. What you see is what you get. Burp takes a bit more trouble than usual with his grooming. He is strangely excited by the presence next door of that flighty Araminta Fettiplace. She isn't remotely his type but he can't help wondering if she is up for it. Just for the hell of it. He certainly is.

Burp hasn't been this eager in a long while. At the same time, he feels a slight pressure in his bladder. He is glad he hadn't had that second pint at *Ye Jolly Yeomen of Days of Yore*. But an urgent visit to the bathroom is required nonetheless. There is nothing worse than dying for a leak when having to make polite remarks about the antique furniture or the inevitable Adam fireplace. He makes a complete circuit of the upper landing in search of a bathroom. Alerted by the noise of rattling handles, Araminta Fettiplace puts her head outside her door.

'Oh, it's you, Mr Burp.'

'George, Araminta. Do call me George. We are neighbours after all. Very close neighbours as a matter of fact, Araminta.'

His winning smile is met with a stony silence and a cold look. He decides to change tack.

'Bit primitive this place. I'm used to having my own *en suite*. I've been looking for the facilities. Don't suppose you happen to know where they are?'

'Mr Burp, I am afraid my mind is on other far more important things. Can't you just feel the drama and history of this place?'

Peregrine Gargoyle now pops out from his room. He has overheard the conversation and wears a knowing look.

'Looking for the facilities? Well, you won't find them up here in a building of this style and period.'

'So where do you think we should look for them, in your learned opinion, Peregrine old chap?'

Gargoyle wishes he hadn't been so quick to parade his knowledge before such an audience.

'Well. I wouldn't like to say. But certainly not up here, and most assuredly not on the *piano nobile*. Have you tried the basement?'

'The basement, you reckon?'

'Well, yes. Although I don't actually mean the basement in the ordinary sense of the word. In a grand Palladian house such as this the basement is in reality the ground floor.'

'A basement on the ground floor? Is that so?'

Gargoyle doesn't respond. This Burp personage has an unpleasant air about him. Why on earth has he been invited to Farthing Abbey? He looks to Araminta Fettiplace for support. The lady obliges.

'Mr Burp, you mustn't expect even the learned Peregrine Gargoyle to know everything. Besides, his knowledge is art-historical rather than domestic. But if anyone can fathom the mysteries of Farthing Abbey, I am sure it will be the formidable P.G., architectural sleuth *par excellence*.'

With this accolade ringing in his ears, Gargoyle cannot fail to warm to the lady. He simpers a weak compliment about the worthy historical romances of Araminta Fettiplace, a lady of whose books he is only dimly aware. Then he wishes them both good luck in their searches. As he closes the door behind him, Burp's relentless questioning continues.

'Art-historical? Is that what you call it? Still, if he's a sleuth, then he should be able to sniff them out. The facilities, I mean?'

Araminta feigns not to hear this remark.

'Goodness me, is that the time? We must be down for tea on the terrace in a couple of minutes. Do excuse me.'

Safely back in her room, Araminta Fettiplace resolves to keep well away from that tasteless oaf George Burp. Instead, she will focus on getting close to Gervase Lloyd-Beauchamp. He is undoubtedly the man of the moment, the one to impress, the person who will unlock for her the secrets of Farthing Abbey.

Peregrine Gargoyle, meanwhile, considers the unexpected tribute to his genius. Architectural sleuth was a bit *populaire* perhaps, but not entirely inaccurate, he has to admit. And he does appreciate the *par excellence* bit. Gradually, his pinched expression softens. His lips purse into a faint smile of curious shape. It resembles a flattened ogee arch he had once admired at Linlithgow Palace in Scotland and whose form he had unwittingly absorbed into his own facial architecture.

Like Araminta Fettiplace, he resolves to make Gervase Lloyd-Beauchamp the target of his efforts. There is, after all, the guidebook to be written and he mustn't lose sight of that. Burp might well be a confounded nuisance, but he could possibly serve as the dull buffoon against whom his own light would shine that much more brightly.

Adrian Lenshood, meanwhile, has picked up Gervase's heavy suitcase with good grace, charmed and mollified by a sweet look from Ophelia. It is nothing precise, but it seems to say 'I am so sorry about this. It's really a fearful imposition. Please do it for my sake.'

Withers leads the way, Gervase at his heels and Ophelia following behind her husband. Adrian brings up the rear. As they descend the staircase she engages the guest conscripted as porter in conversation.

'Mr Lenshood. I hope that bag isn't too heavy.'

'No problem. Absolutely not. I do assure you.'

'Mr Gargoyle says you are his photographic assistant. That must be very interesting.'

'Did he? As it happens, I am the photographer. A photographic assistant would be someone else who worked for me, setting up tripods, changing lenses, film magazines, that sort of thing. I actually take the photographs. Gargoyle just does the words.'

'How very exciting. I do admire creative people. I hope you will find Farthing Abbey an attractive subject.'

'Yes, Mrs Lloyd-Beauchamp, I'm sure I will.'

Adrian is already finding Ophelia Lloyd-Beauchamp a more attractive subject than the house. She carries herself with such grace and elegance. Her slender neck curves most enchantingly as she turns her head with those fiery tresses of red hair. He is intrigued by her tantalisingly wistful, melancholy manner that suggests a rare spirit of sensitivity and otherworldliness.

Withers pauses for a moment by an ornate double-door crowned with an open pediment. He fumbles with a bunch of large iron keys before admitting them to a darkened room. They fall in behind the aged butler who drifts like a spectre through the shadows. There is barely sufficient sunlight seeping in for them to make out an interior full of ornate furniture, lined with gilt-framed pictures.

Withers moves slowly but confidently through the gloom. His feet know the way and guide him rather than his eyes. They pass through two rooms and enter a third, also shuttered. They can dimly discern marble statues on pedestals and shelves of books extending from floor to ceiling.

Suddenly, Withers halts in a corner. Adrian almost collides with Ophelia in the darkness. Like an animal, his nostrils twitch eagerly at her womanly perfume. While waiting for the butler to continue, he remains right behind her engulfed by her alluring feminine scent. He breathes it in greedily. His heart is racing while the butler seems to fumble for something in the bookcase. Gervase becomes impatient.

'What's the problem, Withers?'

'No problem at all, sir. There is a door concealed here in the south-east corner of the Antique Gallery. I am seeking the lever that operates it. I will show you later when I have opened the shutters.'

At last, the secret door in the bookcase opens.

'Why the devil not turn on the lights, Withers?'

'I am afraid there is no electricity, sir. So I keep a candle in the alcove to light the way down the stair to the Cloister Garth.'

Withers strikes a match and lights the candle.

'Cloister Garth, Withers?'

'Yes, sir. The Squire's Bedchamber is located in the old house, the original part which survives from the medieval monastery. This newel stair is the only internal means of communication.'

'Secret staircase, eh? Rather fun, what? Carry on, Withers. Carry on.'

'Very good, sir.'

Down they go, drawn on by the flickering light of the candle held aloft by Withers. Adrian fixes his eyes on Ophelia's silhouette and follows blindly. The spiral stair makes several turns before daylight gradually begins to flood in from below. They emerge one by one out of the gloom into an enchanting cloister.

'This way, if you please.'

Withers ascends a stone staircase, its steps worn over the centuries, up to a stout, nail-studded oak door with hinges like iron tentacles. He lifts the latch, pushes the door open and stands aside to let them pass.

'The Squire's Bedchamber, Mr and Mrs Lloyd-Beauchamp. Welcome home to Farthing Abbey.'

ANCESTRAL BED

They enter the Squire's Bedchamber, musty and cavernous beneath the cracked beams of a timber-trussed roof, its thick stone walls pierced by narrow Gothic windows through which shafts of sunlight cast patterns of delicate tracery on the twisted floorboards. Although the full heat of summer has been beating down all day, still it has not dispelled the clammy chill of the lichen-encrusted limestone.

The furniture consists of a painted cabinet, a large oak chest and narrow wooden table with a straight-backed chair at either end. A polar bear skin does service as a rug, yellow fangs bared menacingly in a wide open jaw, spread out in front of a stone fireplace carved with buxom bare-breasted women in crudely suggestive poses. But one outlandish object dominates the room: an oversize four-poster draped with heavily embroidered curtains. On this all eyes are now directed.

The bed proudly asserts its solitary presence like a single ship sailing on an empty lake or a lone tent pitched in the middle of a field. To Ophelia it suggests no beautiful image of wide-open spaces but a dark vision of confinement in a claustrophobic cell. She shudders at the implications of sharing this marital bed with Gervase. For this is the ancestral breeding pen, the place where countless Lloyd-Beauchamps have been conceived in lusty embraces from which there can be no possible escape.

Gervase views the strange contraption with parallel thoughts of his own. He sees generations of Lloyd-Beauchamps issuing forth from the curtains of the four-poster like actors taking their bow in a theatre. Behind those thick drapes he and Ophelia will soon indulge themselves as nature intends, two naked bodies going about their biological duties in time-honoured fashion. Gervase is powerfully attracted to its dark privacy, secrecy and concealment. He feels the stirrings of desire as he imagines the night ahead.

Adrian, standing behind them, still holding the suitcase, is about to excuse himself and depart when Withers speaks.

'The Squire's Bedchamber was the *frater* of the original Cistercian monastery before the Carthusians took over the Abbey and adapted it to their needs. Since they took their meals in their cells they had no need for a communal dining room. So it became the Abbot's cell with a serving hatch worked into the wall next to the door so meals could be delivered by an unseen hand. And that, sir, was how I served your great uncle, Sir Horace, in his final years.'

No one interrupts. Withers continues in an even more solemn tone.

'This was where Sir Horace expired. I found his body lying here. He was trying to reach the door.'

Withers points with great precision to a spot on the floor, evidently at great pains to be accurate about it, as if it matters very much that they should know exactly where the old squire breathed his last.

Ophelia can contain her anxieties no longer.

'Gervase, do we really have to sleep here? In a draughty old Cistercian refectory? Besides, it might be haunted by Sir Horace.'

Gervase says nothing.

'Surely there is somewhere else, Withers?'

'Ever since 1536, madam, when your husband's forbears converted Farthing Abbey into the family seat of the Lloyd-Beauchamps, this has been the Squire's Bedchamber. There is no other.'

Gervase grins. Even the house seems to be on his side. He reckons at last he's got his wife where he wants her. He doesn't see how she can get out of this.

'Well, the squire is welcome to his bedchamber. For myself I would prefer something less ... less oppressive. Surely, there must be a more comfortable room? In the Palladian Villa perhaps?'

'Madam, there are only four guest rooms in the Palladian Villa and they are all occupied.'

'What about the other apartments?'

'As you will shortly see for yourself, madam, the *piano nobile* of the Palladian Villa was not designed for occupation. So it possesses no domestic facilities of its own. The *garderobe* and other household amenities are all located here in the old part of Farthing Abbey. You will find it more suitable here, madam. I assure you.'

'Does that mean that our guests will have to come all the way over here even to wash their hands?'

'No madam. I have provided each guest with a basin and a jug of water.'

Ophelia falls silent. This gives Adrian the chance to make his excuses. He coughs. Gervase and Ophelia turn round surprised to find him still there. They have completely forgotten his presence.

'Well, here is your suitcase. I'll be off now.'

Withers re-assumes his butler's role.

'Permit me to show you out through the slype, sir. You will find it more convenient to return to the Palladian Villa through the garden. Now, sir and madam, if you please, I will also acquaint you with the general layout.'

They all follow Withers back down the stone steps to the Cloister Garth and on through a narrow passage with a door at the end. Withers pulls it open. Bright sunshine floods in. The medieval gloom does not entirely vanish, however, but withdraws to the remoter recesses of the building where it lurks in dark pockets, biding its time.

'Mrs Lard will serve tea on the terrace in one half of an hour, sir.'

'Thank you, Withers. Thank you.'

Adrian is hugely relieved to be off. As he takes his leave, Ophelia looks a shade paler than before. Briefly, their eyes meet.

'Thank you for your kindness, Mr Lenshood.'

'My pleasure, Mrs Lloyd-Beauchamp. It is my pleasure, I do assure you.'

Once outside, Adrian breathes deep, happy to be in the fresh air, free as a bird to come and go as he will. What was it about the Squire's Bedchamber that makes him now feel like a prisoner emerging from a dungeon? There was a grim mood about the place, the ancient stones dictating their agenda, making people beholden to house, rather than the other way round. Had he detected in Ophelia's parting look a flash of panic, as if that same awareness had dawned on her also?

Still savouring his deliverance, Adrian casts a practised photographer's eye along the south front of Farthing Abbey. Approvingly, he notes the absence of any intrusive elements of the modern age. Such period authenticity is very rare. Then, unintentionally, he falls to speculating about the exact location of the Squire's Bedchamber. He has soon located the window. He reckons Ophelia could make her escape by climbing down the ivy. He would be waiting below in the shadows ready to take her in his arms.

Suddenly, he checks himself. What is he thinking of? Is he seriously planning to carry off the lady of the house? Gervase looks like an absolute brute, definitely not a man to mess with. Adrian seeks to laugh it all off, but he remains uneasy. A highly dangerous thought has already lodged itself in his mind.

As he turns the corner he studies the angle of the shadows and calculates it will not be long before the sun's warming rays cease to shine in through the windows of the Squire's Bedchamber. Inside, it would soon be as cold as a tomb. He shivers at the idea. Why is he thinking such thoughts? What is it to him?

Nor can he understand the logic of the route Withers made them take. It hardly made sense for the noble occupants of Farthing Abbey to usher their equally noble guests through a dark, secret staircase in the library. Unless it was considered part of the fun to disappear through a Georgian bookcase and to emerge within the twinkling of an eye like time-travellers in a perfect Gothic cloister.

Adrian now focuses his attention on the Palladian Villa itself. But he is distracted by the sight of a portly lady arranging cups and saucers on a trestle table. That must be Mrs Lard, about to serve tea on the terrace. He walks over and climbs the short flight of stone steps. The lady is polishing the already shining chrome of a tea urn.

'Good afternoon. Mrs Lard, I presume?'

At this she gyrates slowly, for her days of spinning round smartly are long behind her. She fixes Adrian in a bovine gaze, both unseeing and intense, although not without a dose of alarm. Mrs Lard is not accustomed to being addressed by strangers, let alone by strangers who know her name.

'That's as may be.'

'Withers said you are about to serve tea?'

'About to serve tea in about fifteen minutes.'

Mrs Lard leaves him in absolutely no doubt of her eagerness to see the back of him.

'Right you are, Mrs Lard. I'll see you later.'

Once again Adrian feels a sensation of release. He continues his slow circuit round the house. He turns another corner to arrive back at the Greek Revival west front. He pauses to look at a flowerbed. As he sizes up the blooms for a possible photograph, he spots a bumblebee rolling its furry body inside a giant poppy. He notes the blackness of the pollen that soon covers the bee until its stripes are obscured like a miner in coal dust. The bee flies off, its place soon taken by another that dives right into the poppy.

Like a voluptuary blind to all but its own desires, the insect nuzzles deep into the flesh-red heart of the flower. The sheer abandon of the bee's total immersion in the petals holds him spellbound. Adrian stares into the intensely red flower as into a sensual vortex down which he now wants to plunge, never to surface again. Suddenly, he yearns to trade places with the bee. Even if it were to mean living for just one season, at least it would be a life lived to the full with no regrets and no missed opportunities. He trembles with excitement. He has picked up the scent of something precious.

Adrian scans all around him with a new appetite. There is a thrillingly sharp edge to everything. He hasn't felt so keenly alive before. His eyes take in every detail. Nothing escapes his attention. Half hidden behind some weeds in a flowerbed, he spots a piece of paper. It looks like a pen-and-ink sketch in the elegant style of a previous age. He can clearly make out the soulful eyes of a young woman gazing directly at him through the verdant undergrowth. She seems familiar.

As Adrian bends down to retrieve the drawing, the thorn of a rose stem pierces his thumb. He smartly withdraws his hand and stands up. He watches a bright red bead slowly form on his white skin. He sucks at the wound, relishing the taste of blood. Suddenly he senses a powerful surge of sexual desire. What is going on? But it doesn't last long. A few seconds later, he recalls the drawing that was the cause of his accident. He searches the flowerbed thoroughly. But there is no sign of the piece of paper. It has vanished without a trace.

Peregrine Gargoyle emerges from the Palladian Villa, poised to descend the stair. On seeing Adrian he stops and hails him from his superior vantage point.

'Ah, there you are, Lenshood. Everything OK'

Adrian decides to say nothing of the mysterious drawing, nor of his wounded thumb.

'Yes. Fine. Absolutely fine. Just wait until you see the old part of the house.'

'Well, let us hope it is more impressive than this grotesque Greek front slapped on a fairly decent Palladian façade. Doric demi-columns, if you please! It doesn't bear looking at. I can't think any self-respecting architect could have designed such a thing.'

Gargoyle now adopts a softer tone of voice.

'You didn't happen to find out the location of the facilities in the course of your travels? Not for myself, but the others were anxious to know.'

'You won't find anything in the Palladian Villa. According to Withers, not a water pipe in the place. The bathrooms are all in the old house.'

On receiving this piece of intelligence, Gargoyle beams. His highly educated guess, though rashly offered, was unerringly accurate.

'You are quite sure about that, Lenshood?'

'Oh, yes. Withers was emphatic. But I didn't find out where exactly in the old house. All I can tell you is the only internal access is through a hidden door behind a bookcase in the library and down a spiral staircase. You can always ask Mrs Lard. That's the lady serving tea on the terrace. She looks very knowledgeable.'

Adrian withdraws into the house, while Gargoyle makes his way to the terrace where he actually succeeds in enticing a cup of tea from Mrs Lard. He becomes more favourably disposed to Farthing Abbey, or at least to the Palladian Villa thereof, after discovering the comely Venetian door forming a seductive feature right in the middle of this façade.

Amid the ensuing *mêlée* of renewed introductions and social niceties Araminta Fettiplace is in her element, conducting a conversation with one half of her mouth, while the other half makes short work of a cucumber sandwich. She shakes off Burp who plants himself by Gargoyle and Gervase, where he stands awkwardly like a spare part ignored by the others. His studiedly casual posture suggests an amateur private detective at a garden party trying to pose as one of the guests.

Ophelia hovers on the fringes of the gathering. She is regaining her composure, but the imminent prospect of being trapped all night with Gervase in the four-poster fills her with anguish. Adrian sees his chance and joins her on the terrace.

'Quite a place you have here, Mrs Lloyd-Beauchamp. It has a very special atmosphere.'

'Do you think so? It has come as a bit of a shock, I mean a surprise, finding myself in the role of *châtelaine*. It will take some getting used to. The landed gentry is really much more Gervase's thing.'

He gives her a lingering look of interrogation.

'Do help yourself to a cup of tea, Mr Lenshood.'

'Can I fetch one for you?'

Ophelia does not respond to this offer.

She has been distracted by the approach of two individuals heading towards the house at considerable speed. Setting the pace is a stout woman, wearing heavy tweeds in spite of the heat and shod in stout brogues of polished leather. With her right hand she clutches the leads of four red setters who pull her along like a charioteer in full flight. She reminds Gargoyle, who is also tracking her progress, of the *Quadriga* statue on top of the Constitution Arch at Hyde Park Corner.

Some way behind and pedalling furiously on an ancient black bicycle follows a venerable personage of saintly aspect with sparse strands of long white hair trailing behind him. He wears a Panama hat, crumpled linen jacket and black trousers tucked neatly inside his socks. The starched white collar encircling his neck above a grey cotton bib announces from some distance that this is the vicar coming to call.

ATTIC SPLENDOUR

The final approach of the lady with the four dogs and the vicar on the bicycle has all the intensity of a fiercely contested race, one which the clergyman unexpectedly wins by a short head. This gives him priority to speak, for having dismounted from his velocipede, he addresses the party of tea drinkers assembled on the terrace.

'Good afternoon, ladies and gentlemen. Permit me to introduce myself. Parsnip. As in Reverend Inigo Parsnip. My parishioners call me RIP. Not on account of my funeral services and graveside homilies, but for my Sunday sermons, which do have a soporific effect. Indeed, before you can say parsnips, my entire congregation has usually passed out in their pews. Not that we have much of a congregation nowadays. Still, we are a brave little flock continuing the faithful tradition of Christian worship on this spot for well over a thousand years.'

Reverend Inigo Parsnip waves his dented Panama hat to fan himself.

'Did you know we have a complete list of rectors going back to before the Norman Conquest? Do excuse me. There I go again, wittering on. And I haven't yet come to the point of my visit. When my good wife was alive, God rest her soul, she would edit me down to a proper length. But without her to keep an eye on the clock I just run and run and there's no one to stop me.'

The clergyman pauses to mop his brow with a handkerchief.

'Now this fine lady, and please forgive me for not introducing her straight away, is Mrs Beatrice Worthington, Church Warden, Chair of the Parish Council, Secretary of the Women's Institute and Hon Treasurer of the Castle Farthing Horticultural Society. In short, a pillar of our community, a person to inspire us all as we go about our daily tasks which, however humble, are all equal in the eyes of the Lord. Oh dear, there I go again. Mrs Worthington, perhaps you would kindly take over?'

Reverend Inigo Parsnip steps aside like a music hall compère to concede the stage to Mrs Beatrice Worthington who quickly imposes her presence with a mere turn of the head. The four red setters group themselves obediently at her feet, as eternally watchful as Landseer's lions at the base of Nelson's Column in Trafalgar Square.

'As the Reverend Parsnip was saying. Or rather, was about to say, I should say. We were in the churchyard and we couldn't help noticing the comings and goings up here at the Abbey. Of course, we have all been on tenterhooks since the death of Sir Horace...'

'God rest his soul.'

'Amen, Reverend Parsnip, quite so. Since that sad day we have been praying that a successor would be found. Now we can hardly wait any longer to make the acquaintance of the new master of Farthing Abbey. In short, we have come to pay our humble respects.'

Gervase steps forward, beaming from ear to ear. This is just the ticket, exactly what is needed to set the perfect seal on his inheritance: the holy blessing of the established church, the loyal greetings of the parish. Bring them on. The more the merrier.

'Then you need wait no longer, my good lady. Your prayers have been answered. The lord of the manor is at hand. He walks among you. It is I. I am he. Gervase Lloyd-Beauchamp. At your service. Reverend Parsnip, Mrs Worthington, you are most heartily welcome. Please take a cup of tea on the terrace. Then do join us for a tour of the house. You must stay for dinner, of course. The Lloyd-Beauchamps were always great supporters of the Church.'

Mrs Worthington ties her dogs to the balustrade. Reverend Parsnip skips up the stairs with unexpected nimbleness of foot, light as a communion wafer. With a gracious smile flickering across his cracked parchment of a face, he accepts a cup of lukewarm tea from Mrs Lard who shows him more respect, Adrian notes, than he had been accorded a moment previously.

Gargoyle is glad for this strengthening of the ranks of the serious minded. Ophelia also cheers up in the hope that the presence of these upright folk might have a restraining influence on Gervase later on when he will undoubtedly be the worse for wear.

'You can see our little church over yonder among the trees, near the end of the Scenic Lake.'

Gargoyle's keen eye has already spotted the pinnacles of the church tower. It looks like one of those Gothic follies you find in many a landscape park.

'So what happened to the village? Was it wiped out by the Black Death and rebuilt elsewhere?'

The clergyman swallows a delicate morsel of cucumber sandwich and sips at his tea as daintily as a pied wagtail drinking raindrops from a buttercup.

'With your permission Mr Lloyd-Beauchamp, I shall have to evoke the memory of your ancestor Sir Archibald[1], who built the Palladian Villa. In his day, the village, actually no more than a hamlet, was located right in front of the house. It disturbed him greatly to look out at the mean hovels and their ragged occupants. It was not sufficiently scenic. So one day, he had it all removed, lock, stock and barrel, in order to create the Landscape Park. Only the church remained. For Sir Archibald couldn't touch that. In any case, it made a pleasantly picturesque eye-catcher, as you may see for yourselves.'

'And the village?'

'It was relocated half a mile away. Sir Archibald had two rows of identical cottages built along the main road by the main entrance of the estate. There is a right of way from there to the church, but the footpath can be treacherous in bad weather. The church is really too

---

[1] Sir Archibald Lloyd-Beauchamp (1694-1753)

far from the village, and that poses a problem for some of the infirm among the older folk.'

As this familiar tale of rural England unfolds, the eyes of the audience turn away from Reverend Parsnip to Gervase. Nothing is said, but there is a cooling of the atmosphere. An accusation hangs in the air, implicit in the silence which now ensues.

'I'm not responsible for the ancestors, am I?

'Indeed not, Mr Lloyd-Beauchamp. And let us hope and pray that the sunshine of your good presence will dispel the bad memories which have been casting a gloom over Farthing Abbey for far too long.'

Araminta Fettiplace pricks up her novelist's ears at this reference to Farthing Abbey's chequered past. Before she can enquire, Gargoyle intervenes again.

'Most interesting, Reverend Parsnip, but we must be fair to Sir Archibald. The English landscape garden is one of the jewels of our national heritage. And the new villages, built at the expense of the landowner, were invariably of a higher standard than the wretched hovels they replaced. It was, I think I may safely conclude, a happy union of culture and progress.'

'Well spoken, Gargoyle. We landowners have always taken our social responsibilities extremely seriously. So let's leave it at that, ladies and gentlemen,, Withers will now conduct us through the apartments of the Palladian Villa. But if Mr Gargoyle would care to add any comments, that would be most welcome.'

Gargoyle sighs. All is redeemed. His timely grovel has banished all memory of his earlier gaffe.

'Carry on Withers.'

'Very well, sir. We shall enter by the west front, which is the principal way by which it is intended for the house to be approached.'

'Why can't he just say we are going in by the front door?'

Burp's question elicits no response from Mrs Beatrice Worthington who is standing right next to him. He tries another gambit.

'What this patio really needs is a few tubs of geraniums to brighten the place up, don't you think, Mrs Worthington?'

'It is hardly a patio, you know, Mr…?'

'Burp.'

'I beg your pardon.'

'That's quite all right, Mrs Worthington. George Burp, at your service.'

He isn't sure why he added the last remark, for he has no intention of placing himself at the service of Mrs Worthington or anyone else for that matter. But the lady is nobody's fool. She has already decided George Burp is best given a wide berth.

Withers now addresses the company in a ceremonial tone that succeeds in sounding funereal rather than dramatic.

'The Rococo Vestibule.'

There ensues such a long pause, it seems the butler has lost the script.

'Is that all, Withers? Can't you tell us a bit more?'

Before Withers can respond, Gervase cuts in.

'Well, what do you think Gargoyle? Rather splendid, what?'

'Thank you, Mr Lloyd-Beauchamp. Firstly, for those not conversant with the language of art history, Rococo is derived from the French ...'

'Keep it simple, Gargoyle. Just tell us if it's any damn good or not.'

Gervase has made Gargoyle feel more like an estate agent come to do a valuation than an architectural pundit condescending to deliver weighty and profound aesthetic judgement.

'Well, I haven't had a chance to inspect it closely, but it does seem to be fairly respectable workmanship.'

Gargoyle is no fan of Rococo. He regards it as cheap, flashy and more than a bit suggestive of ladies frilly underwear. He tries to think of a diplomatic way of putting it when Ophelia intervenes.

'Don't put Mr Gargoyle under such pressure, Gervase. Do give him space to consider his views.'

'Thank you Mrs Lloyd-Beauchamp. No matter. I was only going to remark that it is a good example of Rococo plasterwork, although ...'

Gargoyle is again cut short, this time by Withers who opens a door leading off the Rococo Vestibule.

'The Greek Room.'

This is more Gargoyle's line of country. Even before he has seen it, he knows he will describe it as 'a vision of Attic splendour'. He generally does when describing things Greek to a popular audience. It always goes down well and should impress his patron.

They enter a resoundingly neo-Grecian interior with caryatids flanking the doors. A panoramic Aegean seascape is painted on the walls, artfully framed by a *trompe-l'oeil* colonnade suggesting the illusion of a real prospect from the sunny portico of a temple across a harbour to a romantic view of the Greek islands. But on closer inspection Gargoyle finds it overblown, the colours garish, altogether far too grandiose.

Gervase, however, is much taken by it, to judge from the excited way he inspects the mural. He is particularly smitten by two maidens shown naked but for a diaphanous veil of a garment. They enfold one another in a tender, more than sisterly embrace as they watch a galley putting out to sea.

'Well, Gargoyle, how about this eh? Pretty impressive, what?'

'I really can't find words to describe it, Mr Lloyd-Beauchamp. It's ...'

'Yes?'

'It's highly imaginative.'

'Highly imaginative? I hope you'll come up with something better than that for my guidebook.'

This is the first mention of the writing commission. Gargoyle comes over all shy, as if an intimate secret has been made public.

'Gervase, you must give poor Mr Gargoyle a chance. He is a scholar and doesn't deliver off the cuff commentaries.'

Gargoyle is grateful for this but resents being referred to as 'poor Mr Gargoyle'. He consoles himself with the thought that whoever painted the mural in the Greek Room meets his principal criterion for approval. The artist is well and truly dead. Even so, Gargoyle resolves to hint at the flaws and inadequacies of the work. But he has got no further than clearing his throat when he hears the sombre voice of Withers.

'It was painted by young Lawrence, sir. Later Sir Lawrence Alma-Tadema. Charming lad. Done during the summer holidays when he was staying with us.'

Gargoyle's mouth drops open. Withers is old, very old. But old enough to have met Sir Lawrence Alma-Tadema? No, completely out of the question. He can't recall the exact dates of this highly acclaimed Victorian painter of exotic scenes, but he reckons it a chronological impossibility for him to have crossed paths with Withers. Except perhaps in extreme old age just as the infant butler was emerging from the womb? Confused by the mental arithmetic involved, Gargoyle plays his cards warily.

'If it is an early, indeed a juvenile Alma-Tadema, then we may see in it the seeds of his later genius. Already, we have the Classical setting, the grand architectural scale and the ... er ... feminine elements.'

Feminine elements. This is vintage Gargoyle. Adrian, familiar with his turn of phrase, chuckles to himself while Burp whispers loudly in his ear.

'One of Gargoyle's feminine elements has a right handsome pair of knockers. Reminds me of a barmaid in *Ye Jolly Yeomen.*'

Beatrice Worthington directs a look of censure on George Burp. Meanwhile, Gargoyle quizzes Withers.

'By the young Alma-Tadema you say? And you were here at the time? What year might that have been? That is, if you can recall?'

'What year, sir?'

'Yes, the year, Withers. When the Greek Room was painted. What year would that have been? I am sure we would all be most interested to know just how far back in time your memories extend.'

'Ah, time, sir. Most elusive and always such a slippery customer is time.'

Withers slips off the hook. Gargoyle has heard enough to conclude that the butler has gone soft in the head. Nor is he the only one in that category. Reverend Parsnip now emerges from a distant daydream. His reed-like voice comes from a long way off.

'Time. Ah, yes. Time like an ever rolling stream bears all its sons away. They die forgotten as a dream ...'

Reverend Parsnip's recitation hangs unfinished in the air, for Withers has spoken again.

'The Italianate Room.'

Italianate. Gargoyle detests the word denoting a vague hybrid of Roman and Renaissance. For Gargoyle hates vagueness as much as he despises hybrids.

Withers stands just inside the door, waiting patiently for the party to file through. Gargoyle prepares a cool critical look, just to let this bizarre butler know he has been rumbled, at least by this architectural sleuth *par excellence*. The young Alma-Tadema indeed! Who does he take me for? Gargoyle flashes a beady eye as he strides by, barely suppressing the desire to make an acidic comment. But actually it is Withers who speaks.

'The year was 1851, sir.'

Gargoyle arches his eyebrows.

'1851?'

'Yes, sir. You were asking about the year when we had young Lawrence staying with us. It took me a while to recall it exactly. It was 1851. He must have been fifteen at the time. Yes, I am quite sure it was 1851. The talk was all of some great exhibition or other happening up in London. We had a long hot summer here at Farthing Abbey. The Scenic Lake almost dried up. It was most alarming. Most alarming indeed.'

UNCANNY RESEMBLANCES

Withers has more architectural surprises in store for Peregrine Gargoyle.

'Sir Archibald returned from his Grand Tour of 1719 having made the acquaintance of a motley crew of artists. Among them figured a certain Mr William Kent. It was he who designed and painted the interior of the Italianate Room.'

The walls and ceiling of the Italianate Room present the onlookers with an arcaded gallery where gentlefolk in rich Renaissance costumes pose and parade their finery. They look so real they might actually be other visitors like themselves. But as with everything else in the room they are no more than a masterful act of artistic deception.

'Well, Gargoyle. I can see you're impressed. Say something, man. For heaven's sake, let's hear it.'

Gargoyle looks at Gervase, then suspiciously at Withers. Desperately he tries once again to recall names and dates.

'Truly remarkable, Mr Lloyd-Beauchamp. This must be an early *pièce de résistance*. If it is indeed the work of William Kent.'

'What do you mean, 'if'? Withers has been living here long enough to know what's what, eh Withers?'

Like a shark that has been circling for some time, Gargoyle senses the right moment to strike.

'That remains to be seen. Now consider this, Withers, if you please. As far as I recall, William Kent was the *protégé* of Richard Boyle, third Earl of Burlington. Not of Sir Archibald Lloyd-Beauchamp. So he would have been busy at the time up in London, working on Chiswick House for example. And his work at Kensington Palace must have been fairly time-consuming too. So I wonder how he managed to fit in Farthing Abbey on top of all that. Any ideas, Withers?'

Gargoyle fixes the butler in a cold stare and waits. Surely, he has the old fraud neatly pegged in a corner. But Withers appears unruffled. His expression even brightens a shade as he replies.

'Pardon me, Mr Gargoyle, sir. I hadn't realised that you were also well acquainted with Mr Kent. I'm sure you will agree he was a gentleman of a rare and penetrating intelligence, once you could understand that Yorkshire accent of his. Sir Archibald it was who discovered Mr Kent one fine morning in the *Piazza Navona* in Rome and later effected the introduction to Lord Burlington in whose entourage he was travelling.'

Gargoyle hops about like a boxer whose KO punch has been deflected and who now seeks another opening. But it is Withers who lands a deft uppercut to Gargoyle's dangerously exposed, dangling jaw.

'Were you by any chance on that particular Grand Tour, sir?'

Gargoyle stands there, utterly speechless. Here is a deranged old butler asking him if he was in Italy with

Lord Burlington in 1719! What is more, Withers takes Gargoyle's involuntary silence for a yes.

'Well, you were extremely fortunate, sir. The 1719 was the one they always recalled as the very best of all. That is why they stayed in touch for so long afterwards. On account of all the happy memories. And to answer your question, Lord Burlington would often give Sir Archibald the loan of his dear Mr Kent to work at Farthing Abbey whenever he could be spared from more pressing projects in London.'

The longer Withers rambles on, the more Gargoyle's head spins. His normally earthbound mind goes into orbit with wild speculations. Setting aside for a moment the age of the deluded butler, who must now be getting on for 300 years if he had actually witnessed the building of the Palladian Villa, there is still the separate question of those other facts of which he spoke with such authority. If the Italianate Room were really the work of William Kent, then it would redound immeasurably to the credit of one Peregrine Gargoyle if he were the scholar to discover it and write it up.

A vision of awesome splendour now shimmers before him. Farthing Abbey could offer so much more than a run-of-the-mill feature in *Houses and Castles* or the text of the official guidebook. It would be nothing less than that full-blown volume of architectural erudition on which he had set his sights all those years ago. But first he must obtain hard evidence, factual rather than anecdotal. In this business, accuracy is always paramount. One small mistake and a very hard-earned professional reputation could be tarnished forever. One can never be too careful.

So Gargoyle decides not to reveal his hand yet awhile. First he must win the confidence of the eccentric butler and find out what other tasty morsels are to be dished up. There is a coating of honey on his hitherto acerbic tongue when he finally regains the power of speech.

'Most intriguing, Withers. You do have a most original way of presenting the history of the house.'

'Thank you, sir.'

Sensing she is being outflanked by a rival writer, albeit one from an entirely different genre, Araminta Fettiplace decides that now is the time to throw her authorial hat into the ring.

'I have been here for less than a twinkling of an eye but already I feel Farthing Abbey struggling to communicate to me across the centuries. There is a romantic novel just waiting, no demanding to be written. My artistic instincts tell me there is so much more here than architectural detail. I sense a dramatic tale of fiery passion and dark deeds.'

Araminta Fettiplace steps forward and reaches out to touch Withers like a teacher laying claim to a prize pupil. The butler makes no move. The lady's hand on his arm might have been a mere tea towel.

'You and I must find time for a good long chat, Withers. So you can tell me all you know about this truly fascinating house. And we too must have a little talk, Mr Lloyd-Beauchamp. How very astute of you to invite me to Farthing Abbey. If anyone can be inspired by the spirit of the past, it is Araminta Fettiplace.'

Gervase responds with enthusiasm.

'That sounds more like it, I must say.'

Gargoyle clenches his fists. His noble project, unborn as yet, is being upstaged by a self-promoting authoress of tawdry novelettes. How typical of the modern age to prefer a silly made-up story over a serious piece of well-researched non-fiction. Well, let her steal the limelight. He will work in the shadows. Time will tell who emerges triumphant at the end.

They are about to leave the Italianate Room when George Burp draws their attention to a cleverly painted figure in the arcade. It gives a three-dimensional impression of a man clad in breastplate and skirt wearing the crested helm of a Roman centurion.

'Just look at this chap in Roman gear. A dead ringer for Mr Lloyd-Beauchamp, don't you reckon? An uncanny resemblance, I'd say.'

The company gathers round to judge the matter. They look to Withers for an explanation.

'That was one of Mr Kent's little jokes. Sir Archibald unwittingly served as model for this figure. It was intended as a surprise to amuse his patron. The resemblance to Mr Gervase Lloyd-Beauchamp is, as you say, quite uncanny. They might be brothers, or identical twins, the same person even.'

Burp considers his stock much improved as a result of this timely act of observation. Let the likes of Peregrine Gargoyle and Araminta Fettiplace concern themselves with all that airy-fairy stuff. Good old George Burp would always be there to point to the obvious thing being overlooked by the experts. He stands proudly next to the image of Sir Archibald in the guise of Roman centurion, as if he were the artist showing off his work to the others crowded around.

'An incredible resemblance. Very well spotted, George.'

George? Has he heard correctly? Burp basks in the sweet sound of Araminta Fettiplace calling him by his first name.

'Happy to oblige, Araminta.'

Gervase is deeply gratified. This proves he is the rightful heir to Farthing Abbey, of the same kith and kin as the man who built the Palladian Villa. The true blood of the Lloyd-Beauchamps pulses in his veins. He is wrought and fashioned of the same genetic material, directly descended from the one true ancient lineage.

Gervase thanks Burp for discovering his striking resemblance to Sir Archibald by elbowing him brusquely out of the way in order to get a closer look at his own dear image. He then casts about for Ophelia, anxious to impress on her this indisputable proof of his noble pedigree, and the purity of the biological pool in which he had been spawned. But his wife has followed Withers to the next room.

'The Antique Gallery, also known as the Library.'

With the shutters open, Adrian finds it hard to believe this is the same room where he had stood in the dark just behind Ophelia and inhaled her womanly perfume. Now he turns and there she is right beside him. Their eyes meet briefly before she hurriedly looks away. She seems less real in the daylight, somehow lacking in material substance. Although present in the flesh, Ophelia is strangely absent in spirit, as if she were a reluctant resident in her own body.

Withers holds forth once more.

'Young Robert Adam came to stay in 1744. He was barely sixteen but already he showed the keenest interest in matters decorative. Sir Archibald suggested he do some sketches for the Antique Gallery. Really just to keep the boy amused. But the designs turned out to be first rate, as you can judge for yourselves.'

Gargoyle gasps as he surveys the Antique Gallery. He reads at a glance the graceful decor sweeping along walls, doors, ceiling, bookcases and marble chimney piece all cleverly orchestrated within a grand design. Although boyish in its exuberance, it sings out with the true genius which made the Adam Style so fashionable during the 1760s and 1770s. But if this hitherto unknown example really dated back to 1744, it would be a sensational find. His dreams of glory take wing.

Gargoyle is now confused as well as excited. If he were to follow his instinct and continue to challenge Withers on his incredible longevity then the source of all this information might dry up. On the other hand, he must be sure he is not the victim of some elaborate hoax. In the end, he elects for a cunning compromise.

'I am afraid my own memories don't extend as far back as 1744, Withers. But I assume you do have documentary evidence of dates, names and so on. I will need access to all the papers when I prepare my own account for the official guidebook.'

With these words he has also grabbed the writing commission.

'Indeed, yes, Mr Gargoyle. I have done my best to be meticulous as custodian of the Farthing Abbey records. I trust you will find everything in good order. All the papers are kept securely under lock and key in the Archive Room which is situated between yours and Mr Lenshood's.'

Archive Room? This is more than he could ever hope for. Gargoyle has visions of a gold mine awaiting his prospector's shovel. He is about to make a further enquiry, just to make sure he has heard correctly, but George Burp breaks in with news of yet another amazing discovery.

'Good lord, just take a look at this! Here he is again. Sir Archibald. Or should I say Mr Gervase Lloyd-Beauchamp?'

Burp points to a painting over the chimney-piece. In this Sir Archibald wears the attire of an eighteenth century country landowner. He stands languidly, fowling piece under one arm. The other rests on a garden bench on which there sits a lady, presumably his wife. The rest of the canvas is filled with a pastoral English scene. The landscape guides the eye through a ripe cornfield to a noble country house: the

Palladian Villa at Farthing Abbey. Picturesque in the middle distance, on the shore of the Scenic Lake, a circular classical temple coyly beckons.

'Ah those were the days! Roses in the garden, wine in the cellar, fresh linen in the cupboards, golden corn in the fields, and temples of delight arising in the park before our very eyes!'

'Yes, thank you Withers. Very poetic. I must say I do look rather splendid in this one, don't you think? I mean Sir Archibald, of course. And the wife too. Though she doesn't look at all like you, Ophelia.'

They examine the picture. It is indeed Gervase who smugly gazes forth from the canvas, the cocky squire who owns all that is shown in the painting, from the great house in the background right down to the small dog at his feet. But what about the lady at his side? Ophelia inspects the woman seated on the bench, wondering how she fared as the wife of this Gervase of the Georgian age. The prim demeanour of Sir Archibald's tight-lipped spouse gives nothing away.

'Permit me to hazard a guess, Withers. I imagine you are about to inform us that this canvas is an early Gainsborough?'

The mocking edge to Gargoyle's voice goes unnoticed by Withers.

'Precisely so, sir. Just as you say. Mr Thomas Gainsborough really captured the mood of those days, the very spirit of the age, don't you think?'

Once again Gargoyle is lost for words. But none are needed. Gervase has gone on ahead. He strides off purposefully down the Antique Gallery. He glances briefly *en passant* at the marble busts of emperors and philosophers set on pedestals. He marches briskly along as if reviewing a tiresome parade of retainers lined up to receive his blessing. As he reaches the far end, he turns to face the others advancing at the more sedate pace dictated by Withers.

'Rather fun all this, what?'

Gervase is enjoying himself hugely, a little boy opening Christmas presents so much better and more plentiful than he could possibly have imagined. He feels alive, vibrant, aroused. His flesh tingles. Farthing Abbey is in his bones. He is a plant finally returned to its native soil. Here he will take root, flower and bring forth seed. Yes, that's it, he will breed. By Christ and all the saints, he will breed.

Gervase catches the eye of Reverend Inigo Parsnip smiling at him in a knowing manner. He is about to apologise for the blasphemy just committed when he realises it is not strictly necessary to excuse himself for an unspoken thought.

'Well, Vicar. I trust all this is not too secular for your taste. Come on, Withers, look lively! What's next? What's next?'

EXOTIC DELIGHTS

A double door opens on a rich interior lined with blue and white glazed tiles, topped by a frieze of mosaics which add an exotic glimmer of gold and green. In the middle of the room hangs a solitary bronze lantern with an Arabic inscription.

'The Arab Room, sir.'

Gargoyle enters with suspicion. In truth, his aesthetic horizons extend no further east than Greece. This oriental sort of thing is a tad too exotic for his taste. Perhaps for a smallish pavilion in a park by way of a folly it was all very well. But to bring something so outlandishly alien into an English country house goes against the cultural grain. He feels as comfortable as a Methodist minister who has strayed into a sultan's seraglio. So Gargoyle is more than happy to allow Withers to say his piece without further interruption.

'The Arab Room was the creation of the explorer and orientalist Sir Reginald Lloyd-Beauchamp[2]. The tiles are originals purchased on his travels in Isfahan, Damascus and Baghdad. But the overall design was the brainchild of the renowned painter and sculptor Lord Leighton, which he devised in 1875, a full two years before installing an Arab Hall at his own residence of Leighton House in Kensington.'

---

[2] Sir Reginald Lloyd-Beauchamp (1832-91).

The penny finally drops for Gargoyle. Everything in the Palladian Villa is a prototype by a famous architect, painter or designer for work of national importance subsequently completed elsewhere. Farthing Abbey must have served as a veritable nursery for some prodigious talents. Each of the rooms is enough on its own for a lengthy feature in *Houses and Castles*, a learned monograph in some academic journal or even a doctoral thesis for an aspiring academic. But taken together, Farthing Abbey amounts to something absolutely priceless: the architectural equivalent to the tomb of Tutankhamun. Gargoyle's ambitions are now racing ahead. There would be a series of documentary TV films. In these, Peregrine Gargoyle, aesthete and connoisseur, will dispense wit and wisdom as he glides serenely through the apartments, evoking the memory of the persons of uncommon refinement who once trod these halls.

He will discourse with mellow learning on Rules of Taste, bounce elegant epigrams off the walls, with the camera tracking his every move and gesture. He will impress the *cognoscenti* with the depth of his knowledge while bearing the torch of high culture into the hovels of the *Lumpenproletariat*. He will pronounce the sacred words of Art, Truth, Beauty with a resonance befitting the capital letters which graced them in that golden age when these things still mattered so much. Gargoyle's heart is aflutter, born aloft by a chorus of cherubs. But his cautious nature is not to be denied. How has Farthing Abbey conspired to keep its secrets for so long? Suddenly, he is brought back to earth by the imperious tones of Gervase Lloyd-Beauchamp.

'Well, Gargoyle? Come on, man. Don't be shy. Let's have it. What do you think of the Arab Room?'

Not even Gervase's disrespectful manner can hurt him now. Gargoyle is in seventh heaven. To his surprise, he hears his own voice speaking, as if from a long way off.

'Quite magnificent, Mr Lloyd-Beauchamp, quite magnificent! A real cabinet of exotic delights.'

'Well, if you have a taste for the exotic, Mr Gargoyle, then you will surely not be disappointed in the next and final room of the Palladian Villa: the Chinese Boudoir.'

With this, Withers ushers the party inside.

'The Chinese Boudoir was commenced in 1757, the year before Sir Archibald's death. It was a grand obsession that occupied his final days to see it completed. It was not to everyone's taste, but it did make a deep impression on Mr John Nash and even inspired him when he elaborated his own scheme for the Royal Pavilion at Brighton.'

Gargoyle, reeling at the prospect of so many rich pickings in store, can hardly absorb another fact.

'John Nash stayed here at Farthing Abbey, Withers?'

'Indeed so, sir. There is a letter written by Mr Nash himself to Sir Archibald confirming the matter.'

'A letter?'

'Yes. We keep it in the Archive Room, sir.'

So Farthing Abbey had given Nash the Chinese idea for the Royal Pavilion at Brighton, and with a letter to prove it. This is the icing on the cake. Gargoyle is no fan of *Chinoiserie*. But you don't actually need to like a thing in order to sing its praises as a splendid example of its particular genre.

Gargoyle now permits his eager eye to take in the details. Above him, a shimmering semblance of a dome made of painted shells. Porcelain figures of Chinese warriors and musicians shelter in alcoves. The door surrounds are composed of gigantic golden dragons while smaller specimens writhe along the curtain rails and cling to the pelmets. An awesome scaled monster, the undisputed dragon mother, dangles by her tail from the middle of the ceiling, holding in the bared fangs of her open jaw a sparkling chandelier.

Gargoyle decides he will describe the Chinese Boudoir as a 'veritable dragon sanctuary'. Yes, that would do nicely. In fact, he likes the phrase so much, it simply pops out of its own accord.

'A veritable dragon sanctuary you have here, Mr Lloyd-Beauchamp. My heartiest congratulations.'

There is no response from Gervase. His attention has been absorbed by the solitary piece of furniture in the Chinese Boudoir. Rampant and menacing, in the middle of the room, crouches a spectacular *chaise longue* in the shape of a muscular dragon carved in black ebony. The head of the beast is wrenched violently backwards, directing at anyone bold enough to sit on its back a pair of bulbous jade-green eyes. The darting flame of its red tongue complements the rich scarlet hue of the velvet upholstery.

Still Gervase does not speak. His gaze is quite transfixed. He is spellbound. He can't believe his eyes. The dragon sofa is identical to one in a certain house of ill repute in Kowloon which he had patronised times without number during his years in Hong Kong. He stands motionless before this object which reminds him both of the exquisite delights he had enjoyed upon its back and of the neglected wife with whom he had not shared the marital couch for so long.

A thousand thoughts now course through his mind in a confused torrent. What on earth is it doing here in Farthing Abbey? He blinks in disbelief then looks again. But still it is there, exactly as he had known it. He tries to convince himself that perhaps it is one of a pair or even one of a series and thus nothing more than a strange and uncanny coincidence for it to have turned up here.

But deep down, Gervase senses that here lurks his colourful past in the form of this grotesque *chaise longue*. He suspects the dragon sofa might have been waiting here for him all along, perhaps even before his obscene exploits on its identical counterpart in Hong Kong. But for what purpose? Surely he has paid the price? Even so, he knows in his bones that his personal destiny is somehow linked to this particular piece of furniture. He is bound to it as if by an invisible chain.

'Gervase, do you not like your Chinese Boudoir?'

Gervase snaps out of his trance. He feels the full weight of Ophelia's emphasis on 'your' rather than 'our'. The gulf between them is already widening into a chasm even as they stand there. Perhaps the dragon sofa has already begun its work.

The awkwardness of this exchange between Gervase and Ophelia is noted by Adrian, deeply absorbed by every nuance of the persona of Mrs Lloyd-Beauchamp. Araminta, meanwhile, focuses with equal sharpness on Mr Lloyd-Beauchamp. Gervase is not exactly her type. But Farthing Abbey is definitely her sort of place. And there is little she won't do when hot on the trail of a fresh plot for one of her books.

'I bet that *chaise longue* has a few tales to tell.'

Gervase does not react on the surface to Araminta's remark. But he has evidently registered it, for he gives her a swift glance of appraisal before addressing himself to everyone.

'Well, that will do, Withers. As you can see, the Palladian Villa is ... what was it you just said, Gargoyle? A delightful erotic cabinet?'

Gargoyle finds it a trifle embarrassing to correct his host. But he repeats his well-rehearsed phrase.

'Yes, it's a real cabinet of exotic delights and no mistake, Mr Lloyd-Beauchamp.'

It sounds decidedly hollow the second time round. Gargoyle is immensely relieved when Gervase changes the subject.

'How about a stroll outside? I am sure we could all use a breath of fresh air. Withers?'

'Very good, sir. The park is overgrown in places, but a satisfactory circular perambulation can be made around the Scenic Lake to the Temple of Venus. The ground should be dry underfoot.'

They reconvene on the drive with the grandiose columns of the west front behind them. Reverend Parsnip now addresses them as a kindly shepherd might talk to his flock.

'If you are amenable, I suggest we begin by making a small detour to the church. It is hardly out of your way and it would be so gratifying if Mr Lloyd-Beauchamp could visit our humble place of worship on his first day at Farthing Abbey. That would be a most auspicious act and an exceedingly good omen for the future, I am sure.'

'Fine by me, Vicar. Though I'm surprised to hear a man of the cloth speak of omens. Thought stuff like that was not on the menu.'

Reverend Inigo Parsnip gives no direct reply beyond another of his enigmatic smiles.

'Well then, let me lead you all to our wonderful church. We shall take the path through the woods. It will be cooler.'

Adrian holds back.

'If you don't mind, I'll stay behind and make a start on the pics. The light is pretty good right now. Ideal for some of the interiors.'

'Good thinking, Lenshood. But don't forget we want clear views and crisp lines. No soft focus. Nothing fanciful. Visual information before arty personal impressions, remember. The job of your photographs is to record. My words will bring the place to life.'

Gargoyle delivers these patronising instructions as if making a public announcement. The old pedant is clearly showing off to a captive audience. But the idea of Gargoyle's dusty words bringing anything to life is so preposterous it produces a wry smile on Adrian's face as he watches the party set off towards the church in the woods.

TEMPLE OF VENUS

Beatrice Worthington is delayed for a minute or so while she disentangles the knot of leather dog leads attaching her charges to the stone balustrade. Once liberated, the four red setters rapidly pull their mistress straight to the head of the straggling column of sightseers just as they enter a patch of woodland where dead and dying bluebells form a faded carpet between the beech trees.

Withers has excused himself from this small promenade, promising to meet the party at the Temple of Venus, so Gargoyle elects to walk with Reverend Parsnip. He reckons he might pick up a few useful snippets of information from the clergyman. They are followed at some distance by Gervase who has been collared by Araminta Fettiplace who deliberately slows her pace. The romantic novelist is pumping the lord of the manor for juicy morsels of family scandal, though she has already formed the opinion that he doesn't know too much about his Lloyd-Beauchamp ancestors. Gargoyle glances over his shoulder with contempt. Let her amuse herself with the froth of idle gossip, he thinks, confident that his prize will be a treasure of infinitely greater worth than any salacious tittle-tattle she might collect.

Ophelia strolls along distractedly, as if enclosed in a sealed bubble of self-containment. Her faraway look suggests she would rather not share her precious solitude with anyone at this particular moment. That leaves George Burp out on a limb to amble along behind in a semi-detached kind of mode. He takes the opportunity to light a cigarillo and enjoys a couple of puffs before discreetly passing wind.

Nonchalantly, he tosses the spent match into the undergrowth. Then, given the dryness of the weather, he thinks better of it. So he stamps about on the ground to make sure it is out. He hears a sharp crack. Looking down, he spots a vintage clay pipe with a broken stem. He stoops to pick it up and inserts an exploratory finger into the narrow bowl. Immediately, he registers an acute burning sensation and shakes his hand.

The clay pipe is sent flying. He inspects his injured finger which bears the dark traces of the tobacco embers. Who on earth could have left it there? The hot pipe must have been discarded just a moment previously. Yet it is of a type belonging to a previous century. But when he looks for it to confirm the truth of the matter, he can find no sign of the mysterious clay pipe. Suddenly, he feels alarmed. He abandons his search and hastens to join the others.

A few minutes later they emerge from the woodland into a clearing. The church now stands before them. Mrs Worthington ties the four red setters to a post by the lych-gate and is soon busy about the graveyard, dead-heading flowers and ripping up weeds. Gervase breaks off his conversation with Araminta to address the Reverend Parsnip who is contemplating the lichen-encrusted tombstones leaning this way and that.

'Well, Vicar, there must be plenty of Lloyd-Beauchamps lying here in the churchyard, enjoying the sleep of the righteous.'

The look of surprise on the clergyman's face tells Gervase that his remark is wide of the mark.

'I hardly think so. Not in the churchyard."

Gervase arches his eyebrows.

'Not that I am questioning the righteousness of your ancestors, Mr Lloyd-Beauchamp. I merely wish to inform you that they were all buried inside the church, as was invariably the case for the rich and powerful, not out here with the common folk.'

Gervase is relieved it is no more than that. He feels he must tread carefully. He realises he knows very little about his family history. But there is no time to dwell on the matter since Reverend Parsnip now resumes in a more formal tone of voice.

'Pray gather round, ladies and gentlemen. Permit me to welcome you all to the hallowed church of St Dunstan in the parish of Castle Farthing. I won't bore you with the architectural details. I am sure Mr Gargoyle can oblige in that department.'

Reverend Parsnip continues unabashed while Gargoyle blushes, unsure if the ridicule were intended or not. He is all too painfully aware of the ripple of sniggers behind him.

'Suffice it to say that St Dunstan's has everything from a Saxon arch to a Victorian lectern. But a church is so much more than its architecture. It is like unto a holy sacrament, being an outward and visible sign of an inward and invisible grace.'

They file in through the west door, framed by a series of round Norman arches covered with jagged zigzag patterns.

'Like entering the jaws of hell, I always think.'

Just inside the door, the heavy stone bowl of the font is supported on four sturdy columns, each with an impassive carved face. There is no avoiding the gaze of these stern guardians of the baptismal water.

'Delightfully pagan, isn't it? These grim-faced fellows ward off the evil spirits. The old earth magic remains present, lurking just beneath the surface veneer of our modern civilisation.'

No one speaks. Gargoyle, still smarting at the improbable idea he might be thought a bore, refrains from saying anything about the grim beakhead figures which glower down at them from the rafters.

The view east towards the altar is blocked by monumental tomb chests bearing effigies of knights in armour. Carved of finest alabaster, these proud squires point feet first towards the altar like a flotilla of ships sailing blithely down the aisle towards eternity.

'Here they are, Mr Lloyd-Beauchamp. Here are your ancestors. All awaiting Judgement Day just like the rest of us, I would imagine.'

Gervase barely registers this remark. He is hugely impressed by the magnificence of it all. His ancestors certainly knew how to make their presence felt. They have taken over every nook and cranny. Even the floor between the tomb-chests is paved with memorial brasses. Along the walls effigies lie languidly on stone shelves, as if sprawled out on the village green watching cricket. He finds it impossible not to feel cheery in the company of these laid-back Lloyd-Beauchamp squires. Their self-assured breeziness encourages Gervase to make light of this theatre of death.

'Looks like standing room only, eh?'

'Yes, indeed. The church became so full that the Mausoleum had to be built. It was modelled on the Tower of the Winds in Athens. We shall pass close by on our way to the Temple of Venus. But first, let me show you something rather special.'

Reverend Parsnip now points to a smaller effigy lying beneath one of the sumptuous tombs. They cluster round a crude, naturalistic carving of the naked cadaver of an old man with gaunt features and his skin stretched tight over the ribs.

'A *memento mori*. Rich or poor, death means both physical decomposition and spiritual transformation. It's as well to remember you can't take your body with you, don't you think?'

Gervase is in no mood to dwell on his personal mortality. Right now life holds out such promise, he cannot imagine being dead.

'Thank you very much, Reverend Parsnip. I think it is time we pressed on to the Temple of Venus.'

All are relieved to be back in the open air of the churchyard where Beatrice Worthington has finished tidying up her garden tools. She stands at the ready with her four red setters.

'The Temple of Venus? I shall lead the way.'

It does not occur to Gervase that Mrs Worthington, who now sets off at a cracking pace, really has no business offering her services as guide through the grounds of Farthing Abbey. In theory, she is only permitted to use the public footpath as far as the church. In reality, however, she knows her way about the estate as well as anyone.

Where the path crosses a broad alley, Reverend Parsnip pauses briefly and points to a Classical building.

'The Tower of the Winds, Mr Lloyd-Beauchamp. The place where your family has been buried for the past two and half centuries. The Mausoleum was built after the church was full and could take no more cadavers. Your great-uncle Sir Horace is the most recent occupant. Would you care to inspect his tomb?'

Gervase declines. So they continue along a grassy path that snakes artfully through a copse to reveal after a hundred yards or so a vista of exquisite loveliness. The silvery blue water of the Scenic Lake is fringed with reed beds swaying in the gentle breeze that takes the edge off the afternoon heat. On the far shore, Withers can be seen also advancing towards their *rendez-vous* at the Temple of Venus.

Gargoyle seizes the opportunity of getting in a few words of learned commentary, to show them all he is no bore, before that uncannily well informed butler would again steal his thunder.

'Note how the landscape opens dramatically to reveal the Temple of Venus. It may look natural, but it is actually an artificial contrivance, nothing more than a carefully planned surprise.'

George Burp scratches his head.

'I'm afraid you have lost me there Peregrine, old chap. A planned surprise might work the first time. But after that you'd know it was coming. I wouldn't be surprised if the person who planned the surprise didn't find it surprising for long.'

Gargoyle rises to the bait.

'Just so. Now what was it Horace Walpole had to say on the subject? I think I recall something about the delights that surprise the stranger soon losing their charms for the owner who only enjoys his creations when he shows them to his guests. Yes, that was it.'

Gervase takes his cue.

'Well spoken, Gargoyle. Good man. That sums it up nicely. For I intend to open this little paradise to the public, the paying public that is, so that everyone may enjoy all the planned surprises they care to. And if I cease to be surprised, that's my look out, eh?'

Gargoyle is about to continue his lecture on the English landscape garden, but Withers has unexpectedly materialised right behind him. The butler is smiling.

'Mr Gargoyle, it is indeed a pleasure to make the acquaintance of a close personal friend of Mr Horace Walpole. I clearly remember him saying something along those very lines to Sir Archibald at this precise spot. How fares the gentleman?'

Gargoyle is sorely tempted to reply that Horace Walpole is very well indeed, apart from the small matter of having been dead and buried for about two hundred years. But he can ill afford to show Withers the sharp edge of his tongue. He opts for a subtler response.

'Ah, there we go again, Withers. Taking another little trip down memory lane? But let us proceed with the business in hand. May I draw your attention to yonder bold Ionic erection?'

Gargoyle notes the silly grin not just on George Burp's face. He realises that his audience includes some base spirits not attuned to the finer nuances of his archaic turn of phrase.

Ophelia has gone on ahead. She climbs the knoll on which the Temple of Venus perches so prettily. The circular structure is surrounded by a colonnade of the Greek Ionic order. The only access is by a lofty French window, with additional light admitted via three sash windows. Through one of these she now peers in.

She sees a big motorbike, gleaming with chrome, pulled up on its stand. Then her attention falls on two naked figures on the floor. A girl lies on her back. She has a Mohican crest of blond hair died peppermint green sprouting from her shaven head. A swirling tattoo is emblazoned across the pink-white flesh of her left breast. The head of an olive-skinned young man with long black hair, rests between the girl's open legs, using the softness of her inside thigh as a pillow. The couple lie so still and lifeless they might be dead. But there is no sign of violence on their exposed bodies.

Ophelia takes in every detail of the man's nudity. She has forgotten that a naked man can be an object of beauty. Nor can she even imagine sharing such tender intimacy with Gervase. Time stops in its tracks. For a few precious moments she is a million miles away. All too soon, a furious tapping on the window opposite shatters her trance-like state. Gervase is shouting.

'What the hell do you think you're doing? Get out or I'll thrash the living daylights out of you!'

The couple awake. The young man gets up very slowly, taking his time. He fixes Gervase with a long, hard stare. Ophelia notes the supple, languid curves of his body. He has the pose of a perfect Donatello statue and makes no effort to conceal himself. Unlike the girl who quickly covers herself with a studded leather jacket and shouts back at Gervase.

'Fuck off, you filthy pervert!'

As the young man collects his clothes, his eyes meet Ophelia's and hold them fast. A spark of recognition seems to flash. Ignoring the faces at the other windows, which now include Reverend Inigo Parsnip, Araminta Fettiplace, Peregrine Gargoyle and George Burp, the young man continues to look Ophelia straight in the eye. He dresses in a deliberately slow manner while her unblinking eyes remain locked onto his, oblivious to all else. A flicker of a smile moves across his lips as he finally puts on his shirt.

Gervase, red-faced with rage, is about to burst into the Temple of Venus and deliver the promised thrashing, but now he focuses on his wife staring in from the window opposite.

'Ophelia, back to the house! I will deal with this.'

There is soon nothing to deal with. The couple now mount the motorbike. The young man kickstarts the engine. It reverberates alarmingly in the confined space of the Temple of Venus. He nudges open the door with the front wheel, forcing Gervase to stand aside, before roaring off across the grass. The girl twists round to make an obscene gesture. Gervase responds with an impotent shaking fist.

Except for Ophelia, already heading back to the house, they follow Gervase into the Temple of Venus. The air is acrid with the stench of oil and petrol. There is nothing to look at but the walls which are covered with the same fanciful plasterwork as the Rococo Vestibule of the Palladian Villa. Gargoyle examines these swirling shapes, as if they have the power to take him away from the shocking incident and return him to the safe world of art and design.

'As we can see, the Temple of Venus displays a rare degree of artistic accomplishment and ...'

Gervase explodes.

'Spare us the sodding artistic accomplishment!'

Gargoyle winces as if slapped in the face.

'What is the meaning of this outrage, Withers? Do you have any idea what those insolent hooligans were doing here on my property?'

'I expect they are from the council estate, sir.'

'A confounded council estate at Farthing Abbey! What an infernal cheek! Is nothing sacred?'

Reverend Parsnip wears a wounded look.

'Excuse me, *padre*. Just an expression.'

'Surely there is a place for everyone in God's creation, Mr Lloyd-Beauchamp. This is the Temple of Venus and the young man appears to be generously endowed by Priapus. Where is the wrong in that?'

Gervase throws the cleric a sideways look of total disbelief. Burp can't resist a loud aside to Gargoyle.

'Yonder bold Ionic erection. You do have a way with words. That really hit the nail on the head.'

The master of Farthing Abbey can only stand there fuming. Has everyone taken leave of their senses? Where is Ophelia? He recalls sending her back to the house. Why did he do that? Oh yes, his dear wife had been utterly captivated by the young man's nakedness. The little hussy. Or perhaps that was no bad thing. It might warm her up for what is expected for the night ahead. Gervase is now impatient to move on and put the unpleasant incident behind them.

'So let's continue our patrol. I mean our stroll. I trust we shall encounter no more criminal trespassers in my Landscape Park.'

CHINESE BOUDOIR

On his own in the now deserted Palladian Villa, Adrian Lenshood slowly unwinds in silent communion with the house. Without human occupants, it breathes peacefully. The empty rooms come to life on their own terms in a quietly shifting pattern of forms, colours and textures.

All doors having been left open, Adrian feels free as the air to circulate through the apartments of the *piano nobile*. He makes a mental note of an obvious shot from the Greek Room, a fine vista leading the eye via the Italianate Room to the Antique Gallery and straight out through a tall sash window into the fields beyond.

He looks up thoughtfully at the portrait of Sir Archibald over the chimneypiece. Yes, it is definitely Gervase in a previous existence, and no mistake. So Farthing Abbey has fallen into his lap through an accident of birth. The lucky bugger. Then he acquires Ophelia into the bargain. But somehow, she doesn't fit into the scheme of things. Perhaps that is the flaw in the sparkling diamond?

Adrian completes his tour through the Arab Room and the Chinese Boudoir. Duty calls, so he goes to fetch his camera equipment. He has done this sort of job so many times before: shooting tasteful pictures of artificially contrived rooms where you can hardly imagine real people leading real lives. He reckons the

Palladian Villa was designed as a scenic distraction with the sole aim of relieving the congenital boredom of the upper classes. It amounts to nothing more than an entertaining theatrical backdrop to help the rich and restless pass the time of day.

As he starts to work his way swiftly and methodically through the standard shots expected, he feels like a seasoned potter turning out the same old vase for the umpteenth time. There is a quiet satisfaction of sorts to be had, but nothing to get the creative juices flowing. His work done, Adrian drifts back to the Antique Gallery. His gaze lingers on the classical busts of emperors, philosophers and poets. They take him back to a long, hot summer in Rome many years ago when he had photographed the noble marble faces and figures in one museum of antiquities after another. Briefly, he is now tempted to relive those heady Roman days when art had sprung so vibrantly into life. But all that feels so remote, it might have been in another life, and these Classical sculptures in their alien English setting seem entirely out of their element.

Now he abandons tripod and cameras and walks aimlessly through the apartments, letting his legs lead him this way and that, like dropping the reins of a horse for it to graze at leisure. After a couple of circuits of the Palladian Villa he returns to the Antique Gallery. This time he is no longer interested in statues but intent on searching the bookcase for the concealed door leading to the secret staircase. He inspects the leather spines of the thick volumes. The gold letters of obscure titles and names of long forgotten authors gleam enticingly.

Hadn't Withers said something about a lever? Adrian runs his index finger across the top of the books. They all feel real enough, except for one right at the end. It is made of wood. He gives a gentle tug and the spine of the dummy volume tilts towards him on a hinge attached to its base. Behind it he discovers a brass handle. It sits smooth and solid in the palm of his hand. He pulls firmly. The lock is released with a well-oiled click. The bookcase swings open.

Withers had taken a candle from an alcove, but Adrian opts to do without. His right hand reaches out to grasp the stone column of the spiral staircase while his feet tentatively negotiate the steps. He descends like Orpheus into the underworld. It is a curious sensation of non-being, as he dissolves into the darkness, an excitement deliciously laced with fear. As if passing through death into rebirth. Then the gloom begins to thin. A grey light spreads from below. His eyes narrow to the brightness.

He steps into the Cloister Garth and its medieval vaulting cocooned in a natural silence of centuries. The ancient masonry exudes an aura of time-hallowed sanctity, tangible enough to touch the heart of an atheist. For long moments, he remains rooted to the spot, savouring the exquisite atmosphere of this magical place. Then he hears a voice.

'Who's there? Oh, it's you, Mr Lenshood.'

As ordered by Gervase, Ophelia has returned from the Temple of Venus and entered quietly through the slype. She now stands before him in the Cloister Garth. He registers a mystical image: a woman with flaming red hair, milky white skin and pale green floral dress, artistically framed by the Gothic tracery. She is infused with a surreal vibrancy by the grey stone all around her: a perfect pre-Raphaelite vision.

Quite apart from the stunning physical force of her appearance there is something else about her which has radically altered the person he first met only an hour or so previously. No longer closed and opaque, she is somehow amazingly transparent. Her formerly elusive self is now fully exposed to view: a house with doors, shutters and windows flung wide open offering all rooms for inspection. He looks deep into her blue eyes. They do not avoid his but invite him in like limpid pools into which he might plunge endlessly and never reach the bottom.

Immersed in these clear waters everything suddenly makes sense. All doubts and fears are banished. The meaningless of his life is gone. If he had been asked to describe this blessed state, Adrian Lenshood would have been unable to avoid using the word love. But he cannot think, let alone speak. When at last his words do come, it is as if they arrive from a long way off and are spoken by someone else. They convey nothing of the tumult of feelings inside him.

'Hello, Mrs Lloyd-Beauchamp. I've been taking some pictures. Upstairs in the Palladian Villa. Thought

I'd do a quick recce down here. Hope you don't mind. Perhaps I should have asked?'

'Do feel free, Mr Lenshood. It's your job.'

The exchange of politenesses is mechanical, just social sounds with no particular significance attached to them. They face one another in silence for several long moments. Adrian, bowled over by her miraculous intrusion into his dreamlike state, lets himself fall unchecked into the fathomless depths of her gaze. For her part, Ophelia is swimming, perhaps drowning in a different pool. Still under the spell of those tender intimacies revealed to her at the Temple of Venus, she is adrift in the swirling currents of uncharted waters.

'How was the Temple of Venus?'

How can she answer that? Ophelia has no reply.

'Are you feeling all right?'

'Yes, I'm perfectly fine, thank you. I found the sun a bit hot, so I came back to the house.'

A semblance of normality is restored. The magic is dissolving as fast as a thin mist in the morning sunshine. He fears she might be spirited away unless he does something to hold on to the precious moment. Suddenly, he has an inspiration. He will photograph her. No matter that his commission is only for the house, he will do a portrait of the mistress of Farthing Abbey as well.

His mind clicks into gear. This is new territory for him. He is ready to move on beyond those empty interiors, blank-faced statues and still lives. He will capture the complete womanly essence of this wonderful creature. Already he sees his portrait of Ophelia as so much more compelling and vibrant than those hollow images of sterile fashion models that fill the glossy magazines with their anaemic pouts and emaciated bodies. He trembles on the brink of this fresh departure.

'If you can spare the time, Mrs Lloyd-Beauchamp, this would be a good moment to do your portrait.'

'My portrait? Are you sure? No one mentioned that. I didn't know the magazine was interested in me.'

He hesitates, unsure how to overcome her protestations.

'The human angle is always interesting.'

No, that isn't right. Something less vague.

'What is a house without its owners?'

That's better.

'But won't you want Gervase as well?'

Oh dear, she is slipping away.

'I can shoot your husband later. I mean…'

They laugh spontaneously in unison as the same thought crosses their minds.

'Well, I'm not really prepared to pose for anything too formal.'

'No matter. You are fine just as you are. Perfectly fine, in fact.'

Adrian is suddenly wracked with indecision. He aches to portray her just as she is at this very moment standing before him in the Cloister Garth. She looks magnificent in this setting. But he has left his gear in the

Palladian Villa. If he were to go for it now, he fears the divine apparition might simply evaporate in his absence. His agony is acute. For the first time in his life, here is a picture he yearns to take with every fibre of his being. But he dares not go to fetch his camera. At last, he resolves the dilemma.

'The light in the Palladian Villa is good right now. We'll take a look at the possibilities there. Then we'll come back and shoot a few frames here in the Cloister Garth.'

He tries to sound competent and in control.

'I am in your hands. Lead on, Mr Lenshood.'

'Very well then, Mrs Lloyd-Beauchamp. Please follow me.'

In his hands. If only. Then suddenly she is. As they enter the dark spiral staircase, he offers her his hand. She accepts without demur. As they emerge through the bookcase back into the Antique Gallery, Adrian is Orpheus once more, only in this version he is actually returning from the underworld with Eurydice safely in tow. With extreme reluctance he releases her hand. He is on fire, not only where she has touched him, but in his whole body from head to foot. He is walking on air.

'I suggest we look for a promising spot.'

Adrian speaks inconsequentially with a disembodied voice about the eternal problems of light: too little being a bore, but too much in the wrong place no real help either.

'Then there is the background to consider. The Greek Room looks OK, but too much competition from those murals. Not that you would be upstaged by those flimsy creatures, of course. But they are a visual distraction. Same goes for the Italianate Room. Too much clutter.'

He is gaining in confidence.

'Here in the Antique Gallery you stand out so well against these dusty books and old statues.'

'You must get to photograph a lot of people in the course of your work, Mr Lenshood.'

Has he overdone the professional patter? By way of a reply, Adrian contents himself with a gentle shrug as they walk the length of the Antique Gallery and enter the Arab Room.

'A bit too gloomy.'

They proceed to the Chinese Boudoir where the sun floods in through the tall west-facing window. The dragon sofa basks in its rays.

Adrian puts down camera bag and tripod.

'This is it. Perfect.'

While Adrian fiddles with lenses and film magazines, Ophelia perches on the dragon sofa and waits. The heat of the sun has permeated the velvet upholstery. Now it enters her skin and embraces her with its warmth. She feels drained of all shyness and inhibition. She offers herself calmly to the camera as if she were no more than a beautiful vase of flowers to be arranged at the whim of a stranger.

'Is this all right?'

'Yes, that will be fine. No. You're a bit too stiff. Lean back a little. One leg resting on the *chaise longue*. Let the other trail.'

He is amazed how readily she complies with his wishes. She looks ever more magnificent. Her pale green dress strikes a defiant note against the scarlet sofa. There is menace in the dragon's head with its jade eyes and red tongue just behind her, poised to strike. Yes, he will compose a picture of power and beauty.

How different she now appears to the Ophelia just encountered in the Cloister Garth. There she was still a shade unreal, ethereal, virtually abstract. Here in the Chinese Boudoir she is resoundingly material, a creature of flesh and blood with a tantalising hint of decadence. That is just how he will portray her: sensual, provocative, carnal as a courtesane.

Her eyes are half closed, like a cat dozing in the sunshine. He can sense the shape of her body beneath the thin summer dress. His eyes feast on the sight of her. He drinks in every detail.

Still he doesn't release the shutter. It's as if the whole world has stopped turning. Time stands still. Then a shoe falls off her dangling foot. In the sultry silence it sounds like thunder.

'Don't move. I'll get it.'

He advances towards her. No sooner has he reached the *chaise longue* than he falls to his knees. With one trembling hand, he picks up the fallen shoe. He takes hold of her slender ankle in the other. The touch of her flesh is electric against his. His senses are numbed. He drops the shoe. It hits the floor with a dull thud. She doesn't stir.

Without a word, he removes the other shoe. As he does so, he plays tentatively with the hem of her dress and watches his hand brush softly against her skin. She lies there, offering no resistance. Holding himself in check, fearful she might tell him to stop, he imagines the thrill of uncovering her inch by inch, tenderly stroking his fingers across her body, caressing her breasts and kissing every part of her beautiful nakedness before finally taking his pleasure.

But all that occurs in the realm of thought. Still he remains motionless kneeling beside her. Then he can restrain himself no longer. His hand moves of its own accord. It is irresistibly drawn to the cool skin of her calf and advances slowly beneath the flowery petals of her dress until it rests lightly on her thigh. He can hardly believe he is doing this. In a sense he isn't. It's as if something is happening through him. He is not the doer, merely the instrument of a higher force. As for Ophelia, still she doesn't move. Is she in a trance? Or feigning sleep?

Incredulous at his boldness and her compliance, he takes hold of her knickers and slides them down to her ankles. Animal instinct guides his cheek to rest softly on her silky thigh. He nuzzles up to her delicate flesh. Surely she will now tell him to stop. But then he feels the tips of her fingers play with his hair and press gently on his head. Seeking their own fulfilment, his lips caress her womanhood. It is sweet and wet as a wounded peach.

As blind in his desire as that voluptuous bee he had watched earlier cavorting in the poppy Adrian explores Ophelia's open flower. Anticipating her wish, his tongue plunges deep inside her, thirsting to drink all her honey from the source of her femininity. Her body comes to life. Languorously she writhes, moaning softly in harmony with his movements like a finely tuned musical instrument. Adrian feels a crescendo of orchestral proportions gather force. He takes Ophelia up and down the scales until she can bear it no longer. Finally he brings her over the top. Gasping for breath, she dissolves in a series of rhythmic convulsions and releases passions trapped inside her for so long.

Adrian aches for release himself, but something holds him back. He is stunned, overawed by the immensity of what he has done. For the first time in his life, he has let go completely and allowed his body to act without hindrance. The sense of liberation makes him dizzy. He feels the novel satisfaction of giving himself totally to a woman's pleasure. He tells himself there will be opportunity for himself later. Next time she will be as yielding to his pleasure as he was to hers. How could she be otherwise? He is certain he has laid up a rich store for himself. So for now, he is proud and happy to have been the instrument of her happiness.

Ophelia lies there in a state of bliss, dreamily aware of nothing but the head of a young man nuzzling between her thighs. Something vast and mysterious has happened. A dream has become reality. The ocean swell on which she now floats is wide and deep. It swallows up all individuality. The name of the person who has just so delicately aroused the most intimate folds of her flesh is of no account. As for her own identity, it too is equally immaterial. Right now she is no longer the person formerly known as Ophelia Lloyd-Beauchamp. She has no more substance than that wisp of a smile on the Mona Lisa's face. She knows she can never ask for more than this. She wants to hold it fast and let everything else vanish from the face of the earth.

Caution has been flung to the winds. Anyone entering the Chinese Boudoir at this moment would discover the mistress of Farthing Abbey in erotic communion with a magazine photographer. But as far as they are concerned, the only witness to their private scene is a camera on a tripod whose shutter has remained discreetly closed throughout.

They have no inkling how much time passes before they are startled by the sound of footsteps. Someone is entering the Rococo Vestibule. Ophelia sits up, pushes Adrian away, smoothes her dress, slips on her shoes. Then she makes for the door, pausing briefly on the threshold, only to leave him with a quizzical, non-comprehending look before vanishing into the Arab Room whence they had come. It all happens with an abruptness that shocks him to the core.

He strains to catch the echo of her fading footsteps as she scampers off through the Antique Gallery. In his mind's eye he tracks her down the staircase to the Cloister Garth and so to the Squire's Bedchamber where tonight in that ugly four-poster bed Gervase Lloyd-Beauchamp will surely lay claim to what is rightfully his. Already in his hour of glory, Adrian experiences the painful pangs of burning jealousy.

His ecstasy is short-lived. Ophelia leaves behind a gaping void. Had it all been a dream? But it is real enough. He sees that from her silk knickers dangling suggestively from the red tongue of the dragon at the head of the *chaise longue*. Gratefully he reaches out to take the tiny garment, presses it to his cheek and kisses it tenderly as if it were the most precious of lover's tokens. At this moment the door opens.

It is Gargoyle.

LANDSCAPES OF THE MIND

I t seems to Adrian Lenshood a particularly cruel trick of fate that the sour odour of Peregrine Gargoyle should violate the Chinese Boudoir even while Ophelia's perfume hangs in the air.

'Ah, Lenshood, there you are. I really don't see the point of photographing the *chaise longue*. Perfectly hideous. Not the sort of thing our readers would wish to see. And what is that in your hand?'

Adrian hastily pushes Ophelia's knickers deep into his trouser pocket.

'Nothing. Just a cloth for cleaning my cameras.'

'Well, don't hang about, Lenshood. We are due for cocktails in the Long Gallery at seven.'

Once Gargoyle is gone, Adrian looks at his watch. It is a few minutes past six. Less than an hour and he will see her again. He doubts whether he can wait much longer. He picks up his camera gear and trudges upstairs. The air in his room is stifling. He leaves the door open to encourage a reluctant breeze. He peals off his shirt. On his way to the washstand, he finds himself suddenly illuminated by a powerful cluster of sunbeams streaming directly through the circular window. Like a star on stage he is caught right in the middle of this golden spotlight. It feels like a giant finger of destiny singling him out.

The more he thinks about it the less he can believe what he has done. He has behaved in a way he would never have dreamed possible. For a brief moment back there in the Chinese Boudoir he was totally at one with himself. He has taken the plunge, the animal in him has burst out from its civilised shell and followed its desires heedless of the consequences. Adrian still feels a lingering glow of excitement at his own dare-devilry. After that erotic encounter in the Chinese Boudoir, surely he is capable of anything?

As the sun plays pleasurably on his skin, Adrian yearns to feel Ophelia's touch on his naked body. He still has the taste of her in his mouth, her smell fills his nostrils. He knows it will not be long before all that fades away into nothingness. He now regrets he has not claimed his prize. Nor did he shoot a single picture of her. He must have been utterly bewitched to let even that small consolation slip from his grasp. Suddenly, his new found confidence is punctured. He sees himself as a complete loser. The grim realisation makes him shiver from head to toe even in the stifling heat of the sun.

Peregrine Gargoyle, passing at this moment along the landing, catches sight of Adrian through the open door. He can't help but look at him. Try as he might to tell himself that his rapt contemplation of the photographer's naked torso is simply an aesthetic experience on a par with viewing an antique statue in a sculpture gallery, he does not entirely succeed in convincing himself this is so. The same malaise that unsettled him in Adrian's flat that morning returns with far greater force. At last, he pulls himself together and taps smartly on the door.

'You left your door wide open. Lenshood. Rather careless of you.'

Adrian does not respond.

'Well, I thought I should point it out. There are ladies about.'

Gargoyle pronounces the word 'ladies' as if it signified a real threat.

'Do make yourself smart for dinner, Lenshood. We'll meet downstairs at seven in the Rococo Vestibule. Don't be late.'

With that, Gargoyle scuttles away, anxious to conceal the confusion he can feel stamped on his face. Adrian shuts his door, pours cold water into the basin and immerses his head. His thoughts revert to Ophelia. Never before has he progressed with such speed and intensity of purpose from formal introduction to total intimacy. Without her underwear in his possession, he might be tempted to think it has all been a dream, a mere fantasy sprung from an over fertile imagination. Even so, it feels as flimsy as the small, thin piece of silk now lying weightless in his hand.

He reruns through his mind the entire scene in the Chinese Boudoir. Frame by frame, he watches himself go through each amazing detail as if peering into a flickering what-the-butler-saw machine on a seaside pier. Then he curses himself for being no better than a cheap voyeur prying on himself. His seduction of

Ophelia, if that is what it was, now feels even more remote and unreal.

Soon he will have to resume his official role of photographer. Ophelia will doubtless assume her guise as the squire's lady once more. He considers his options. What is he to do? How should he behave? The bold voice of the new Adrian Lenshood prevails. He must finish what has been started while the memory is still fresh. He will take her properly before the evening is out. Somehow, somewhere. No matter how difficult or dangerous the circumstances. With that resolved, at least in theory, he dresses hurriedly for dinner.

Araminta Fettiplace is already downstairs. Washing in a basin of cold water is not her idea of country house living. But Farthing Abbey has class. It is the real thing. She makes a tour of the Palladian Villa, imagining herself as one of the erstwhile mistresses of the place. A glimpse of her reflection in an ancient gilt mirror tells her she looks the part. The stately apartments appeal to her taste. The most exciting ingredients are there, all under one roof: Greece, Italy, Arabia and China. The setting offers endless promise.

The secrets of the house will surely reveal themselves to her in due course. Failing that, she can always be suitably inspired to invent them. But something tells her that may not be necessary. Already, her unwritten book has been conceived. More than that, it has taken root inside her like a fully formed baby waiting its moment to be born. For the first time in her career, romantic novelist Araminta Fettiplace feels the raw power of something primal about to express itself through her. This time she will not have to craft a fiction from her own imagination. The material would write itself. As if she were merely the outlet for a real story whose outlines she can as yet only dimly discern.

Blithely confident her novel is already in the bag, she races fast forward to the feature film with star-studded cast. It will set her up for life. These are no idle dreams. Araminta Fettiplace knows such things are very much in the realm of the possible. Farthing Abbey – even the title has a pleasing Jane Austen ring to it – will bring about a quantum leap in her literary reputation. It is nothing less than her vehicle to a higher sphere, the sweet chariot come at long last to whisk her away.

She paces slowly through the Antique Gallery and stops in front of the Gainsborough portrait. One day she might be a *châtelaine* herself. Why not? Only she would not be as self-effacing as Sir Archibald's demure-looking spouse. Then her eyes widen. She has seen something in the painting she hadn't noticed before. A book, just like one of her own recently published novels, lies on the bench. And is that not her name on the cover? She blinks in astonishment. Surely not? The canvas must be at least two hundred years old. She leans forward to verify the matter.

'Admiring the jolly old squire?'

Araminta spins round to face a grinning George Burp. It is awful to be brought back to earth with such a bump.

'Some people have all the luck, don't they?'

What possesses the ridiculous man to wink at her like that?

'Mr Burp. You gave me such a start. You really shouldn't creep up like that on unsuspecting people.'

'George, remember. I'm sorry if I startled you, Araminta.'

'Very well then, George. If it makes you happy.'

So desperately does she want to resume her examination of the painting that she promptly turns her back on him. But this time there is nothing there. Nothing at all. No sign of any book on the bench. She is utterly confused. Might she have been mistaken?

'Everything OK?'

She does not respond immediately. George Burp wonders what had grabbed her attention. Araminta glances at her watch.

'Oh, is that the time? We had better join the others in the Rococo Vestibule. It's nearly seven.'

Together they pace to the end of the Antique Gallery where the concealed door to the secret passage is still open.

'That's a short cut to the conveniences. Must say I don't fancy having to go down there in the middle of the night.'

Araminta breathes a sigh of relief he does not dwell further on his nocturnal habits. In silence they pass through the Italianate Room to the Greek Room, where Peregrine Gargoyle is engrossed in an examination of the mural featuring the two ladies in diaphanous robes on a terrace. His attention is directed to a minor figure, he hadn't spotted before, in the person of a Greek youth who has stripped off for some form of athletic activity. To Gargoyle's astonishment, a shy smile spreads gently across the painted face of the youth. Gargoyle squints incredulously at it through his half-moon spectacles. It is a perfect likeness of that beautiful boy at boarding school to whom he had been so strongly attracted.

'Inspecting the feminine elements, are we?'

Gargoyle spins round to find George Burp and Araminta Fettiplace looking at him intently. Alarmed to be caught thus engaged, he makes great show of assessing the entire mural with academic detachment.

'Well, I suppose it could possibly be an early Alma-Tadema.'

Gargoyle steals another glance at the mural. But now his smile is gone and with it the Greek youth too. The figure is no longer a boy but of yet another maiden. Could there be some illusionist trick with which he is not familiar? He immediately dismisses the idea.

'But most unusual all the same.'

'Farthing Abbey is turning out to be quite a little gold mine for the connoisseur, isn't it, Peregrine?'

Gargoyle is flustered. What does Araminta Fettiplace mean by that? Can she read his mind? These novelists with their intuition are not to be trusted. He decides to play down his interest.

'Well, I suppose there are certain aspects, some interesting features, diverse miscellaneous matters that might possibly repay the bother of looking into. I will have to see what remains to be seen.'

'So you are impressed?'

'It is a bit too soon to say anything definitive on the subject. Ah, Lenshood, there you are.'

Adrian greets the group.

'Hello. And how did you all enjoy the church and the Temple of Venus? So sorry I couldn't join you.'

Burp responds on their behalf.

'Well, the church was fine and dandy, apart from it being stuffed full to the rafters with all those Lloyd-Beauchamp stiffs. You'd think they'd have had the decency to let the peasants pray in peace without piling up all those dead toffs in front of the altar. I reckon Parsnip thinks so too, but the parson musn't upset the squire, now must he? So where is the good Reverend, by the way?'

'The Reverend Parsnip and Mrs Worthington will be joining you shortly in the Long Gallery.'

The answer to Burp's question comes from a long way off. Withers stands in the doorway of the Rococo Vestibule. The sun wraps his silhouette in a golden aureole, while the long shadow of his body spreads like a dark stain across the elegant marble floor.

'Shall we proceed?'

Gargoyle, with exaggerated olde worlde courtesy, makes way for Araminta to exit. He follows close behind, turning his back abruptly on Burp. As they descend the stair, step by step in time with the slow pace of the butler, Burp gives Adrian his account of the promenade.

'You really missed out on something special at the Temple of Venus, I can tell you.'

'Never mind. I'll take a proper look tomorrow morning.'

'No, that's not what I mean. There was a bit of a rumpus when we turned up. We found this young couple lying there, completely starkers. They'd been on the job. Only just finished off with a wee spot of cunnilingus for afters, I reckon. Lloyd-Beauchamp was livid. Threatened to give the young man a damn good thrashing. Is there any other kind, I wonder? Anyway, the fellow was pretty cool, what with all our faces pressed against the windows and them two caught with their pants down. But the cocky bloke just gave us all a look as he put his trousers on, then started his bike....'

'His bike?'

'He'd parked his motorbike in the Temple of Venus, hadn't he? Then he rode straight out of the door and over the lawn with the girl hanging on the back.'

'Good lord! I really have missed something.'

'Old Lloyd-Beauchamp was hopping mad. Lord of the manor went puce when he spotted Mrs L-B. She'd been standing there gawping through the window longer than anyone else. She couldn't take her eyes off what she'd been looking at, I can tell you.'

'Ophelia? I mean ... er ... Mrs Lloyd-Beauchamp?'

'Yes, her. Who else? Well, he only packed her off straight back to the house like a naughty schoolgirl.'

'Perhaps she was in a state of shock?'

'Who knows? Well at any rate, you really missed something there. And you should have seen the bike. What a beauty! One of those machines that can go up the side of a mountain. What a racket it made! Enough to waken the dead.'

'But who were they, this couple?'

'That's just what old Lloyd-Beauchamp wanted to know. Withers wasn't too forthcoming, but I reckon he knows more than he was prepared to let on.'

The medieval aspect of Farthing Abbey now comes into view.

'Behold the roofline full of dramatic incident'.

Gargoyle is delighted to deploy a firm favourite among his stock phrases. It always feels freshly minted to him no matter how often he uses it. Adrian is familiar with this particular Gargoylism from his casual browsing through the pages of *Houses and Castles*.

'And here we have the perfect spot from which to survey the Landscape Park.'

It is indeed an idyllic vista that opens before them. A broad avenue runs straight as an arrow to a distant obelisk, a feature Gargoyle might possibly describe as 'a bold Baroque flourish in a setting of quintessential Englishness'. The rest of the park is pseudo-natural with trees dotted seemingly at random, while the Scenic Lake coils smoothly out of sight to suggest a broad river flowing towards a distant ocean.

'Looks like Capability to me, Withers?'

'Capability, sir?'

'I mean to say the Landscape Park was doubtless designed by Capability Brown.'

Withers pauses in reflection.

'Do you mean perchance Mr Lancelot Brown?'

'Yes, the very same.'

'A most extraordinary gentleman. He once tore a strip off the head gardener for planting roses. Flowers were anathema. He said he wanted no disgusting display of art in the garden. Those were his very words. Now, if only dear Mr Repton had come on the scene earlier. He was charm and politeness personified. Those delightful red albums of his with their before and after sketches. He was working with Mr Nash at the time. Such a pity Sir Archibald couldn't afford their West End prices.'

Gargoyle's heart skips a beat.

'So Humphry Repton actually produced a *Red Book* for Farthing Abbey?'

'Indeed he did, sir.'

'Where is it, Withers? The *Red Book*? Where?'

'Along with all the other documents relating to Farthing Abbey. In the Archive Room located between your room, Mr Gargoyle, and Mr Lenshood's. Now, if you permit, pray let us continue. Mr and Mrs Lloyd-Beauchamp wait on your presence in the Long Gallery.'

The reference to Ophelia's marital status brings home to Adrian the harsh reality. With foreboding he views the prospect of the evening ahead. How he aches to be alone with her once more as that wanton creature he had embraced on the *chaise longue*.

They process through a gated entrance enclosed within a pointed arch. As he sets foot again in the Cloister Garth where he had established that first tentative contact with Ophelia no more than a couple of hours previously, Adrian stumbles and almost falls.

'Daydreaming again, Lenshood? I must say, you do look a trifle flustered. Someone should take you in hand.'

He doesn't like the sound of what Gargoyle might be implying. Not one bit.

SUMPTUOUS REPAST

The Long Gallery makes a huge impact on Gargoyle. It is by far the loveliest he has ever encountered. The creamy white plaster ceiling contrasts pleasingly with the dark wainscot of the walls like the icing on a wedding cake. Gervase and Ophelia stand at the end, awaiting their guests who advance in close formation behind Withers. They smile in unison. Their greetings are formal and collective.

'Good evening, Mr and Mrs Lloyd-Beauchamp. Don't you think mahogany spelled the death of English furniture making?'

With a sweeping theatrical gesture, Gargoyle indicates his admiration of an imposing oak sideboard of Jacobean vintage.

'And the Long Gallery, how exquisite! What a ceiling! I really must congratulate you, Mr and Mrs Lloyd-Beauchamp, on being the proud owners and worthy custodians too, I am sure, of Farthing Abbey.'

While Gargoyle continues to overflow with a rare display of bubbly enthusiasm, Withers circulates among the guests with a silver tray bearing crystal goblets filled with champagne.

Adrian tries to rally his flagging spirits with a touch of the silk talisman that he carries in his trouser pocket. Already he has begun to doubt whether he will be able put his bold plans of sexual conquest into operation. In this grand setting, Ophelia and Gervase appear inseparable. She looks remote, unapproachable, an impregnable fortress.

His fevered thoughts are interrupted by the arrival of Mrs Beatrice Worthington and the Reverend Inigo Parsnip. The former reaches out to grasp the hands first of Gervase, then of Ophelia. She pumps them purposefully for a good, long while before releasing them. Then she examines them both at unusual length and with an expert eye, as might a judge of canine breeds at Cruft's Dog Show. Ophelia finds her steady, detached and enquiring gaze uncomfortable.

Ophelia looks for relief to Reverend Parsnip. The hatless cleric is wearing a dark suit that accentuates the snowy whiteness of his hair. He seems curiously lacking in physical substance. His presence amounts to perhaps no more than a stray feather blown in by the wind. Yet there is something deeply reassuring in his aura of holiness so much more potent than with any ordinary clergyman. There is even a suggestion of something pre-Christian, almost a whiff of white magic about Parsnip. His eyes sparkle with a youthful brilliance that belies his years.

'Mr and Mrs Lloyd-Beauchamp. *Mea culpa*. I must take full blame for our late arrival. I am not as spritely on my pins as once I was. It is indeed an honour to be invited to your first dinner at Farthing Abbey.'

'Very good, Vicar. Quite so. Have a glass.'

'Thank you most kindly. It is an exceedingly long while since I last stood here in the Long Gallery, well before Sir Horace finally took to his bed. This was once a monks' dormitory, you know. Just imagine some sixty or so snoring Cistercians snoozing here in this very room. Of course, that was before the Carthusians took over the establishment. England was then awash with abbeys and priories such as this. Now the godless roam all over the face of the earth and ...'

Reverend Parsnip pauses as if he has decided not to say something that was on the tip of his tongue.

The ensuing silence is broken by Withers who announces that dinner is served in the Privy Parlour. Gervase offers Araminta his arm. Gargoyle follows suit with Mrs Worthington. Adrian is about to offer his services as escort to Ophelia. Surprisingly, Reverend Parsnip beats him to it, so he trails disconsolately behind with that other social outcast, George Burp.

'Got the hots for Lady Ophelia, have we?'

Adrian can't believe he is so transparent. And to Burp of all people.

'Only joking, Adrian old chap. Now don't look so glum. I bet there's some good grub and plenty of booze to get stuck into.'

They process to the end of the Long Gallery and enter an oak-panelled chamber. The low ceiling is richly decorated with a thick crust of ornamented plaster.

'Your Privy Parlour is most charming, Mrs Lloyd-Beauchamp. We are privileged to be your guests.'

They take their seats around the table. Reverend Parsnip recites grace.

'For what we are about to receive, may the Lord make us truly thankful. Amen.'

'Thank you, Vicar. Now let the juices flow!'

Before they can start on the food, George Burp draws their attention to the portrait behind Ophelia. All eyes focus on yet another stunning likeness of their host[3]. This time Gervase is kitted out in dashing Tudor costume of doublet and hose with an ostrich feather sprouting from a brimmed hat shaped like an inverted flowerpot. In the background, shimmers a spectral image of Farthing Abbey, as yet without the Palladian Villa. Gervase strains to get a better look of himself.

'Well spotted, Burp. I reckon that makes your hat trick. I wonder how many more of me there are about the place. Gosh, don't I look splendid in that outfit? Rather fun, what?'

'Most comely of limb. It is such a shame men nowadays don't show a leg, Mr Lloyd-Beauchamp. Your ancestor was obviously proud of his. And with good reason. A remarkable likeness.'

Araminta's compliment, calculated only to curry favour, has turned out far more fulsome than she desires. Gervase gives her a predatory look. Araminta shrinks before his unsettling stare. Now her card is well and truly marked. She is relieved when George Burp changes the subject.

---

[3] Sir Owen Lloyd-Beauchamp (1516-79).

'I expect you'll be pretty busy running the place when you open to the public. Ever done this sort of thing before, Mrs Lloyd-Beauchamp?'

'I don't really know about that, Mr Burp. I am sure Gervase will take charge. After all, Farthing Abbey is his family inheritance, not mine.'

Gervase gazes down the table through the dancing orange flames of three candlesticks to Ophelia at the other end. She has a new glow about her. Perhaps it is a trick of the light or just the cumulative effect on him of all that champagne and the *Manzanilla Barbadillo* that accompanies the walnut and mushroom soup.

'What's that you're saying about me down there?'

'Mr Burp was just asking how I'm going to run the place when it's open to the public. So I told him that's your job.'

'I intend to make it his job too. Why do you think we've asked you along, Burp? You are here to advise on tourism marketing and all that stuff. Well, we might as well get our money's worth and have your thoughts straight away. Let's hear you.'

Burp noisily slurps a final spoonful of soup before wiping his mouth with the back of his hand.

'Very well. I'm not sure how you'll take this. But here goes anyway. It's fairly simple actually. Now, I'm sure Farthing Abbey is of great historical and architectural interest, as our friend Gargoyle here keeps telling us. But the plain fact is ordinary folk aren't too bothered. Couldn't give a hoot. It's period atmosphere, shopping and attractions they're after. Then somewhere for the kids to play. And a decent teashop, of course.'

Gargoyle chokes at the affront. Burp continues unabashed.

'A little bit of family history is OK. But you mustn't overlook the servants. How hard they worked and for so little. Ordinary people can relate to that. I bet old Withers here can tell you a thing or two about domestic exploitation by the upper classes.'

Araminta Fettiplace is distressed to hear her grand pageant reduced to an insignificant side-show.

'Really, Mr Burp. Doubtless, there are fascinating stories from below stairs. But the glamour of the Italianate Room, the pomp of the Antique Gallery are so much more exciting than your rather low-life take on social history, don't you think? My romantic novel will lift the lid on the noble upper echelons of Farthing Abbey. In the most tasteful possible way, of course. I intend to start just as soon as Mr Lloyd-Beauchamp and Withers will allow me to tap their personal memories.'

With fish knife poised to skewer out a succulent piece of pink-white lobster flesh, Gervase responds.

'Thank you, Araminta. I place myself at your entire disposition. So what do you say to that, Burp?'

George Burp has profited from the diversion to stuff a large chunk of lobster in his mouth. But the conversational ball has landed back in his court sooner than expected. He takes a quick gulp of the nicely chilled *Pouilly Blanc Fumé* 1986 and swallows hard.

'Speak up Burp, be frank.'

Burp takes another gulp.

'Well, I suppose the average punter might be interested in what your ancestors got up to. Especially if you have any rogues or villains skulking in the woodwork. Dirty deeds, double-dealing and outrageous acts always go down well. After all, that's what we common folk have come to expect of the nobs up at the big house.'

Gervase listens silently to this unflattering inventory. Burp is decidedly an awkward customer, a bolshy sort of character who badly needs cutting down to size. But an inner voice tells him that if behaving badly goes with the territory of lord of the manor, then he is admirably qualified for the job. Perhaps even, it is something to be proud of.

'All right, Burp. That's quite enough. You've made your point.'

Burp blithely sails on regardless.

'One more thing. What really matters at the end of the day is somewhere to park plenty of touring coaches close to the house and enough toilets to cope with pensioners' outings. That, more than any amount of history, will guarantee you a steady flow of business.'

His voice tails off as he realises what he has said. An embarrassed silence hangs over the table. George Burp prises a final chunk of lobster flesh from its horny carapace and stuffs it between his teeth as if to put a stopper in his troublesome mouth.

Gargoyle can contain himself no longer.

'A coach park? A coach park indeed! Oh, base villainy! Vandalism! Utter vandalism! The historic landscape is as precious as the house itself. Destroy the setting and the jewel in the crown loses its sparkle.'

Reverend Parsnip attempts to take the sting out of the debate.

'Pay and display in all around I see. The infernal combustion engine shall inherit the earth. I do agree with Mr Gargoyle insofar as what we have here at Farthing Abbey is beautiful in its way and deserves to be cherished. But I also admit to a deep nostalgia for the older landscape of prehistory which expressed the natural forces that once regulated the lives of all, whether rich and poor.'

Gervase doesn't relish a discussion on the qualities of the estate prior to coming into the possession of his ancestors. As far as he is concerned, the most important fact about land is the simple matter of who holds the title deeds in his tin trunk.

'That's all very well, padre. But you must be the first to admit that land needs to be owned by someone in order to be properly cared for. Just look at the Church of England. Thousands of acres producing a tidy profit to maintain the owners. That is surely the example for us laymen to follow.'

'I am not advocating an immediate return to non-ownership, Mr Lloyd-Beauchamp, merely reflecting that things have not always been ordered as they are today. The landscape itself was once a vast temple in its own right. There were no limits to the human imagination just as there were no boundaries on the map. Indeed, there were no maps at all. Except in the mind. The big questions merged into one another. Fertility of the soil meant procreation of the species. Sex, death and the afterlife were all part of one vast intermingling of human experience. Monasteries were often founded on sites of earlier ritualistic significance. So I wouldn't be surprised if Farthing Abbey was in the dim and distant past a site of quite extraordinary potency, a hotspot of earth magic, a place that really got the hormones humming.'

Gervase is beginning to get annoyed.

'Humming hormones? Sex, death and the afterlife, Parsnip? I'm not so sure your bishop would recommend all that lot in one go.'

Araminta eyes the clergyman with curiosity. Those mystical ideas of the pre-Lloyd-Beauchamp landscape have charmed her. She can easily imagine the white-haired cleric as a Chief Druid invoking some elemental earth magic on this very spot several millennia ago. She also reckons Reverend Parsnip might know a thing or two about more recent goings on of a private nature at Farthing Abbey. She is about to draw him out when the main course of roast spring lamb arrives and Gervase seeks to lighten the conversation with a spot of banter.

'Well, Parsnip, you must be relieved we haven't put you on the menu tonight. Just the peas and carrots. I'd say that's pretty damn decent of us, what?'

'Very gracious of you, I am sure, Mr Lloyd-Beauchamp. I really must confess I always feel a bit apprehensive at mealtimes.'

Conviviality is thus quickly re-established, aided by the superbly mellow *Château Cissac* 1982.

'Do you keep dogs, Mr Lloyd-Beauchamp?'

'Not at the dinner table, Mrs Worthington.'

Gervase's attempted witticism falls flat. He has no inkling how to convey humorous intent. Beatrice Worthington, her favourite conversational topic rudely rebuffed, devotes her energies to her dinner and makes no further attempt to speak.

'Well, Lenshood, how about you? What do you think of it?'

'Excellent, Mr Lloyd-Beauchamp. Very tasty.'

Adrian has followed Gervase's exhortation to let the juices flow. He has been drinking everything Withers pours into his glass. As the alcohol goes to work, he unwinds like a clock with springs uncoiling.

'Pay attention, Lenshood. I don't mean the food. The house. What do you think of the house?'

'Oh, I'm not really the right person to ask. Photographers are not required to think. As Gargoyle is always pointing out.'

'Never mind Gargoyle. Don't you think that Farthing Abbey makes a pretty picture?'

Gargoyle smarts. Why does everyone have it in for him? Adrian, meanwhile, downs another sip of claret and composes himself.

'Well yes, I do think Farthing Abbey makes a pretty picture, as a matter of fact. Furthermore, I do consider it is the essence of good architecture to be picturesque. By that I mean that a fine building should inspire a painter or indeed a photographer.'

'A very pretty speech, Lenshood. And what about Mrs Lloyd-Beauchamp? Don't you think she makes a pretty picture?'

Adrian chokes on his wine.

'What's the matter, Lenshood? Don't be shy. It's a simple question.'

Adrian flushes to the roots. He is thankful for the soft candlelight that tones down his red complexion. Does Gervase suspect something? He dares not so much as glance at Ophelia for fear he might betray them both. He attempts to look Gervase in the eye and encounters the blank stare of a man too drunk to know what he is saying.

'Unless of course you don't have an eye for that kind of beauty, Lenshood? Far too arty and intellectual for your own good, I shouldn't wonder. That's the trouble nowadays. But I'm a simple man. Red blood flows through my veins. I know my job. I am not ashamed to go forth and multiply. Living and dying is all I have to do. Human beings, at the end of the day, add up to no more than so many kilos of cosmic compost. What do you say, Parsnip?'

'It is not possible by definition to discuss the ineffable, Mr Lloyd-Beauchamp. A higher purpose cannot always be discerned.'

Gervase is about to say, well 'eff the ineffable', but a last vestige of respect for a gentleman of the cloth holds him back.

'So, Lenshood, what do you say to that. You look like the sort of chap with plenty to say about higher purposes.'

Why is Gervase singling him out? Caution tells him to tread carefully. Bravado urges the opposite. A bold statement would silence his loathsome host and show Ophelia what he is made of. Adrian feels all eyes on him. He takes a deep swig of claret to fire his courage.

'Very well, Mr Lloyd-Beauchamp. Let me see now. Without a higher purpose, there can be no hope, for example, of human beings making the necessary sacrifices to save the planet.'

Whatever made him say that? It sounds totally wet and ridiculous.

'Save the planet, Lenshood? Sentimental twaddle. Are you out of your soft little mind? The bloody planet doesn't need saving, at least, not by us. On the contrary. Once we humans have made it uninhabitable for ourselves, then the planet will save itself very well without us making a mess of everything. So, the sooner we destroy it, the sooner your beloved planet can be saved. And the sooner Parsnip's precious prehistoric landscape will return. Well, what do you say to that?'

Adrian withers under the force of Gervase's angry challenge. His aggression is palpable. But Adrian senses this is his moment of truth. He would have to stand up for himself, if he is not to look utterly pathetic in the eyes of Ophelia.

'Mr Lloyd-Beauchamp, I must object. If everyone thought like that, then the human race would be worth no more than ...'

Adrian does not get to complete his sentence. A loud fart reverberates through the Privy Parlour. George Burp is the object of intense public scrutiny.

'Well, there's another small hole in the ozone layer to help things along. Just pretend it's one of your own, and it won't seem half so bad. That's what my dear old father always says.'

Reverend Parsnip now intervenes, as if picking up the thread of a conversation on a matter of some importance.

'That reminds me. Let me see. How did it go?'

A saintly smile lightens Reverend Parsnip's face.

'Ah, yes. I have it.'

The cleric addresses the assembled gathering.

'The man who farts conquers the man scented with frankincense.'

Reverend Parsnip glances up to see a circle of silent faces looking at him in amazement.

'An old Lebanese proverb. I came across it recently. I was looking up 'fart' in the Oxford English Dictionary. And a most instructive experience it was too. As a verb, it is defined as 'to send forth as wind from the anus'. Has a certain biblical resonance, don't you think? And that is when I came across the proverb which I have just quoted.'

Gargoyle pushes back his chair in protest. He is not alone in thinking the elderly cleric has taken leave of his senses. Gervase, drunk as he is, cannot bear to see his dinner party on such a slippery downhill slope.

'But that's exactly the sort of thing naughty little boys get up to, Parsnip. Looking up dirty words in the dictionary. May I enquire what was the precise object of your research?'

'My research, Mr Lloyd-Beauchamp? Ah, yes. Yes, indeed. Thank you so much for reminding me. I was researching a small matter that should interest you. In some old documents Farthing Abbey is written as Ferting or Farting Abbey. I merely wondered whether the Victorians had inserted the 'h' to make the name more respectable just as they put the 'h' in the Isle of Rum to make it non-alcoholic.'

George Burp sees a chance to redeem himself.

'Now, that's just what you need, Mr Lloyd-Beauchamp. If the place were to be called Farting Abbey, you would get acres of free publicity. You won't be able to keep the punters away. You'd have queues tailing back to the *Happy Eater* on the bypass.'

Gervase listens open-jawed to George Burp. Then Reverend Parsnip speaks once more.

'But I am sorry to disappoint you. It seems the name is derived from the Old English *ferthing* or *farthinge* meaning a measure of land. So Farthing Abbey it is, I am afraid. I would be happy to pen a small footnote on the subject for Mr Gargoyle's guidebook.'

Gervase is only half listening. The wine has addled his brain. He catches Araminta Fettiplace's eye and flashes a lascivious grin. She returns it with what she thinks is a cool flicker of a smile. It comes across as more than she intends. It's as if someone has turned up her controls. Gervase drains his glass in a single gulp. Yes, she is definitely asking for it.

Adrian studies Ophelia. He is looking for little nuances of behaviour to give sustenance to his amorous ambitions. She seems yet more beautiful and mysterious than before, dreamily detached from all that is going on around her. She appears to float on the surface of reality like a leaf on the stream. She hardly bothers to say a word, as if she were not quite of this world, or perhaps not of this era. Her red hair, which had previously struck him as distinctly Pre-Raphaelite now looks decidedly Tudor. He suspects she might, like a sorceress, be able to change her appearance at will.

Adrian's head is reeling. He is in a befuddled limbo, buoyed by hopes, a prey to doubts. Dinner will soon be over, Ophelia spirited away from him. They are now on the dessert of raspberries and clotted cream. Clotted, he reckons, is a good word to describe his present state. He downs his glass of *Château Lafon* 1979 so quickly Withers promptly refills it. He decides he is going to go the distance. Why not?

There is a brief lull in the conversation. Withers resumes his position at his master's elbow. Araminta sees her opportunity.

'Mr Lloyd-Beauchamp, now that Withers has a free moment, don't you think it might be interesting to ask him about the private doings of your ancestors? I bet he has a few tales to tell.'

'Well, what do you say to that, Withers?'

'You would not find that appropriate, sir.'

There is a firm finality in the butler's voice. Gervase is immediately persuaded not to push the matter. He has had enough surprises for one evening. He dismisses Withers and rises unsteadily to his feet.

'I propose we break now for a post-prandial promenade or a visit to the jolly old garderobe. The freedom of Farthing Abbey is yours. Port and walnuts back here in half an hour. That means a bit more talk and we can get stuck into the serious drinking.'

CLOISTER GARTH

As they rise from table, Burp catches Adrian's eye and draws him aside.

'If you want my advice, old chap, never take on a man like Lloyd-Beauchamp. Not unless you can stick the knife right in the jugular. There won't always be folk around to bail you out.'

This remark is overheard by Araminta Fettiplace. Does this mean George Burp's flatulent intervention had been deliberate? As for Adrian, he is not really listening properly. He is aching to get away and communicate a message to Ophelia.

'Right. I'll try to remember that. Thanks.'

He turns to find Ophelia advancing towards him. How he longs to re-live even a tiny part of that delicious intimacy. Her first words delight him with their directness.

'Back there in the Chinese Boudoir ...'

She looks over her shoulder to make sure no one is within earshot. This is it. Her declaration. Adrian wants to touch her and only restrains himself with the utmost effort. His heart beats like a drum. He desperately wants to tell her how much it meant to him. But first he must allow Ophelia to say her piece.

'I don't know what came over me. It wasn't at all what I intended. You must forget what happened. Everything.'

One illusion is shattered.

'I think I left behind a certain item, my ...'

Adrian pats his trouser pocket.

'Fear not, Ophelia, I have your 'item' in a safe place.'

She frowns at the mention of her first name.

'Mr Lenshood, I require it back. Please.'

Another illusion goes up in flames. She has not left him any lover's token.

'As a matter of urgency, you must understand.'

She blushes.

'I must not be compromised in this way.'

His hopes thwarted, Adrian is now prompted by a low cunning. If she wants her 'item' back, then she must meet him in private. In the meantime, he will cling to that tiny piece of silk as the one weak bond that holds them together.

'It's not possible now. We'll have to meet later. I'll give it to you then. In any case, we must talk. I can't leave things like this.'

Adrian sees Gervase approaching. He has to act quickly.

'Listen. I'll go on ahead to the Cloister Garth and wait for you in the spiral staircase. Come just as soon as you can.'

He mumbles this garbled message out of the corner of his mouth as he walks away. Ophelia watches him depart. Gervase now addresses the assembled company with a booming voice.

'Anyone fancy a peep in the Squire's Bedchamber? Most important room in the house. Well come on everyone. Let's go and see where the little Lloyd-Beauchamps are made.'

Withers is summoned. The butler opens a small door in the wainscot, half concealed behind a tapestry running the length of the wall. It shows a hunting party riding to hounds. A terrified deer is being dragged to the ground by a murderous mastiff. They pass through this scene of carnage one by one.

A hush falls over the party as they gather round the four-poster in the Squire's Bedchamber like pilgrims at the shrine of a saint. Gargoyle prowls about the room, peering into the dark corners feebly illuminated by the two candlesticks, one held by Withers and the other by Burp, who has been conscripted as an extra torch-bearer.

'After the Black Death, when the fortunes of Farthing Abbey were at their lowest ebb ...'

While Withers witters on under the flickering candlelight, Gervase homes in on Araminta. He has been finding her an ever more tempting a proposition as he worked his way through the wines. Normally, he has a preference for women of a boyish allure. But under the smooth candlelight he admires the mellow curves of her mature body. She is a ripe, juicy fruit into which he longs to plunge his teeth. He signals his presence by squeezing her elbow. Then he gives her bottom a rough pinch, as if testing the pressure of a bicycle tyre. She promptly removes his hand. Gervase remains hovering nearby for a second strike.

Araminta reckons she knows how to deal with Gervase. He is seriously drunk, but still hardly likely to embarrass her in front of his wife and house guests. So there is no cause to act the startled virgin. Besides, she has to play him along until she has all she needs for her novel. In the meantime, it is not entirely unprofitable to experience the master of Farthing Abbey trying to claim his *droit de seigneur*. It could even be seen as a piece of vital research that might yield some authentic material.

Gargoyle takes advantage of a lengthy pause in the lecture by Withers to embark on some independent sightseeing. What he glimpsed earlier that evening has whetted his taste buds. Now is the time for a real spot of architectural sleuthing. The moment he sets foot in the Cloister Garth, a hop and a skip find their way into his measured step. Try as he might, he can't suppress his excitement.

From his hiding place in the spiral staircase, Adrian hears Gargoyle's footsteps. Thinking it is Ophelia, he rashly advances to meet her. His shock at seeing his colleague sends him scuttling sharply back into the shadows. Fortunately, Gargoyle's attention is fully engaged elsewhere.

The fan vaulting, dimly visible in the shadows, holds him riveted. His eyes probe the darkness to examine the delicate pattern of ribs that spread out above him like a spider's web. Spellbound he admires this miracle of the mason's craft to transform inert, heavy stone into something as light and alive as gossamer. It reminds him of fireworks bursting in the sky, a single moment petrified for eternity. It touches both his heart and his intellect. Gargoyle suspects he is on the verge of another momentous discovery. He hastens back, all aflutter, to the Squire's Bedchamber and silently joins the company listening to Withers who has now reached the end of his talk.

'Very interesting, Withers. But permit me to enquire about the vaulting in the Cloister Garth.'

'Certainly, sir. I shall be happy to oblige. A band of masons came to us one day with an idea for a new kind of vault. Something to resemble an open fan or a dove's tail. They weren't sure exactly how to describe it. The Abbot was intrigued and granted them the means to realise their project. His faith was rewarded. It turned out to be a great success. No sooner were they finished here at Farthing Abbey than they packed their saws and chisels and set off for the great Abbey of St Peter in Gloucester, where they were commissioned to build something in similar style but on a much grander scale.'

'Thank you, Withers. Thank you very much. Thank you very much indeed.'

With an air of triumph, Gargoyle now seeks out Gervase, whom he can see lurking just behind Araminta Fettiplace.

'Did you hear that, Mr Lloyd-Beauchamp? You are the proud owner of the earliest fan-vaulting in England. And by the very same masons who built the cloister at Gloucester! So you won't be wanting any pensioners' coach parties once word about this gets around. There are several books of potentially huge significance to be written about Farthing Abbey, Mr Lloyd-Beauchamp. And I place myself entirely at your service. This is far too exciting for words.'

Gervase has not been listening. His roving hand is poised for another advance on Araminta.

'Far too exciting? What's that you say?'

Gargoyle now addresses himself once more to the butler.

'Withers, please conduct us to the Cloister Garth forthwith.'

'Is that in order, sir?'

'What's that, Withers?'

'Mr Gargoyle proposes we now proceed to the Cloister Garth.'

'You can all proceed wherever you jolly well please. Port and walnuts back in the Privy Parlour in half an hour.'

To Gervase's intense annoyance, Araminta promptly slips away from him and follows in the wake of Withers, Gargoyle and Burp. Then he is waylaid by Beatrice Worthington and the Reverend Parsnip who have just taken their leave of Ophelia.

'Ah, Mr Lloyd-Beauchamp, there you are. Mrs Worthington and myself would like to thank you for a splendid evening. But sadly, we have to renounce the pleasure of sipping port and cracking walnuts together. I do have the early Matins tomorrow.'

Gervase is glad to see the back of them. He speaks with barely concealed relief in his voice.

'I'm sure the pleasure would have been all ours, Reverend Parsnip, Mrs Worthington. But if you really must go, then good night to you both.'

'And a very good night to you, Mr Lloyd-Beauchamp. A pleasure deferred is a joy forever, as the saying goes.'

Gervase, to whom the concept of a pleasure deferred is quite alien, arches an interrogatory eyebrow at the cryptic cleric. Ophelia, for her part, is extremely alarmed at the imminent departure of the vicar. His presence, she feels, has been keeping some sinister forces at bay.

'Do you really have to go Reverend Parsnip? It seems we have hardly had time to talk about anything.'

'Ah, time. The ever-rolling stream waits for no man, my dear lady. Thank you once again for a delightful evening. Shall I reserve the Squire's Pew for communion at eleven?'

Gervase doesn't know how to reply to this.

'Er, very civil of you, Parsnip, I'm sure. Thank you so much for coming. Good night to you both.'

After they have departed, Ophelia immediately excuses herself and joins the others. Gervase is desperate to get back on the trail of Araminta Fettiplace. But the Cloister Garth might be a bit crowded for what he has in view. He decides to take a pause for reflection.

Gervase passes back through the Privy Parlour and re-enters the Long Gallery. The crimson afterglow of the late midsummer evening sunset tinges the thick plaster of the barrel ceiling a bloody hue. The flesh-red passage draws him on, as if into a vast gullet that swallows him whole. Farthing Abbey now unmasks itself as a living creature with physical appetites of its own. How, Gervase wonders, has the house survived so long, but by feeding off his predecessors and digesting them one by one? It will consume him too. He feels that it is only a question of time.

He paces up and down the Long Gallery while he ponders his own transient role in the grander scheme of things. He stops by a stone Jacobean chimneypiece rampant with figures of bare-breasted women striking suggestive poses. He devours them with his eyes, runs a tingling finger over their voluptuous curves. They feel alarmingly real. The wood carvings have aroused him. He shrugs in mute acknowledgement of an eternal truth. The flesh is what matters. Serving its demands is all that is asked of him. What else is there for him in life but to plant his seed and do some damage along the way?

Gervase finally wrenches himself away. His mind is made up. He descends the stair to the Cloister Garth where he sees Gargoyle busy ingratiating himself with Ophelia like a fawning courtier. She is only half listening, while Withers points the candlestick into the deep recesses of the stonework. A few steps away, Burp gazes into space as he puffs at a cigarillo. Gervase lurks in the shadows. A stratagem takes shape in his drink-sodden mind. He does not have to wait long to put it into effect. When Araminta emerges from the garderobe, he springs out of the darkness and takes her firmly by the arm.

'Got you, Araminta, old girl. It's me. Gervase.'

Before she knows what is happening, Araminta is being pushed none too gently in the small of the back towards the inky blackness of the spiral staircase. She stumbles on the stone steps. Gervase hisses at her to keep quiet as he hauls her to her feet and prods her forwards.

'Mind the flaming steps.'

'Really, Mr Lloyd-Beauchamp. Steady on. This is hardly the time or the place for ...'

She feels Gervase's hand caress her bottom.

'Come on, you saucy filly, there's a good sport. You know you want it. We'll go somewhere more comfortable next time. But I've got to shag you right now. *Noblesse oblige*. Or something like that.'

Araminta struggles to free herself. Gervase holds her tight. He pushes her up the stairs. When she is a couple of steps above him he thrusts his hand up her dress, grabs her knickers and wrenches them down to her ankles. Off they come. Gervase seizes the garment and holds it aloft like a battle trophy, as if he has taken the enemy colours. Momentarily free from his clutches Araminta kicks out wildly from her superior vantage point. Her heel connects with something solid. Gervase's head? A groan of pain tells her it is precisely that. Then all goes quiet. Nothing moves. Her attacker must be out for the count.

Araminta's heart is beating fit to burst. She gasps for breath. Beyond that she can hear nothing except for the dulcet tones of Gargoyle somewhere in the distance waxing lyrical about the fan-vaulting. A minute or so pass while she figures out what to do next. She is terrified of going back down to where Gervase lies, possibly dying in a pool of blood. Perhaps he is dead? Has she killed him? But she is even more terrified of climbing further up the spiral stair where she senses yet another unwelcome presence lurking in the darkness. Then she hears sounds of Gervase stirring.

'Look, Araminta, old sport. Everything OK? Just a spot of fun. High spirits. No harm done. Talk later. I'm off now.'

Gervase picks himself up, pressing Araminta's knickers like a bandage against a badly bleeding nose. He staggers off through the Cloister Garth. At this moment Ophelia, who has at last torn herself from Gargoyle's lecture on fan-vaulting, comes hurrying towards the spiral staircase. She almost crashes into Gervase. But he doesn't even notice her. He seems anxious to conceal himself as he rushes past, hiding his face behind what looks like a strange frilly handkerchief.

Ophelia imagines the worst. Gervase has had words with Adrian Lenshood. Perhaps he has uncovered her guilty secret. There has been violence. She hurries on, half expecting to find Adrian's body on the floor. Instead, a distraught, dishevelled Araminta

Fettiplace comes tumbling down the spiral stair just as she starts to climb it. The romantic novelist falls sobbing into her arms.

'My dear Araminta, you look as if you've seen a ghost!'

Araminta is about to tell Ophelia about Gervase and his assault, then decides she had better keep quiet.

'A ghost? Yes, a ghost. That was it. It must have been a ghost. Very spooky.'

Ophelia quickly makes the connection between the lady's distress and her husband's hasty retreat. She fully understands what Araminta declines to tell her. But having unwittingly created a convenient little ghost fiction to explain matters, Ophelia lets it rest at that.

The two women remain enfolded in one another's arms while Ophelia tries to calm the victim of her husband's violent lust. Araminta clings to her as if her very life depends on it. She feels this woman's body moulded close against her own, breast to breast, stomach to stomach. Suddenly, an intended kiss of comfort on the cheek brushes Araminta's lips instead. Their mouths meet. Now their tongues are touching. Their hands switch, seemingly of their own accord, from soothing pats to softer caresses. Their flesh melts into one another. Ophelia is powerless to stop herself. It feels like the Chinese Boudoir scene all over again only with a different partner and one of her own sex.

Araminta starts sobbing again. Both women seek retreat to the safer ground of their respective roles as victim and comforter. The burning fuse fizzles out. Yet they remain for a few moments more entwined in a looser embrace, slowly detaching themselves from what so nearly might have been.

Ophelia trembles from head to foot. The strangest things are happening to her in this house and she doesn't know why. Except that somehow Farthing Abbey seems to be playing a part in it all. Suddenly, she snaps completely out of the sensuality of the moment. Adrian! He must be right there behind her, waiting in the spiral stair. He must have been there all along.

'Come along now, Araminta. Let's get you all cleaned up. I'll take you to the garderobe.'

Adrian bemoans his rotten luck. Not only has he been denied his lover's tryst, Ophelia has almost made love to another woman right under his nose. He curses Farthing Abbey and all its works. No sooner has he done that than he receives a chilling reply to his puny, petulant insult. A soberingly cold, eerily damp breath falls like a wet cloth on the back of his neck. He races in panic from the spiral stair.

IN VINO VERITAS

C onsiderably shaken, Adrian hurries back to the Privy Parlour. There is no one about. A solitary five-branched candlestick stands on the oak table. The bottles of port and pewter dishes filled with walnuts look curiously unreal, as if they are merely objects posing for a still-life painting. There is a tangible air of suspense about the empty room, suggesting the temporary absence of revellers from long ago who will soon resume their convivial gathering.

Adrian turns to see Withers and George Burp enter the room, each bearing a candlestick. Between them marches Peregrine Gargoyle, carrying himself with all the pomp and circumstance of a medieval bishop in procession. It is an amazing sight.

'You have every reason to be amazed, Lenshood. I have made a most exciting discovery. The Cloister Garth possesses England's earliest fan-vaulting. Be sure to take plenty of pictures first thing tomorrow morning. I can't begin to tell you now how important it is.'

George Burp has other things on his mind.

'Thought I heard a bit of commotion just now. Wonder if you heard anything from wherever you were, Adrian?'

Adrian goes straight on the defensive.

'A commotion? From wherever I was? What do you mean? Better ask Araminta. What I mean is, I'm sure it was her I overheard just now saying she had seen a ghost or something.'

Adrian is saved from further confusion by Gervase who enters the Privy Parlour, pressing Araminta's knickers to his wounded face. Her shoe struck him below the right eye. The bleeding has stopped, but there is no doubt it will be a real shiner.

'What's that you're saying about a ghost? That must have been what made me stumble just now. I almost did myself a serious injury bumping into some damn piece of Gargoyle's infernal Gothic stonework. Practically put my eye out.'

Gervase hastily stuffs Araminta's knickers into his trouser pocket, but not before Adrian has recognised the garment for what it is. The two of them are, he reflects, fellow travellers at least in one respect.

'Some ghost that, Mr Lloyd-Beauchamp. Must be very painful.'

There is a mocking tone of disbelief to Burp's voice.

'Where did you say you saw it?'

'I didn't say I actually saw anything, Burp. That's the thing about ghosts, not always visible. But I sensed something spooky come at me out of the shadows.'

'Something spooky, eh?'

Ophelia and Araminta now appear. Gervase does not hesitate to invoke the phantom spectre as his own personal assailant, while seeking to make peace with the victim of his assault.

'So what's all this about a ghost, Araminta? Think I've had a pretty close encounter myself. Got this knock as I took evasive action. Still, no harm done. Trust you are OK. Reckon we could all use a drink.'

Gervase deftly marshals his guests, boldly placing Araminta by his side. George Burp takes the seat next to her. Ophelia is sandwiched between Peregrine Gargoyle and Adrian Lenshood. Thus ensconced, the latter quickly forgets the frustration and then the fear born of his lonely vigil in the spiral stair. But Adrian feels no warmth in Ophelia's proximity. There is a distinct chilliness about her.

Once more the genial host, Gervase makes sure the port passes swiftly from hand to hand in order to drown the memory of recent events. It seems to do the trick. Araminta begins to look as if she might even be enjoying herself. But she maintains a safe distance from Gervase. Instinctively, she gravitates to the reassuring proximity of George Burp who relishes being the beneficiary of her feminine closeness as she edges towards him. Like a wily old fox, Burp has spotted the gaping hole in the chicken wire of her temptingly exposed little coop.

'So did you get a good look at this ghost of yours then, Araminta?'

'Not really, George. Whatever it was, it certainly gave me a shock. I wouldn't be surprised if Farthing Abbey were haunted.'

'Haunted, you reckon?'

'Quite possibly. We must ask Withers. He would know.'

Gervase calls for the butler.

'Sir?'

'How long have you been here at Farthing Abbey, Withers?'

'I have always been here, sir.'

'Well, that should be long enough to know if there are any ghosts in the place, what?'

'Ghosts, sir?'

'Yes, Withers, ghosts. Ghosts, as in things that go bump in the night, spirits of the departed, spectres that walk through walls, dead ancestors with heads under their arms. You know the sort of thing.'

'There are none like that here, sir. The previous occupants of Farthing Abbey all conduct themselves with due propriety.'

'Previous occupants. Due propriety. That's a good one.'

Gervase guffaws, but his jocularity is forced. It makes a hollow sound. Withers has made him feel uncomfortably close to being a 'previous occupant' himself. Seeking to change the subject, he comes out with the question that has been troubling him ever since that unpleasant encounter at the Temple of Venus.

'Withers, I have been meaning to ask you about that young hooligan and the girl at the Temple of Venus.'

'Hooligan, Sir?'

'Well, what do you know about them? I must say you didn't seem entirely surprised. Who are they?'

Withers hesitates, choosing his words carefully.

'I have never seen the girl before, sir.'

'So you have seen the insolent youth then?'

Withers gives the faintest assent with a lowering of his eyelids.

'Well then, Withers. Out with it, tell us what you know.'

The butler remains silent.

'Come on, Withers.'

'It is a long story, sir.'

'No matter. We have all the time in the world. Fetch yourself a glass and pull up a chair.'

Still Withers hesitates.

'That's an order, Withers. And bring more port.'

Withers returns bearing a silver tray with a single glass and a bottle of port, which he places by Gervase. After further prompting, the butler pours himself a small measure. Then he walks solemnly to the foot of the table. Steadying himself with one hand on the vacant chair, he directs his gaze directly at Gervase at the head of the table.

'I shall willingly imbibe a glass of port, sir. But I prefer to remain standing, if you will permit. It is more seemly thus.'

'Very well. Now come on, Withers. Tell us all you know.'

Withers resembles an actor struggling to remember his lines.

'Something wrong, Withers?'

'No, sir. I am merely considering in which year it would be more appropriate to commence. In 1741 or in 1991.'

The butler stands before them in frock coat and wing collar, furrowed face framed by silver hair. He speaks in softly enunciated tones that would have been soporific, were not his listeners hanging on his every word. He has opted to begin at the earlier date.

'In 1741 we received a visit from *Signore* Paolo and *Signore* Pietro Francini. Italian *stuccadori* or artisans in plaster, as they explained themselves to be. They were promptly engaged by Sir Archibald. The master had a penchant for all things Italian as a result of his various travels. The Rococo Vestibule in the Palladian Villa was duly decorated by them.'

'Do get to the point, Withers. I think we have had enough history. The yobbo with the motorbike in the Temple of Venus.'

'Ah yes, the Temple of Venus. Indeed, the Francinis decorated the interior of that edifice too. But Sir Archibald then declared he had not consented to the additional expenditure. Heated words were exchanged and the master ordered them to remove themselves forthwith. They resolved to set sail for America where their talents would be properly rewarded. It was a sad end to a happy collaboration. For one glorious summer they brought the radiant sun of Italy to shine down on Farthing Abbey.'

Withers pauses, savouring the sweet memories of those happy days.

'Come on, Withers. Do get on with it.'

'Very well, sir. There the episode might have ended. But there was also a young lady companion to Lady Lloyd-Beauchamp, a most beautiful creature. She was stricken with love for *Signore* Paolo Francini. Her feelings were heartily reciprocated. They would meet often in the Temple of Venus. They made promises of matrimony.'

At last, thinks Araminta, the love story. The very stuff of her romantic novel. How she wishes she has a tape recorder.

'The lady was exceedingly distraught when her beloved was dismissed without notice. She begged him to take her with him, but he said he would send for her later. Amid much anguish, they parted. Neither of them knew she was then with child. The last she heard from *Signore* Paolo was from Bristol where he intended to take ship for America. In this note he repeated his promises and begged her to be patient.'

All eyes and ears are on Withers.

'Knowledge of the lady's condition became public some weeks later. At the same time news arrived that the vessel on which the Francini brothers were sailing had been wrecked off the Irish coast. Sir Archibald summoned the lady and condemned her as a common slut. Then he informed her, quite wrongly, that her lover had been lost at sea. Finally, he confronted her with a choice. Get rid of the child and submit to be his mistress or be married off to a filthy, obnoxious swineherd who lived in squalor in a miserable hovel.'

Horrified, they look at Gervase. How could he? The spitting image of Sir Archibald downs another glass of port in a single gulp and glares back defiantly at his silent accusers.

'I don't know why you are all looking at me. It was nothing to do with me. Anyway, do you think that Francini fellow would have married her? He was probably doing a runner. Only an Eytie, after all. But the story isn't over yet. There is probably a happy ending, isn't there Withers?'

'A happy ending? No, sir. I am afraid not. To oblige her to reflect on her situation, Sir Archibald locked the unfortunate creature in the Squire's Bedchamber. Lady Lloyd-Beauchamp was away at the time. All that evening the master drank copiously before going to take his pleasure. But the lady refused to be his mistress and begged for mercy. Ignoring her tearful pleas and overcoming her brave attempt to reject his advances, Sir Archibald forced his attentions on her with extreme violence. Her pitiful screams could be heard in the Servants' Hall.'

Horrified, Ophelia is even more resolved than before not to spend a night in the Squire's Bedchamber. The room is cursed. For her part, Araminta listens spellbound to this real-life bodice-ripper. It goes against the refined character she would have liked for Sir Archibald in her story. But there is no helping that.

'I will spare you the sordid details of what happened in the Squire's Bedchamber. But when Sir Archibald had sated his lust, he turned on her with foul abuse, thrashed her for being a wanton and a harlot. Her torment did not end until the master fell asleep in a drunken stupor.'

Again all eyes fall on Gervase, who stares blankly past them. He is looking intently at the painting of Sir Owen Lloyd-Beauchamp hanging behind Withers. A smug grin spreads across the face of his Tudor ancestor, as if approving the dastardly deeds of his Georgian look-alike, Sir Archibald. Gervase can hardly believe his eyes as the portrait now gives him a sly wink and raises an arched eyebrow as if egging him on to equally impressive acts of devilment. Gervase wonders how Sir Owen had made his wicked mark, but thinks it wiser not to enquire under present circumstances.

'The young lady took advantage of Sir Archibald's inebriated slumber to make her escape. But she had no thought of deliverance. Believing her lover to be dead and knowing her own honour to be sullied, she went directly to the lake and drowned her sorrows. Her unborn child perished with her. Her body was never given a Christian burial. Sir Archibald had it weighed down with stones and left it lying there on the bed of the lake. To cover his tracks he put the story about that the lady had run off to join her lover. You were enquiring about ghosts, Mr Lloyd-Beauchamp. She is one whose spirit has not yet been laid to rest.'

Gervase now adopts a more conciliatory tone.

'That's a tragic tale, Withers. Really very tragic. But I still don't see the connection with our intruder on the motorbike.'

'Well, sir, the young man first appeared at Farthing Abbey in the summer of 1991. Out of nowhere. We, that is your great-uncle Sir Horace and myself, became aware of his presence from certain signs of habitation at the Orangery where he had installed himself. One day, Sir Horace spotted the young man from the window of his chamber and sent me to find out who it might be. I instantly recognised a living replica of *Signore* Paolo Francini. Identical in every respect, the same face and olive skin, the same black hair. And the way his dark eyes sparkled when he smiled. It was the very same expression. It was him.'

Gervase gives a snort of derision.

'Well, he left it a bit late, don't you think? 250 years is a bit long for any girl to wait. What did he want?'

Withers continues unperturbed.

'He didn't want anything, sir. Nor did he have any idea why he was here. It was a curious encounter. I related every detail of our conversation to Sir Horace who concluded that this was indeed *Signore* Paolo Francini come to fetch his lady and to have his account for the Temple of Venus settled. The *stuccadore* had returned exactly as he had promised. Sir Horace immediately resolved to make amends for any obligation on the part of his ancestors.'

'Did he present no demands, this young man?'

'Not exactly, sir. I only know that they met briefly and that Sir Horace granted the young man permission to stay.'

Araminta is intrigued to hear more.

'And what did he do with his time, the young man?'

'That is another strange thing. He seemed content to do very little. He passed the time of day idling by the Scenic Lake, mostly near the Temple of Venus. He revealed himself to be an artist of sorts, for I sometimes saw him sketch. He spent a whole summer here. Then in late September he disappeared. But the following year he was back with the bluebells and again he left with the swallows. And this year, he is with us once more staying at the Orangery.'

'Summers at Farthing Abbey appear to have become quite a routine for our young friend, don't they, Withers? Does he always treat the Temple of Venus as a private love nest? And as a garage for his motor bike into the bargain?'

Ophelia recalls her first sight of the young man. So, he is Italian, just like that Donatello statue he so resembles. And an artist too. Suddenly, Farthing Abbey has something that appeals to her.

'Calm down, Gervase. We mustn't act hastily. There is perhaps a slight misunderstanding to be cleared up. That's all.'

'Slight misunderstanding? Yesterday, I didn't even know I owned a bleeding Orangery, and now I discover an Italian vagrant posing as the re-incarnation of an eighteenth century plasterer squatting in it!'

Gervase turns back to the butler.

'Tell me, Withers. Did Sir Horace sign a lease or anything permitting this young rascal to stay?'

'Not to my knowledge, sir.'

'Well, in that case you can tell him to pack up and clear out. This little swallow will be migrating early this year.'

Gervase draws breath. But no one dares fill the angry silence.

'And another thing, Withers.'

'Yes, sir.'

'I'm sure I'm not the only person here who would like to know how you have been the witness to all this and so much else besides. Have you discovered the secret of eternal life?'

Gervase's rude tone has no noticeable effect on Withers.

'Eternal life, sir? I don't know how to answer that. You see, I have always been here. Always. That is all I know.'

Gargoyle now attempts to turn the situation to his own advantage.

'Mr Lloyd-Beauchamp, if you will permit. I think I may have a logical explanation. Withers has clearly spent many years on his own at Farthing Abbey deprived of all contact with the outside world. I would suggest he has absorbed the history of the house to such a point that he has imagined himself to be present at all sorts of events that didn't actually happen and then mixed them up with things that really did. Under such circumstances, fact and fiction so easily blend together. It is not unknown for people to believe they were alive at moments in the past that were clearly too remote to be humanly possible.'

Now Gargoyle reaches out to claim his prize.

'I for one would rather put my faith in the documentary evidence of the Farthing Abbey archives than the recollections of someone who can't possibly have witnessed all the events he describes. The archives, Mr Lloyd-Beauchamp, are the key to this mystery. And if I might be given the key, I will take it on myself to resolve matters conclusively.'

Adrian Lenshood has been exploring another angle.

'I know it might seem absurd, but say the young man in the Orangery is a re-incarnation of Paolo Francini. Then could not Mr Lloyd-Beauchamp also be a re-incarnation of his ancestors he so strikingly resembles? And isn't it also conceivable that Withers has lived more than one life here at Farthing Abbey? Only in his case, he has preserved the memories from his previous lives. Come to think of it, we might all be re-incarnations. I wouldn't be surprised if Withers has encountered some of us before.'

Gargoyle is about to pour scorn on this re-incarnation theory that has diverted attention from his own more sophisticated explanation of things. But then Withers looks Adrian straight in the eye.

'Indeed, I do recall you very well, Mr Lenshood, sir. In the reign of Good Queen Bess you were a moderately accomplished painter of portrait miniatures. Also a composer of amorous sonnets which gained you the repute of a lovesick swain.'

Gargoyle laughs derisively.

'Lovesick swain? How very revealing, Lenshood.'

'And you Mr Gargoyle sir, were a Cistercian brother who rose to be in charge of the Farthing Abbey scriptorium. A stickler for accuracy and neatness. Once you even expelled our most talented scribe for penning a small personal comment in the margin of a manuscript. You said posterity would not be interested in his private ramblings.'

Gargoyle takes the rebuke stoically. He thoroughly approves of the disciplinary action taken by his medieval *doppelgänger*.

Withers now turns to George Burp.

'You were a groom, Mr Burp. A rough and ready character, though too much given to drink and unreliable in your accounts with blacksmiths and farriers. You were made redundant in the spring of 1905 when Sir Percy Lloyd-Beauchamp purchased his first Bugatti.'

On the edge of her seat, Araminta braces herself to hear the worst.

'And you, madam, were a buxom milkmaid during the Regency. Ever generous with your favours. Mr Nash took quite a shine to you.'

Araminta blushes. So much for her lofty social ambitions.

'Will that be all, sir?'

'Certainly not, Withers. What about Mrs Lloyd-Beauchamp?'

Withers gives Ophelia a tortured look but he says nothing.

'Come on now, Withers. You mustn't keep the lady waiting.'

Still Withers holds his tongue, speechless and ashen-faced.

'I am much fatigued, sir. If that is all, I shall bid you good night.'

Gervase, suddenly fearful of hearing something that will not reflect well on Ophelia and thus on himself, allows Withers to withdraw. The butler duly retires, leaving behind six stunned people and a number of empty port bottles.

'Well, that put you lot in your place, I must say. Breeding will out, you know. But no need to look so glum. The night is young. It's far too early for bed. Anyone fancy a spot of wrestling?'

MANLY SPORT

Gervase is serious about the wrestling.

'A harmless bit of manly sport. Just the thing to round things off. You've stuffed yourselves with food and drink at my expense. Now let's see if you can keep it down.'

Peregrine Gargoyle, George Burp and Adrian Lenshood look at one another with varying degrees of alarm.

'Surely one of you must fancy your chances?'

Gargoyle quickly counts himself out of the reckoning.

'Really, Mr Lloyd-Beauchamp, this is a most entertaining proposition. But I shall have to decline. I'm a bit old for that sort of caper. Even in my previous life it seems I never did anything more strenuous than manage the scriptorium. So it wouldn't be much fun wrestling with an aged Cistercian such as myself. Perhaps one of the other gentlemen?'

'So that leaves a drunken groom and a lovesick swain. Can't say I like the sound of that last chap very much. Any reason why I shouldn't start with you, Lenshood?'

Adrian feels as helpless as the lamb that has just caught the glint of the butcher's knife. He reviews his options. If he were to decline for no good reason, he would look pathetic. Ophelia wants to intervene on his behalf, but she hesitates, fearing that would only arouse her husband's suspicions. Meanwhile, Gervase removes his dinner jacket. Gargoyle, who has been so quick to excuse himself, now urges Adrian on.

'Nothing wrong with a bit of manly sport, Lenshood. Might do you some good. And I am sure Mr Lloyd-Beauchamp won't hurt you.'

'Glad to hear you've come round to the idea, Gargoyle. I'll take you on last. After the others have tired me a bit.'

Gargoyle bites his tongue. Slowly, Adrian removes his jacket. There is a sadistic look in Gervase's bloodshot eyes shining hard as humbugs in a mask-like face flushed with drink.

'Prepare to meet your fate, Lenshood. Gargoyle, Burp, grab a candlestick. Come on, ladies, I can promise some good sport.'

Seizing a candlestick himself, Gervase stalks out, leaving the others to follow in his wake. Adrian, trembling at the prospect of what lies in store, wonders why he should be singled out. Does Gervase know about the scene in the Chinese Boudoir? Has Ophelia confessed? Surely not, or he would be as good as dead already. But it is too late for such questions. Gervase has halted in the middle of the Long Gallery.

'Right, Lenshood. Let me size you up. I'm a bit heavier. But you've got youth on your side. Should be a fair contest.'

'That depends on the rules.'

'Rules? Well, I never. Of course you can have some rules. What rules do you normally fight under, Lenshood? You can choose.'

Adrian can hardly believe it. The man is hopping mad. What rules are there? He looks up to see yet another portrait of one of Gervase's ancestors gazing down at him with undisguised scorn. He reckons reincarnations of this loathsome strain are likely to go on plaguing the world until Judgement Day. There will always be a malevolent Lloyd-Beauchamp waiting to pounce on a defenceless Lenshood.

'I'll leave that side of things to you, Mr Lloyd-Beauchamp. After all, this is your little game. You can decide on the rules.'

A tone of defiance has entered Adrian's voice. He is going to make a scrap of it after all.

'Very well. I propose the Indian bear hug, Lenshood. It's very simple. You seize your opponent round the middle and lift him off the floor. Best of three wins. Start when you like.'

Indian bear hug? Can this be serious? Adrian stands there nonplussed.

'Well, come on Lenshood. Show us what you're made of.'

Adrian eyes Gervase with repugnance. He has been hoping to embrace Ophelia before the night was out. Now fate offers him Gervase instead. Steeling himself for the awful clash of bodies, he makes a clumsy lunge forward. To his surprise, Gervase takes no evasive action, but allows himself to be grabbed. Then, overriding his puny hold, Gervase applies his own manlier grip. Adrian feels weak and impotent against him. His main sensation is nausea as he inhales a foul cocktail of sweat, drink, cigars and half-digested food. Gervase steadily squeezes the breath from his body. He thinks he is going to pass out. He wants to throw up.

Isn't the idea to lift his opponent off the ground? His efforts produce no result. Gervase might as well be nailed to the floor. Why on earth doesn't the bastard put him out of his misery? But he knows that his suffering is an essential part of Gervase's game plan. After what seems like an eternity, Gervase concludes the proceedings by hoisting him a few inches off the ground. It is accomplished as easily as if he has been lifting a child. Round one is over.

'Well, Lenshood, you must do better than that in the next round, or we'll have to begin all over again.'

Adrian's heart sinks. Gervase has read his thoughts, for he longs to get it all over and done with.

'Me to go first this time, Lenshood.'

Gervase enfolds him in a smothering bear hug. Adrian responds in like manner, but it is useless. Perhaps if he were to shift his weight a bit? He leans to the right, then springs for all he is worth to the left. Gervase follows his double move with consummate ease and then carries on where his exhausted opponent leaves off. Off they go, leaping down the Long Gallery, arms bound tightly around one another. Under the flickering candles, their cavorting has a staccato effect, like two drunks dancing the polka.

Eventually they come to a halt. Now Gervase puts a painful squeeze on Adrian. It seems to last forever, until finally he hoists him off his feet and then drops him like a dead weight. His knees buckle and he collapses into a crumpled heap on the floor. It is all over. Thank God. Adrian looks up to find a beaming Gervase extend a hand.

'Excellent contest, Lenshood. I would never have guessed you were so agile. Let's shake on a good fight.'

As he bends to help him to his feet, Gervase hisses in his ear.

'I haven't finished with you yet, Lenshood. Not by a long chalk.'

Gervase turns away, leaving Adrian a prey to the direst thoughts.

'Right, Burp, you're next. But first, another drink. This is thirsty work. Withers has some champagne stashed away up by the dresser. Go and fetch it, Gargoyle. There's a good man.'

Gargoyle cuts a very poor figure as a butler. He returns with a bottle of champagne that he holds nervously as if it might explode in his hands. He proffers it uncertainly to Gervase.

'Bollinger 1948! Do you know what this stuff is worth? And I'm serving it to peasants like you, Burp! I expect ale with no hops is what your ancestors would have knocked back in some smelly hovel while my lot were sipping claret up in the big house.'

Gervase grabs the champagne from Gargoyle's trembling hand. As if wringing the neck of a chicken, he unwinds the wire and twists the cork. He lets it fly unchecked. The small missile strikes the ceiling with force and detaches a solid chunk of plaster that falls noisily onto the oak floorboards. Gargoyle bends down to retrieve the precious fragment of Jacobean strapwork and cradles it in the palm of his hand.

'Don't fret, you old fool. Plenty more where that came from.'

Gervase splashes the vintage Bollinger in a haphazard shower over a handful of glasses. Gargoyle makes a brave attempt at dignified butlering serving Ophelia and Araminta while Gervase helps himself. Burp, however, refuses the offer of a drink.

'What's the matter, Burp? Is the drunken groom upset? You must never take offence at the truth. We all have our place in the great scheme of things. It's in the genes. We Lloyd-Beauchamps trace our bloodline right back to the Norman Conquest.'

'I'd keep quiet about the Normans, if I were you, Lloyd-Beauchamp. Anyone who claims descent from that bunch of land-grabbers, robber barons and bully-boys is no better than a bandit himself.'

'So that's your grievance, is it? One of the Saxon dispossessed, Burp? Well, too bad. There are always winners and losers. Fairness has nothing to do with it. It is the fate of you Saxon underdogs to lie down in the dirt, and for us Normans to stand on your necks. Nothing personal in it. Just the way of the world.'

The two men draw closer, eyeball to eyeball, pacing to and fro like stags doing the parallel walk.

Gervase's blood is up.

'I'm going to wipe the floor with you, Burp.'

'Take my advice, Lloyd-Beauchamp. Don't start pissing until you've undone your flies.'

'You've quite a tongue in your head, Burp. I can tolerate a bit of lip. But only up to a point.'

'Too late to patronise me now, Lloyd-Beauchamp. I've met plenty of your type before. All very impressive in your straw hats and fancy blazers, but a bunch of pansies when it comes to the crunch.'

They glare at one another with undisguised loathing. Suddenly, like Sumo wrestlers, they fling themselves into combat.

They look evenly matched in terms of height and weight. But Burp is the older of the two by several years. However, the exertion shows first on Gervase's face. The bout with Adrian was nothing more than a warm up. The two men rock and sway as each tries to lift the other. This is the real thing. Burp, sensing he is really up against it, summons his last ounce of energy. In doing so, he releases a thunderous fart. Gervase, momentarily distracted, is suddenly hoisted aloft.

Gervase is furious.

'That was wind-assisted. Two can play at that game, Burp.'

'Never force a fart, Lloyd-Beauchamp. Or you might get more than you bargained for.'

'Why, you disgusting wretch! I'll teach you a ...'

Gervase throws himself with blind fury into a second clinch that might have crushed the life out of a man less robust than George Burp. But his initial burst of strength fuelled by anger is quickly spent. Burp rallies himself for a final effort. He squeezes as hard as he can while hauling his opponent several inches from the ground. Then he drops sharply and unceremoniously. Gervase stumbles about as drunkards do and drops a knee to the floor before recovering his balance. Two to nothing. Gervase is white with rage.

'Damn your eyes, Burp. I challenge you to a re-match. To an immediate re-match.'

'Not tonight Lloyd-Beauchamp. You look a bit unsteady. See how you feel tomorrow.'

Gervase snarls venomously. He seizes a candlestick with one hand. For a moment it looks as if he is going to resort to armed combat. But Ophelia is his target. He grabs her roughly by the wrist and drags her off to the Squire's Bedchamber.

After a long silence, Gargoyle addresses Burp.

'Don't you think you went a bit far? After all, Mr Lloyd-Beauchamp is our host. He only intended a bit of harmless fun.'

Burp eyes Gargoyle with acute distaste.

'It would have been your turn next, Peregrine, old chap. You should be thanking me for saving your rotten old hide.'

Adrian realises he has let the entire evening pass without arranging to meet Ophelia. And now she has been dragged off by that brute of a husband. Some schemer he has turned out to be. But suddenly, Ophelia reappears before them. And without Gervase.

'I just wanted to ask you all for your understanding on account of my husband's... I mean I am sure he intended no harm. So may I wish you a comfortable night. I trust you will find the way back to the Palladian Villa easily enough in the moonlight.'

Adrian seizes his opportunity.

'It has been a splendid evening, Mrs Lloyd-Beauchamp. In spite of everything. And it looks like a wonderful night with a clear sky and a full moon. Before retiring, I think I shall take a few pictures from the Temple of Venus. There should be some magical reflections in the water, I expect. An opportunity not to be missed, don't you think?'

This is about as far as he can go in front of the others.

'What a delightfully romantic notion, Mr Lenshood. Please feel free to do as you please.'

With that she is gone.

At least Adrian has told her where she might find him. But she has not given him the slightest hint she will come. Unless that reference to a delightfully romantic notion was a coded message. It leaves him with the wild hope Ophelia might after all attend a lover's tryst.

'That's a downright queer notion of yours, Lenshood. I don't think we need any moonlit shots for *Houses and Castles*. I suggest you get a good night's rest after all your exertions.'

'All the same, Gargoyle. I do have other outlets, you know.'

By the time they let themselves out through the slype, Adrian has convinced himself Ophelia will come to him. He imagines her approach, a pale figure of ethereal beauty bathed in moonlight. Everything is possible. The night is young, still full of destiny and boundless promise. The universe is limitless. Romance is in the stars.

Araminta Fettiplace takes George Burp's arm for the short walk back to the Palladian Villa.

'I say, George, you put on quite a show back there. You are a man of surprises, I must say.'

'Why, thank you kindly, Araminta. I reckon there will be a few more surprises before the night is out.'

'Oh, really?'

'Didn't you notice the evil glint in that pompous bastard's eye?'

THE ORANGERY

The moon-drenched scene of lake, lawn, trees and water is steeped in the artificial glare of a surrealist painting. The Palladian Villa, by day the most imposing object in the landscape, has faded to a scenic backdrop, so flimsy it might sway in the gentle breeze like a piece of canvas. The dark sky breathes with a life full of nocturnal menace. Strange things might be on the move, perhaps the occupants of the tomb chests in the church have stirred and grave slabs are shifting. All it needs is the sound effect of a hooting owl to complete the picture. Instead, the tortured shriek of a peacock comes wailing across the black mirror of the Scenic Lake. The four figures now approaching the Palladian Villa stay close to one another.

'Infernal din those peacocks make. Can't think why they keep them at stately homes. I'd throttle them if I had my way. Didn't they once eat them stuffed with weasels or something nasty?'

Burp is whistling in the dark. He has been brought up in a tiny terraced house with neighbours right and left. Here at Farthing Abbey, with the nearest human habitation out of sight, he feels as vulnerable and exposed as if camping on the vast Siberian steppe with wolves sniffing at the ropes of his tent.

'Rather you than me for that moonlight walk by the Scenic Lake, Adrian.'

They climb the steps of the Palladian Villa and enter the Rococo Vestibule. A radiant light floods down through the glass dome and shimmers off the white plaster of the walls. For several moments they stand in reverential silence at the foot of the staircase, bathing in the moonbeams cascading over them like a waterfall.

Gargoyle leads the procession upstairs. They bid one another good night across the balustraded landing. Four doors open and close in unison. Within minutes they all are in bed except for Adrian sorting out the equipment he will need for his moonlight photography. Already he regrets his plan for a stroll by the Scenic Lake. Of course, Ophelia will not come to him. Why should she? Yet the moon is there to urge him on, insisting in its sly, whispering way that dreams are as real as anything else you might care to think of in this confoundedly unreal world.

Adrian slips camera bag over his right shoulder and tucks tripod under his left arm like a gamekeeper's shotgun. It gives him the illusion he is not entirely defenceless. He walks stealthily along the landing and down the stairs. The moonlit interior looks even more awesome than before. The swirling arabesques of the plasterwork seem to start moving the moment he takes his eyes off them. The open front door invites him to step forth as if obligingly held by an invisible butler. Did they not shut it? But the die is cast. There is no turning back.

There is not a cloud in the blue-black sky sparkling with tiny stars like distant diamonds. The path towards the Temple of Venus is well lit by the moon. Only a few trees artfully positioned by Capability Brown cast their shadows. That will be his best route, not the shady woodland track via the church. He sets off slowly, treading softly, trying to be calm and collected. The gravel crunches deafeningly beneath his feet. Loud enough to awaken the dead. Every creature with ears must already be alerted to his presence.

He surveys the medieval monastic buildings of Farthing Abbey, a hotchpotch of ancient masonry draped with creepers. A reddish-orange light obscured by flickering shadows fills one of the Gothic windows. That must be the Squire's Bedchamber. He hopes Gervase has collapsed in a drunken stupor and will sleep like a log until morning. Then Ophelia will be free to come to him. He does not care to speculate what might otherwise be going on. He presses on towards the Temple of Venus.

The scene of marital strife unfolding within the Squire's Bedchamber is predictable. Gervase, inflated by drink and deflated by his various humiliations, feels as useless as a beached whale. He is master of Farthing Abbey, but nothing and no one responds to his will. He has suffered an assault by that shameless Fettiplace woman who has been leading him on all evening. Then there was the public ignominy of being outwrestled and grossly insulted by that lout Burp.

Ophelia remains remote as ever. If he had hoped that Farthing Abbey would bring them closer, then he must think again. Even here, in the Squire's

Bedchamber, she rejects him yet again and slips out of his tired, clumsy embrace. He orders her to bed, thinking they might at least sleep alongside one another. She shies away from the four-poster. It frightens and repels her. Gervase lashes out with a torrent of abuse.

'You frigid bitch! You think you're so pure and perfect. Floating high and pure above everyone. But you're just like the rest of us really. You should have seen yourself gawping at that naked yobbo. You couldn't take your eyes off him, you filthy slut! At least I'm honest about myself. I'm a man of flesh and blood.'

There have been angry scenes before. This is different. Ophelia can no longer pretend she is immune to the desires of the flesh. The dam inside her had burst that very afternoon in the Chinese Boudoir. The floodgates opened. She shudders at what Gervase might do if he were to find out about her spectacular fall from grace with Adrian Lenshood. No, better not even think of it. He might read her guilty thoughts. So she lets her husband continue down the wrong track.

'So you're not denying it? Took quite a fancy to our Italian squatter, didn't you? Well, I think I'll go and queer your pitch before you get up to anything. If I'm not going to have the pleasure of my own wife, I'll make damn sure that trespassing hound isn't in any condition to either. The scoundrel will regret the day he set foot on my land.'

Gervase stumbles over to the oak chest. He flings open the lid and rummages about. There is a shout of triumph as he lays hand on a suitable instrument of chastisement. He brandishes aloft a long leather whip once used by coachmen to crack over the manes of their galloping horses. It responds to the jerk of his arm with a fiery sound that reverberates in the Squire's Bedchamber like a pistol shot.

'This'll tickle his tender parts, the insolent dog!'

Gervase storms out into the night. Ophelia is filled with foreboding. In this murderous mood, Gervase would be capable of anything. Instinct tells her to go for help. But she can hardly call out the guests on account of her drunken husband rampaging in the park with a horse whip. Besides, she reasons that Gervase in his present state might not even find his way to the Orangery in the dark.

But what if he did? Then she remembers Adrian. He had said he would be taking pictures by the Temple of Venus. Perhaps he can help restrain Gervase and avoid a tragedy? She grabs hold of the remaining candlestick to light her way down to the Cloister Garth. She has taken only a few steps when a chill draught blows it out. Now in darkness, she gropes through the slype. The wooden door swings open on its creaking hinges. Gervase is out there somewhere on the rampage. There is no time to lose.

Adrian, meanwhile, has almost reached the Temple of Venus at the head of the Scenic Lake. He crosses a low stone bridge spanning a narrow stream that serves as an overflow. As he looks back across the water towards the house, the view is magnificent. He has at least been right in that respect. The moon and a galaxy of stars hang over the dark silhouette of Farthing Abbey, all gloriously reflected in the smooth black watery mirror. For a moment he forgets he has come here as a pretext for meeting Ophelia. He will take some pictures for his own pleasure.

He sets camera on tripod and is about to start work when he hears something like a box of firecrackers going off in the direction of the church. Then, all of a sudden, his heart leaps with joy. He spots Ophelia rushing along on the other side of the lake. She is coming to meet him after all. His heart races. A few minutes later, she is by his side.

'Have you seen Gervase? We must get to the Orangery! As fast as we can. You go that way. I'll take the other route.'

It is a strange request. She says no more before running off. What on earth has Gervase to do with their rendez-vous? In a flash, he thinks he understands. An angry husband is on their trail. He and Ophelia are to take refuge in the Orangery. He has a vague idea which way to go. Hurriedly, he packs his camera gear. There is a path leading into a dark copse. He plucks up his courage and follows it. His heart thumps in his chest. His throat tightens with fright.

The night air has not sobered Gervase. The alcohol propels him along at a blistering pace. He has reached the crossing of the paths from where he can see the Mausoleum. A sharp pain in his side forces him to stop for breath. Again he cracks the whip several times and curses his evil fortune, swearing vengeance on all who dare thwart his purpose. The sight of the Mausoleum makes him shudder. But a morbid curiosity gets the better of him. He limps up the grassy path, drawn on by an irresistible force towards the octagonal temple. He hesitates at the entrance. He peers through each of the windows on either side of the door. Finally, he steels himself and steps inside.

The moon shines strongly enough for Gervase to see that the main wall is composed of square compartments, each sealed with a stone slab and inscribed with the names and dates of one or other of his various Lloyd-Beauchamp forbears. He follows the sequence from Sir Archibald (1694-1753), builder of the Palladian Villa right down to his immediate predecessor Sir Horace (1905-1999).

The next compartment is unmarked. That will surely be his. The stark inevitability of his own death takes the wind out of his sails. His grave is waiting for him, a cruel reminder of the harsh finality poised to crush all his desires and ambitions. What is the point of eking out his time on earth any longer? He is doomed to be the last of the Lloyd-Beauchamps. No fruit will spring from his loins. With no offspring to carry on the family name, his life has failed in its essential purpose. His bed is made. He might as well lie in it now.

Gervase touches the blank slab where all too soon his name will be engraved. He removes the stone and runs his hand around the modest entrance to his future tomb. Then he turns away in anger. So that is all he has to look forward to? Being stuffed in some damn hole in the wall of a spooky Classical temple, doubtless to be visited by herds of common tourists who would calculate his age from the inscription and figure out whether or not he had enjoyed a good innings.

Gervase stalks up and down in the Mausoleum like a caged tiger. He stares out from each window in turn. But wherever he looks he can see nothing but the utter failure of his life. To hell with it! Not yet. He will not die until he has taken his revenge on everyone. Then he remembers the immediate thorn in his side, that cursed young man in the Orangery who seems to have some mysterious claim on him.

Clenching the coachman's whip, Gervase marches off once more into the night. Guided by some animal instinct, he finds his way to the Orangery. It is a brick structure covered in ornamental stucco with greenhouse windows on three sides extending from floor to ceiling. As he covers the last few yards, he creeps as silently as possible, thinking what a scandal it is that a man should have to go about like a thief in the night to enforce his legal rights on his own land.

He peers inside. Close to the door stands the motorbike with tools scattered about. The one windowless wall is covered from end to end with a huge panorama outlined in charcoal on the smooth plaster. This looks like the sketch for a mural to be painted in later. It portrays a fantasy landscape dotted with various garden buildings. Gervase thinks he can recognise the Temple of Venus. But the drawing is incomplete. A large area remains blank, having been crudely brushed over several times with whitewash.

Gervase strains to locate the young man. He wants to take his victim by surprise. In a corner he can make out a sleeping bag on a mattress. It looks empty and lifeless. Perhaps the intruder is out on the prowl and will return at any moment? Gervase spins round to check behind him. But all is quiet. No sign of anyone. Then he sees the sleeping bag move a fraction. Only a trick of the light made it appear empty. He gloats over his helpless prey about to suffer a rude awakening.

Gervase pushes open the door and braces himself to hand out a damn good flogging. He makes a mental count to ten, unleashes the whip with the precision of a veteran coachman to crack like a detonator a few inches above the sleeping head. The effect is immediate. The contents of the sleeping bag convulse into life and attempt to stand up only to lose balance and fall down again. Once more Gervase cracks the whip over his head. The glass panes rattle in their frames. Again the sleeping bag tries to stand up. Again Gervase sends it spinning to the ground with another furious whiplash.

The young man rolls over to shelter behind a large urn on a plinth. As he does so, Gervase lands a stroke of the whip that rips into the sleeping bag and sends up a shower of feathers. Once behind the urn, the sleeping bag unzips itself. The young man, naked but for a thin cotton vest, advances towards Gervase. He wants to say something. But then the long leather thong lashes out again and wraps itself several times round his neck. The words die in his throat.

Choking for air, the young man lurches forwards to strike his assailant in the face. Gervase takes the blow on the chin and throws a counter punch to the midriff. The young man buckles at the knees and crashes to the floor. There he lies, quite still, both hands clutching at the whip curled tightly round his throat. For several seconds Gervase stands staring at the limp body at his feet. Then he turns and flees. It is as if his legs have acquired a life of their own and bear him off at a gallop.

He knows not where he is heading.

LADY IN THE LAKE

gain Ophelia hears the cracking of the whip. Now she fears the worst. She runs on through the woodland with greater urgency, blind to the beauty of the moon casting its mournful light through the leafy canopy of branches overhead. Just as she struggles the last few yards up to the Orangery, Gervase comes charging out, face transfixed with a wild, unseeing expression like a man possessed. He brushes past her as if she were not there. She pays him no further heed as he races off down the hill and vanishes among the trees.

Ophelia enters the Orangery. She quickly takes in the scene. The young man lies lifeless on the floor. Both hands clutch at the whip wrapped like a python round his throat. Prising his fingers apart, she unwinds the leather thong and puts an ear to his chest. Her own lungs are pumping fit to burst. Her heart beats so noisily she can hardly hear a thing. In the moonlight his skin already has the pallor of a corpse.

Tilting back his head, she inhales deep gulps of the night air and exhales with all her strength into his open throat. She repeats the process over and over again. At last, there comes a stirring of breath from his nostrils. She keeps going until she collapses exhausted at his side. Putting her ear again to his chest she can now hear the faint sound of a heartbeat that is not her own and the shallow rhythm of lungs returning to life. She weeps with relief.

But what next? The dark weal around his neck looks sinister, as if it might be throttling him still. Going for help would mean a long walk back to the house and leaving him unattended. What if Gervase were to come back and finish the job while she was away? There is nothing for it but to remain here by his side until he is out of danger.

Ophelia sits down on the floor. Within seconds, the cold of the tiles penetrates her dress, numbing her flesh. She stands up and stares down at the young man wearing nothing but a cotton vest. He must be freezing too. She will have to keep him warm for the rest of the night. She looks about for something to lay over him. The slashed and tattered sleeping bag with its feathers bursting out has been ripped to shreds. Then she sees a thin mattress in the corner. It is too far for her to carry the young man, who still shows no sign of regaining consciousness.

So she drags the mattress over to where he lies and with great effort slowly pulls him onto it. She pauses for breath. The half-naked body has a poignant quality, like a wounded warrior or a fallen statue. Bathed in moonlight he might have been fashioned from a block of antique marble. The illusion is perfect but for that incongruous vest which proclaims this is no inanimate piece of chiselled stone but a real man. She delights in the beauty of this Adonis whose head she now cradles gently in her lap.

As she runs her fingers through his tousled hair, she feels the stirrings of a deep and mysterious love. The sight of this handsome stranger lying there abandoned to her tender mercies sends a surge of desire coursing through her veins. But there is more to it than that. When he finally responded to her kiss of life she felt it was like giving birth. Now she watches over him as might a mother attending a sick child.

Again she looks about her for something to cover his body. Seeing nothing, she unfastens her long gown and steps out of it. She lays it over him and stands there motionless for several minutes, while the moon shines in through the tall windows illuminating her nakedness. Shivering, she lies down next to the young man and wraps him in her arms.

She is glad he is sleeping. Five minutes ago she was desperate for him to wake up at any price, just to show he was alive. Now she wants above all that he should slumber on. It would be useless to express any of this in words. This nocturnal anonymity is so much more real, infinitely more precious. They are far better off like this, not yet knowing one another. Who needs a name in the night?

He shifts in his sleep as Ophelia snuggles up to him pressing an ear against his back to hear the rise and fall of his breath soothing as the sea sighing in the shingle. She is filled with a deep certainty. For the first time in her life, she senses the presence of her own true self. At long last, she has become the person she is intended to be. Time and place no longer exist. She surrenders to the magic of those sweet moments before sleep. Dawn would arrive all too soon.

As Ophelia slips into a dreamless sleep every detail of this encounter in the Orangery passes before her. But there is one thing she has missed. If she could rerun the scene back to the moment just a couple of minutes earlier when she stood there completely naked in the moonlight, she might now observe someone else present in the wings, a forlorn face gazing in at her through the window.

The unseen face belongs to Adrian Lenshood. Having spotted Gervase heading back to the house, Adrian has finally arrived at the Orangery with high hopes of finding Ophelia alone. With mounting expectations he approaches. How thrilled he is to discover Ophelia standing there in the moonlight, posing naked as an artist's model. He admires the provocative way she displays her body like a work of art. He thinks it is all for him. Eagerly, he absorbs every ounce of her perfection. Then he sees that other person lying at her feet. Mortified, he watches as she lies down beside the young man and presses her body so passionately against his. He does not doubt they are already lovers.

The elaborate edifice of Adrian's fantasy fragments into a thousand pieces. The full measure of his sad situation now strikes him. He has been discarded while still an unrequited lover. Even a cuckolded husband cuts a more dignified figure. To play the role of ardent suitor to a lady who bestows her favours on some unknown vagrant is a gross act of betrayal. It is a humiliation without parallel. Within a few hours he has been elevated to the role of passionate lover only to be cast aside and finally reduced to acting the voyeur, nose squashed against the window. In the hot sun of the Chinese Boudoir, Ophelia was his for the taking. Now under the cool moonlight of the Orangery she gives herself to another.

Adrian watches in agony as Ophelia reaches out in her sleep, takes the young man's hand and holds it to her womanhood. Yet still he does not turn away from a sight that torments him on the red coals of sexual jealousy. He will accept without flinching his suffering in full. There is more to come, for he now notices the sketch occupying the entire wall of the Orangery. Immediately, he recognises this as a brave and confident production. It has a boldness of vision and a strength of line that are more than promising. If the young man is as accomplished a painter as he is a draughtsman, then this will surely be a masterpiece.

The resounding artistic talent on display makes Adrian painfully aware of his own limitations. Photography has served him well enough but he knows it is a poor second best to art, a mediocre substitute for the real thing. With his camera he will never be taking off on such soaring creative flights. He is doomed to remain earthbound, while the lucky few with wings and the courage to use them will carry all before them and scoop up every prize on offer, including the fair Ophelia. He now accepts he is thoroughly beaten.

Adrian tears himself away from the Orangery and trudges off down the hill. He wonders how, in his previous incarnation as painter of Tudor miniatures, he coped with his miserable lot. Probably no better than now, he reflects. A composer of amorous sonnets, a lovesick swain must amount to a pathetic creature at any period of history. Now that his dreams have been so brutally shattered, his senses are numb. His faltering steps lead him at random through the wood down to the Scenic Lake. He lays down his camera gear on the bank like a heavy burden he can carry no longer.

He gazes across the lake reflecting the full moon bright and clear. The very same moon he so fervently admired just a few minutes earlier now seems to mock his existence. He scoops up a handful of pebbles and hurls them angrily into the water, destroying the yellow circle. But within seconds the moon comes wobbling back fully intact in one whole piece and is laughing at him once more. Furious, Adrian advances into the water, sends forth ripples in ever widening circles. The reflection of the moon breaks once more into tiny pieces. The stars cavort wildly in the firmament. He is playing havoc with the very heavens. He is up to his waist and still he continues further into the lake until the water reaches his chest. A faint inner voice warns him to turn back. A strange compulsion urges him on, to have the courage to keep going, to meet the destiny calling out to him from the depths of the lake.

Then something catches his eye. It is floating just beneath the surface. As it drifts closer, he stares at the submerged body of a lady in flowing dress, her long hair trailing like sea-grass. Now she reaches forward to embrace him. Powerless to resist, Adrian is in the act of delivering himself into her outstretched arms. Her pallid skin is eerily illuminated by the moon. Every detail is etched with the utmost clarity. At the last moment, he recoils at the sight of her moonlit face. The lady in the lake is none other than Ophelia Lloyd-Beauchamp.

Already he feels the chill touch of her fingers on his. He fears it is too late. But suddenly the spell is broken. Adrian knows he doesn't want to die. He wants to live. To live more than ever before. And to live life to the full. He splashes about in wild panic, swallowing water as he fights to free himself from her embrace. But still he can feel the lady in the lake tugging at his arms and legs, trying to drag him down.

He kicks out violently. His movements are weak and sluggish. He tries to swim away but his waterlogged clothes and shoes weigh him down. Somehow he manages to struggle back to shallower water. Now he is able to wade. He presses on with increasing speed, splashing, stumbling, slipping and finally falling flat on his face as he makes it to the bank. Here, no clammy hand can claim him. He lies exhausted on the ground by his camera bag. He clutches it like a dear old friend. He is out of danger. He will live.

Yes, he really will live. A rush of strength and vitality follow hard on the heels of his brush with death. By some miracle he is a man reborn. It feels as if his former self has actually died in the arms of the lady in the lake. Someone else has taken over. So it's goodbye and farewell to yesterday's man, the lovesick dope who handed over the title deeds of his emotions on the strength of a quick spot of cunnilingus with the squire's lady on a *chaise longue*. Yes, that ridiculous creature has passed away. Well, good riddance.

Oblivious to everything that has gone before, the Adrian Lenshood who now dries himself off by rolling in the long grass of the Landscape Park is a different creature, a man of purpose, one who would set his own agenda. He will now take those pictures of Farthing Abbey by moonlight after all. That is what he said he was going to do. That is what he will do. Mindless of the cold, he sets to work straight away.

The shot of moon and stars over the dark silhouette of Farthing Abbey could be the perfect cover shot for a beautiful book to lift his photography into the realm of art. That would show that slut Ophelia Lloyd-Beauchamp he had better things on his mind than an adulterous tryst with a faithless mistress. Once more, he puts up his tripod and takes out his camera. But before he has taken a single picture, he begins to turn over in his mind the implications of that near fatal encounter with the lady in the lake, Ophelia's identical sister is still lurking out there, patiently lying in wait to draw someone else down into her watery tomb.

Then he has a vision of a more nightmarish scenario. The young man, supposed by Sir Horace and Withers to be a re-incarnation of that Italian *stuccadore*, can be no ordinary mortal. More likely, he too is a spirit from beyond the grave. But what is his purpose, now that he has returned from the dead? Surely not to claim payment for the Rococo plasterwork in the Temple of Venus? More likely to abduct a living replacement for his drowned mistress of two and a half centuries ago. None other than Ophelia herself. Who else?

So this is the sinister being in whose arms Ophelia lies even now. He sees a gothic horror story of monstrous proportions unfolding. There is nothing for it but to return forthwith to the Orangery and confront her with the awful truth. He will rescue her from a fate worse than death, indeed from the devil himself. Regardless of his own injured feelings, he must do his duty. Had not Ophelia, hardly an hour previously, summoned him to meet her in the Orangery? The new Adrian Lenshood forgets his moonlight photography and goes heroically into action.

ILL MET BY MOONLIGHT

G ervase has found his way back to the house. He is no longer fully conscious of the murderous assault he unleashed on the young man in the Orangery. There is other, more important business to be settled before he can rest for the night. His unwilling wife must be brought to heel. He doesn't require her love. Penetration and planting his seed are all that matter. A violent urge to have his way with Ophelia in the ancestral bed, by brute force if needs be, now drives him on.

Gervase stumbles through the slype into the Cloister Garth, tearing his shirt on an iron stud in the oak door. His dinner jacket he has already abandoned somewhere in the park. It takes him a long while to find the narrow staircase leading up to the Squire's Bedchamber. He trips over twice, bruising his knees and elbows on the hard stone steps. But he doesn't feel any pain. The curses he utters are on account of the huge effort it requires to get back to his feet.

He comes crashing into the Squire's Bedchamber and makes for the four-poster. Ripping back the drapes, he tumbles onto an empty bed. It is cold. Ophelia has not slept in it. Not knowing what he should do next, he lies there on his stomach and groans feebly. He is at the end of his strength. It is tempting to let go entirely.

For several moments Gervase hovers on the verge of passing out. Then he hears a sharp crack as the oak bed adjusts to his weight. Something dreadful gnaws at his subconscious. The four-poster makes another loud crack. In a flash, he recalls the coachman's whip. Things come flooding back in a confused torrent. Has he killed the young man? If so, what next? Should he dispose of the body? Perhaps drag it to the Mausoleum? Stick it in a spare compartment? But he can't just lie there and do nothing. He must return immediately to the scene of the crime. He pulls himself together and sets off back to the Orangery.

At the same moment, Adrian hurries along towards the same goal. Having emerged from his slough of despond, he clings fiercely to his new mission in life. He rehearses in his mind the calm, dignified phrases he will use to inform Ophelia that her identical image was drowned in the lake two and a half centuries ago and that she is now sleeping with a long dead Italian *stuccadore* whose real intent is for her to share his grave as well as his bed. At the back of his mind is the idea that, having wrested her from the clutches of death, he will be re-instated in her favours.

Adrian arrives at the Orangery and approaches the window. As before, he presses his nose against the glass. The sleeping couple, bathed in moonlight, lie on the mattress, enfolded in a loose embrace, bodies entwined in the flimsy twist of cloth that was once Ophelia's evening dress. Adrian's resolution wavers. Suddenly, he no longer has a clue what he would say or do if he were now to intrude on their intimacy. He shuts his eyes and attempts to sort out his troubled thoughts.

Gervase reaches the Orangery from the other side and stares into the opposite window. He can hardly bear to look, fearing what he might see. His gaze alights first on the angry curl of the leather whip discarded on the floor like a dead serpent. Every last detail of his attack returns with shocking vividness. Then he spots the young man on the mattress. Gervase stares long and hard, until he is entirely satisfied that he is not seeing a corpse but a sleeping figure breathing normally. So he hasn't committed a murder after all.

Relieved of any burden of guilt, Gervase surveys the scene with more detachment. Only now does he notice the woman sleeping next to the young man. He hadn't been aware of any woman on his last visit to the Orangery. Where the hell has this little tart sprung from? His blood is up once more. He decides to scare the living daylights out of the pair of them. Why not? After all, it's a free country and he is on his own land.

Gervase takes a closer and realises this is not the crude strumpet he had seen in the Temple of Venus. She has no blond and green mohican crest. He feels a surge of admiration for the young philanderer who can switch so quickly from one female to the next. A man after his own heart. He hopes one day he might have a son of his own who would be a chip off the old block and give the local fillies a run for their money. Thus his rambling thoughts turn to Ophelia. Why couldn't his own wife follow the example of this cheap slut, presumably another one from the council estate, and simply do the business like any bitch on heat?

Gervase's jaw drops. The woman on the mattress is Ophelia. His wife is lying in the arms of that filthy squatter. His blood boils. He should have killed the blighter when he had the chance. He raps angrily on the window. This does not rouse the sleeping couple, but it stirs Adrian out of his reverie. His eyes now look across to meet the angry gaze of Gervase on the opposite side of the Orangery. Between them lies the lady who has eluded their dreams and desires that evening.

Gervase's wrath refocuses on the softer target in his sights. Adrian senses the danger. He will have to run for his life. He scuttles off into the night. Gervase goes after him. Once he has dealt with Lenshood he will do what needs to be done in the Orangery to avenge his honour. By God, he will!

Gervase is not in great shape, but Adrian's flight is hampered by the camera gear weighing him down. Gervase soon catches up and brings him down with a thumping rugby tackle. Adrian's vague notion to use the tripod as a last ditch weapon in hand-to-hand combat proves as hopeless as everything else he has tried that evening. He can only strike out with his one free foot, which strikes Gervase on the nose.

Coming on top of the previous injury inflicted by Araminta, this only aggravates Gervase's foul mood. He lunges after Adrian. This time he holds him fast and reels in his kicking victim. He secures his prisoner by crushing the breath out of him with his entire body weight. Adrian feels the life seep from his limbs as in a python's embrace. He dreads to think what might come next. He smells the hot stinking breath of his tormentor on his face. He wants to vomit.

'What the hell do you think you're up to snooping around here in the dead of night, Lenshood? Taking dirty pictures of my wife for the newspapers? Is that your little game? Or have you got the hots for her too? Don't think I didn't notice those lecherous looks you've been giving her all evening. Why don't you answer, dammit?'

Adrian has no breath left in his body.

'Perhaps you were hoping to have a quick thrust at her yourself, eh? That's it, isn't it, Lenshood? Well, she's busy right now, so you'll have to play with me instead. Or have you been at her already and come back for seconds? Greedy little bugger.'

Something in Adrian's agonised expression tells Gervase he has, albeit unwittingly, hit somewhere near the mark.

'So that's it? Well, you can begin by telling me exactly what's been going on. I'm going to make you squeal, Lenshood. I'll crush you until the pips squeak. We can take all night if necessary. Confess all before I wring the bloody stinking truth out of you. Talk, dammit, talk!'

Squashed under Gervase's full bodyweight, Adrian waves a limp arm like a wrestler submitting. Gervase heaves himself to his feet, hauling up Adrian by his collar and pressing him violently against a tree with one powerful hand squeezed tightly around his windpipe. The other forms a clenched fist, poised to strike him in the face. Still Adrian can't speak. Gervase loosens his grip just enough for him to draw air.

'I want the whole truth out of you, Lenshood. It will be far worse for you if you don't tell me everything.'

Gervase's cruel eyes convince Adrian he means business. But how much does he already know? Why had he made those threats back in the Long Gallery? He can't think straight any more. It is all becoming a frightening blur. The pressure on his windpipe tightens.

'Out with it Lenshood! This is your last chance. Speak!'

Adrian nods weakly. Yes, he will tell. He will tell all. To hell with it. What does he owe Ophelia? Nothing. Now that he has been rejected as her lover, he wants to unburden himself, to purge painful memories. At last, he brings himself to speak.

'I haven't made love to your wife, if that's what you mean. It wasn't like that at all.'

'Well, what was it like then? Come on, Lenshood, spit it out.'

Gervase tightens his grip. Adrian almost passes out. No use holding out any longer. The game is up. Adrian is ready to come clean. Slowly but surely, he spills the beans. He relates the entire scene in the Chinese Boudoir. He tries to minimise the blame of either party. She was as surprised as he was. He did not force his attentions on her. Nor had she seduced him. He had merely done what he sensed she wanted him to do. He had been unable to resist. It had just happened.

'Was that all, Lenshood? Sure you didn't get your filthy end in?'

Adrian shakes his head as vigorously as he can.

'Quite sure, are we? If you're lying...'

He repeats his denials. Gervase laughs bitterly in his face.

'Well, what does that make you, Lenshood? Some kind of throwaway sex appliance? Do you oblige any woman who lifts her skirt?'

Gervase continues to grip Adrian by the throat while he considers the implications of this new knowledge of Ophelia as a carnal creature with lustful desires of her own. His curiosity is aroused. He wants to know everything about her depravity. He forces Adrian to describe the scene again with due attention to every detail. Whenever Adrian dries up, Gervase squeezes his throat to get him to cough up more. When he has finished, Gervase makes him replay the entire scene once more from timid beginnings to gushing climax on the dragon sofa.

Hearing another man describe his sexual antics with his own wife arouses him in a way he couldn't have imagined possible, even with all the deviant erotic delights sampled over the years. Adrian, painfully aware of his assailant's mounting excitement, fears what might happen next. Finally, Gervase's mood reverts to anger.

'You bloody fool, Lenshood! Just look what your dirty little habits have led to. No wonder every dog within barking distance is after her now. This damn business in the Orangery, it's all your fault. You'll have to be punished, you do understand the need for that?'

Adrian realises his frank confession has achieved the opposite of what he hoped. The man is barking mad. There is no telling what he might do. Gervase will probably finish him off. How he wishes he had stood his ground and maintained a dignified silence. He would have saved Ophelia's honour as well as his own.

'Punishment, do you hear me, Lenshood?'

Gervase squeezes Adrian's mouth in a vice-like grip.

'You deserve to have your filthy tongue cut out, roasted on a spit and fed to the dogs.'

Adrian trembles.

'I'll think of something to scare you shitless. Perhaps you think I'm bluffing, Lenshood? Out in Honkers even the cockroaches rushed for cover when I loosened my belt.'

Gervase falls silent for a moment.

'Punishment should match the crime, don't you reckon?'

Gervase mulls over the possibilities.

'Sauce for the gander, sauce for the goose.'

Another ominous silence.

'Yes, that's it. I'll teach that pretty little mouth of yours to behave itself in future, Lenshood.'

What his tormentor has in mind, Adrian does not wait to find out. With a surge of strength that surprises him, he jerks his right knee with extreme force up into Gervase's scrotum. He hears a howl of pain. The grip on his throat loosens. He follows up with the left knee into the same place. The throttling hand is removed.

Once free, Adrian does not hesitate. He makes off as fast as his legs can carry him. With every staggering step, his hopes rise that he will get clean away. Should he should head back to the Palladian Villa or try to escape completely from this wretched place? But he has lost all sense of direction and can only run blindly for dear life, crashing wildly through the thick undergrowth beneath the trees.

He reaches a grassy avenue. He stops for breath on the fringe of the wood and gulps in deep lungfuls of cool night air. He peers through the branches. No sign of Gervase. He thinks he is free. Then his heart sinks as he sees the lumbering figure of Gervase Lloyd-Beauchamp still hot on his trail, unerring as a bloodhound on a scent. Adrian takes to his heels. He sprints across the open grass towards the safety of more woodland. As he runs, he lifts his eyes to the heavens as if seeking guidance from above. Thus his gaze is fixed on the clear night sky when the ground suddenly opens up beneath him and swallows him whole. He falls headlong into an abyss, bangs his head against a stone and knocks himself out cold.

Gervase, closing in for the kill, can't figure out how his prey has vanished into thin air. In vain, he scans the moonlit meadow for any sign of movement. Nothing. He curses himself for letting even the pitiful Lenshood get the better of him. Now the rigours of the evening take their toll. He feels an alarming pain in his chest. Could it be a heart attack? He knows he has to give up the chase. In any case, he has lost interest in the photographer. What does it matter if the occasional interloper takes a fancy to his wife? Just as long as nothing serious comes of it. He reckons he can at least trust that wimpish apology of manhood to have been truthful on that score.

He has far greater cause for concern about what he witnessed in the Orangery. There lies the real threat. He has turned the full fire of his anger on Lenshood because he couldn't face confronting Ophelia *in flagrante*. Gervase Lloyd-Beauchamp now slumps to his knees and looks up at the stars. They tell him nothing he doesn't already know. The master of Farthing Abbey is a contemptible cuckold.

His violence abates. Gervase has no more energy. He is a spent force. He can go no further. That cursed business in the Orangery will have to wait until morning. His desolate thoughts now turn to the empty four-poster that waits as cold and cheerless as his grave in the mausoleum. An exhausted and broken man, Gervase Lloyd-Beauchamp trudges wearily back to the Squire's Bedchamber. His dreams lie in tatters. The ancestral chickens are coming home to roost.

WITCHING HOUR

Gargoyle lies awake in his bed. He has hardly slept a wink the whole night. His brain buzzes with eager speculation about the Archive Room which would furnish all the material for his architectural history of Farthing Abbey. After years of journalistic drudgery he will soon be elevated to the pantheon of eminent authors. Perhaps a knighthood is in prospect. Sir Peregrine Gargoyle. Why not? Why not, indeed? His is the sort of name to adorn a title even more than the title can adorn it.

The moonlight shines obliquely into his room and suffuses it with a soft luminescence. This does nothing to calm a fevered mind churning over the delightful possibilities this way and that. Meanwhile, his restless body tosses and turns seeking a comfortable position for sleep. Finally, Gargoyle can take it no longer. He sits bolt upright in bed and gazes fixedly at the wall. He focuses all his energies on it, as if by sheer mental concentration he will be able to view the treasures stored on the other side. If only he had the key. Now he has a thought. Perhaps the one in his own door might fit the lock of the Archive Room?

It is worth a try. Clad only in his striped flannel pyjamas and carpet slippers Gargoyle tiptoes over with mincing steps and gently removes the iron key. He puts on his silk dressing gown. Then he opens the door and steps furtively onto the landing. He moves softly towards the locked door of the Archive Room, feeling more like a burglar approaching a strong-room than a researcher delving into historical records. But he is not going to steal anything, merely to take a look at some old papers. What harm can there be in that?

Still Gargoyle hesitates. It is totally out of character for him going about in this clandestine fashion. By nature he is a conformist, a respecter of rules, a harsh judge of those who transgress. But such is the attraction of Farthing Abbey and all its mysteries he is as powerless to resist as an ardent young lover who has picked up the scent of his beloved. He hasn't come this far merely to turn back, his curiosity unrequited.

He inserts the key. At first, it doesn't engage properly. He fumbles about. A metallic clunk announces that the mechanism has surrendered. Gargoyle now falls prey to doubts about entering this tabernacle of secret knowledge. Yet even while his scruples order him back to bed, already his hand is turning the knob. He pushes softly at the door. By slow degrees it swings back with a squeak of protest and a degree of resistance, as if something heavy is leaning against it. He applies his shoulder firmly to the task and pushes harder. Steadily the door opens. The moment the gap is wide enough to admit him, he takes a deep breath and slips inside.

The Archive Room is unfurnished. The moon floods in through the curtainless window onto bare floorboards. Gargoyle's nose twitches like that of a rabbit in a forbidden vegetable patch. He sniffs a couple of times, then again with greater relish. A smile spreads across his face as he savours an exquisite perfume of vellum, parchment, India ink, goose quills, gutta percha and sealing wax. He breathes it all in with the delight of a gourmet who has gained access to the kitchen of a master chef.

He had hoped to find shelves crammed with books and documents all neatly filed in leather wallets or stuffed in thick manilla envelopes. He had anticipated ancient deeds, plans, elevations of buildings, estate maps, inventories, cost estimates, letters in copperplate handwriting from craftsmen and architects, perhaps even the slim volume of a sketch album which would be Repton's *Red Book*. But the sole contents of the Archive Room consist of some half dozen wooden chests standing on the floor.

A quick inspection confirms that the chests are securely locked. Gargoyle hisses with frustration. Then he views matters in a more positive light. In spite of his disappointment, it is comforting to know the archives do exist, that they are not the figment of Withers's fertile imagination. First thing in the morning, he will go and take permission from Gervase Lloyd-Beauchamp to have the chests opened up for a rough assessment of their contents.

With mixed emotions Gargoyle decides to leave the Archive Room. He has taken a single step towards the door, when his blood curdles in his veins. Withers stands before him. The butler has his back to the door, barring the exit. He has been caught in the act. The shame of it is simply too awful for words. But now embarrassment turns to fear. Withers isn't standing on the floor but eerily floating a full foot above the ground. And it isn't exactly the real Withers either, but a skeleton wearing the butler's uniform whose eyeless sockets stare blankly out of a smooth skull which gleams menacingly in the moonlight.

Gargoyle cowers before the ghostly apparition. Then, summoning up his courage, he makes a dash for the half open door. No sooner outside, he pulls the door shut behind him with a resounding bang. A spine-chilling rattle of bones reverberates against the woodwork. A second slamming marks his speedy arrival back in his own room.

In his panic to escape, Gargoyle has left his own key in the lock of the Archive Room. He must go back for it, if he wants to cover his tracks. He steels himself to slip out and retrieve it, when he catches the sound of another door opening. Through his empty keyhole Gargoyle observes the bulky figure of George Burp emerging to investigate the disturbance. He has an idea. After a few seconds have elapsed, Gargoyle steps forth onto the landing with a look of surprise that is not entirely feigned.

'What the devil is going on? Who's there? I say, Burp, is that you? What's all that racket about?'

'Search me, Peregrine. I'm trying to find out for myself what's going on.'

While Burp peers down into the stairwell to see if anyone is about, Gargoyle darts along to the Archive Room, locks the door and deftly slips the key into the outside pocket of his dressing gown. For the sake of plausibility, he then makes great show of testing the handle before turning to face George Burp who is eyeing him suspiciously.

'Well, this door seems locked and bolted. Perhaps it was Lenshood coming back from his moonlight photography?'

They advance to Adrian's room and tap on the door. It swings open and they step inside. No sign of the photographer. The bed has not been slept in. The pale moon shines through the solitary circular widow. It creates a macabre scenario, like being inside the skull of a Cyclops. Gargoyle recalls Adrian standing there a few hours earlier, with the afternoon sun caressing his torso. He finds the memory unsettling, and for reasons he cannot and will not yet bring himself to think about.

'Takes his photography seriously, young Adrian, doesn't he? Must have been out taking snaps half the night already.'

'Most uncharacteristic behaviour, I assure you.'

Just as they are leaving Adrian's room, they hear Araminta's voice from across the landing.

'Oh, it's only you two. Thank God for that. I've been lying in bed, petrified, scared out of my wits. I thought it might be ....'

Breathless, Araminta continues.

'Just now I heard footsteps on the landing. Thought it might be that ghost again. Or even an intruder creeping about. Then it sounded like someone trying to pick a lock. After that it went quiet and then there was a loud slamming and finally another door opened and shut.'

Gargoyle looks distinctly on edge, shifting his weight nervously from one foot to the other. George Burp doesn't notice. He is otherwise engaged as he watches Araminta's every gesture.

'Doesn't sound like much of a ghost to me, Araminta. I thought real ghosts could walk through walls and had no need for keys to open locks, and to slam doors and such like.'

Burp aims to be reassuring, but his discrediting of the ghost theory only serves to unnerve Araminta the more. Gargoyle sees a way to cloud the issue further.

'That may well be true, Burp. But there are poltergeists and spirits of a playful nature who delight in making noises just for the sake of it. Especially in an old house like this. It could have been one of them.'

Burp eyes Gargoyle with suspicion.

'Well, I dare say it was. But let's check the other rooms just to make sure no one is lurking.'

They do the rounds and find all the other rooms securely locked. There is nothing for it but return to bed with the mystery unsolved. Gargoyle mumbles a tetchy good night and quickly regains the privacy of his room. He swears to himself that never again will he act on an impulse. Impulses always mean trouble. Always.

George Burp and Araminta Fettiplace remain on the landing. Neither is eager to return to an empty room and lie awake in anticipation of more bumps in the night. So it comes about entirely of itself that George Burp, clad in his flannel pyjamas, asks Araminta Fettiplace if he might have a few words in private. And it is without demur that the lady opens her door and beckons him inside. She indicates him to sit in the only armchair while she perches on the edge of the bed.

'Now, about that ghost, Araminta?'

'Yes, I was terrified. I heard these footsteps from across the way. It was probably just outside Peregrine's room ...'

George Burp cuts her short.

'No, Araminta, I don't mean that ghost. I've a pretty fair idea who that was. I mean the other one. The previous ghost. The one you said you saw back there in the Cloister Garth after dinner. I wonder if you know anything about that particular spook, the one that gave Lloyd-Beauchamp one in the eye? Quite a blow. Delivered by someone fighting to defend herself. What do you reckon? Am I getting close?'

Araminta Fettiplace sees he has her cornered.

'Well, George, I don't know how you've guessed. I must say you are a cunning old fox. Well, you might as well know it all. It was me. I mean, I did it. He tried to have his way with me in the Cloister Garth. Dragged me up a dark staircase. Violent stuff. I kicked him in the face. That's about it. Sort of thing that happens at all the best dinner parties, you know. I was frightened just

225

now he might be paying me another surprise visit. Perhaps he was.'

George Burp looks her over as he speaks.

'Well, I can't say I would blame him for that, Araminta. Not that I'm trying to excuse him. The man's a reptile. What I mean is that I wouldn't blame him for trying it on. You've been giving him every encouragement. Just because the bastard owns a stately home, and you need it for one of your yarns, doesn't mean you have to flirt with him like that. You were coming on a bit strong, you know.'

Araminta Fettiplace stands up indignantly.

'Mr Burp, you have a damn cheek, muscling your way into my room and then insulting me. I would say you are the one coming on a bit strong. I think you had better leave.'

'Suit yourself. No skin off my nose. I'll be off.'

Burp gets up from the armchair. He pauses at the door.

'I hope you will be able to get some rest now. Good night.'

She watches him open the door. Suddenly, she is afraid to be alone.

'No, please don't go, George. You are right of course. I have been behaving badly. Quite deserved to have my bodice ripped by the squire. Though it was much worse in reality than in my books. Not that it did him any good, mind you. And I am grateful for your concern. Would you sit with me for a while?'

George Burp slowly returns to the armchair and sits there without a murmur. He wonders what his next move should be.

'You see, George, my writer's antennae started twitching the moment I set eyes on Farthing Abbey. It's not some casual fancy I'm talking about. This is entirely different to the plots I usually concoct. There are real human stories here. Like that poor sad lady who drowned herself in the lake. Normally, I get my material from my imagination. But suddenly, it's coming at me from all sides already written. I am merely a receptacle waiting to be filled with news of actual happenings. I have never experienced anything like this before. It's almost like taking down a piece of dictation from long ago. I have a strong feeling there is yet to be a dramatic *dénouement*. Something sinister is lurking here at Farthing Abbey, some sort of evil retribution waiting to happen, perhaps a curse that must be exorcised.'

Araminta Fettiplace now rattles off a series of questions.

'So many mysteries to be cleared up. What about all those identical Lloyd-Beauchamps popping up every other century? And old Withers? How can you explain away everything he seems to have lived through? Then there is the romantic character of the young stranger on the motorbike. Where does he fit in? I've got to get to the bottom of all that. So you can't really blame me for trying to make my mark with Gervase, can you? After all, he is undoubtedly the key to everything.'

Burp bridles at the mention of his name.

'I think I let him off too lightly.'

It proves a good ploy to remind her of his triumph.

'I think you were magnificent, George. You certainly showed him who is the boss when it comes to a scrap.'

An inspired look now comes into Araminta Fettiplace's eyes.

'I've just had a brilliant idea. For a subplot to the novel. I intend to interweave some of my own material. Just listen to this. That pretty dairymaid. The one John Nash took a shine to, remember?'

'Meaning your good self, I suppose.'

'No need to be quite so literal, George. Now, I reckon the dairymaid would make the ideal viewpoint character. The perfect heroine for today's taste, don't you think? Not born to wealth and fame, but upwardly mobile, someone who makes it to the top. A person ordinary people can relate to in our more egalitarian times. That should appeal to you.'

George Burp sees his chance and grabs it with both hands.

'Appeal to me? I reckon she does. And I don't suppose there might be a small part for the drunken groom? Perhaps she fancies him?'

The conversation has taken an unexpected turn. George Burp leans forward. He is about to take her hand. Araminta recoils.

'Be realistic, George.'

He sinks back in the armchair.

'What do you mean?'

He looks crestfallen. Why not throw him a few crumbs of comfort?

'Well, perhaps a minor amorous dalliance.'

'A minor amorous dalliance? Sounds promising.'

Oh dear, she has gone too far. He is grinning at her. He thinks it's in the bag.

'On the other hand, better not. I would imagine the drunken groom will worship his darling milk maid from afar and devote himself selflessly to her cause. From behind the scenes and in his rough and ready manner, of course. Anything more intimate would be quite unsuitable. Most inappropriate. This has to be a rags-to-riches story, don't you see? From rustic dairy to Palladian Villa. Not to the stable loft.'

'So what happens to the drunken groom?'

'Oh, I don't know. It doesn't really matter, you see. My readers will only be concerned with the fate of the heroine, you understand. That's the way it is in literature, I'm afraid. Winner takes all'

George Burp quickly registers these harsh truths. He is somewhat disappointed. But at least he will be spared unnecessary effort. He lets Araminta Fettiplace ramble on at length about the complex tradecraft of romantic fiction until he begins to nod off. Finally, a rhythmic snoring alerts her to the fact that her audience of one has fallen asleep.

What now? It doesn't seem right to wake him and send him back to his room. Besides, after all the alarms of the night, it is comforting to have George

Burp by her bedside like a trusty old watchdog. But he doesn't look too comfortable. So she takes the eiderdown off the bed and spreads it over him. As she does do, she gives him a tender look that tells him he isn't such a bad sort, although sadly not in her league.

At this moment, George Burp opens his eyes to the sight of Araminta Fettiplace in her negligée, cleavage exposed, leaning over him. She has thought better of his offer. He reaches out without a word and draws her powerfully towards him, covering her wide-open mouth with his own. Holding her captive in his lusty embrace, he carries her over to the bed, lays her down and immediately throws himself on top of her. With amazing speed, he pulls up her nightdress, then unhitches his pyjamas and enters her

Before she knows what is happening, George Burp is having his way with a petrified Araminta Fettiplace. Her squeals of protest are swallowed up unheard by his wet, hungry kisses. It is all over in a flash. The very next thing she registers is a warm wet sensation on her thighs and the sudden shrinking of his loins. His passion quickly spent, George Burp allows his full weight to slump unchecked upon her. He promptly falls asleep. There he lies, like a comatose sunbather on a quivering airbed. Araminta Fettiplace struggles for breath beneath him.

It takes all her strength to roll his heavy body over to one side. After that, she remains motionless, mortified with shame and stunned by the shocking suddenness of it all. Her mind slowly grapples with this awful situation. Surely she did not give him any grounds for believing this is what she wanted? But since it was all over so quickly, she wonders whether anything really happened. So perhaps it didn't even count. She reflects that it could hardly have been worse with Gervase.

Frozen with shock, Araminta is unable to move. She rests her head on the edge of the pillow while listening to the soporific cadences of Burp's various body noises. For what seems an eternity, she lies there lamenting the crudeness of today's men who can never match the lofty ideals so nobly embodied in her historic fictions. A dreamless sleep releases finally Araminta Fettiplace from further ruminations on the shabbiness of humankind in this base modern age.

ARTIST AT WORK

By the time everyone has settled down to sleep in their various locations, little remains of the short June night. Before long, the dawn chorus begins. It is a tentative affair at first, with just a handful of soloists tuning up. Then it quickly swells to the full orchestra. Soon, a wild symphony of birdsong surges up with glorious abandon from all over the Landscape Park of Farthing Abbey.

Meanwhile, the night sky turns by slow degrees from inky black to dark blue, purple and magenta. Next, the horizon glows and a tongue of red flame, precarious and uncertain, flickers behind the trees silhouetted on the hilltop, a burning ember licking timidly at the grate. Finally, a great hush falls as a band of fire flares up and ignites the skyline.

Ophelia wakes to the caress on her skin of the morning sun as it floods in through the windows of the Orangery. Along with her dress, she has cast off her previous existence. She feels primed and ready to begin all over again with a blank sheet of paper. She is a lump of primal clay ready to be moulded, an empty vessel waiting for fresh life to be poured into her. She has returned to her starting point and is deliciously poised to begin anew.

It takes her a while to remember where she is. Then she does. The dazzling light prevents her from opening her eyes. She extends a hand to touch the young man who slept in her arms. Finding nobody, she withdraws her hand and places it between her legs where she held his in her sleep. Where is he? She doesn't want to find herself alone. Perhaps it has all been a dream? Then she hears a voice.

'Must you fidget so? Lie still. Stretch out your arm just how it was before. That's better. Now keep quiet. I'll soon be finished.'

Long minutes pass in silence. It becomes so quiet she fears he might have gone off and forgotten her. As she strains to hear, she can just detect the faintest scratch of pen on paper. At last, he speaks.

'Well, that's it. At least for now. You can relax.'

Hand shielding her eyes, she squints at the young man through the sunlight. He is inspecting the results of his labour in a sketchpad.

'May I see?'

'Certainly not.'

The gruffness in his voice alarms her.

'It's only a rough sketch for something much bigger. I think I shall do more drawings of you. Perhaps for a series of lithographs. *Thirty Six Views of Mrs Ophelia Lloyd-Beauchamp*. Would you like that? Your intimate beauties displayed in all the best drawing rooms.'

Is he making fun of her? He seems to see her merely as an abstract object to be reproduced in a series of multiples. Perhaps something like Andy Warhol's prints of Marilyn Monroe?

'How do you know my name?'

'Who else could you be?'

'And you, who are you? What is your name?'

'You may call me what you like.'

'Surely you must have a name? Everyone does.'

'Don't you think your name is quite long enough for the two of us, Mrs Ophelia Lloyd-Beauchamp?'

Her question has been turned back at her like a sharp instrument. She strains her eyes against the sun to get a proper look at this uncivil young man, so very sure of himself. He is now leaning against an urn, wearing nothing but a white cotton vest. Forgetting her own nakedness, she is shocked to see he hasn't bothered to cover himself. She notes the thick weal, now dark and swollen, around his neck.

'I should like to apologise for my husband. Gervase can get very violent when he is angry.'

'There is no need to apologise for him. He had every right to be angry and violent. Having knowledge of your adultery, as he did.'

Ophelia is not at all prepared for this. Everything she says produces an entirely unexpected result.

'My adultery?'

He doesn't bother to reply to this.

'What do you mean, my adultery? Right up to the moment Gervase attacked you last night, I had never set eyes on you before. Except for those few seconds in the Temple of Venus. And then you were ....'

He says nothing to help her bridge the awkward silence.

'... fully occupied at the time.'

Her words sound desperately coy and banal. She flounders on.

'So I really don't see where adultery comes into it. The point is that Gervase intends to evict you. To him you're a trespasser, a squatter. Of course, I'll do what I can to help. But I can't promise anything.'

He laughs drily.

'Why should you want to help me? I don't think Mr Gervase Lloyd-Beauchamp is going to evict me. As for your adultery, your husband immediately sensed your intent. Even if you were unaware of it yourself at the time. Isn't that enough? Men are intuitive in these matters. You could say his attack was a pre-emptive strike. But in the event all he did was deliver you to me that much sooner.'

Ophelia bridles at the insufferable arrogance of this insolent young man almost ten years her junior. In his presence she feels all at sea. What he says is all the more annoying because she cannot entirely deny he has a point. Did she not undress and lie down naked beside him of her own free will? Did she not take him in her arms? But adultery, surely not? Yet she finds it impossible to be sure of anything. His overbearing confidence crushes any certainty she might have. She hardly dares ask the question now forming itself in her mind, namely whether he made love to her during the night. She would have remembered something as important as that, surely?

'You must let me speak to Gervase. He can turn very nasty.'

'Speak to him about what? My eviction? Or your adultery?'

He is at it again. He seems to enjoy taunting her with that word, as if its mere pronunciation were tantamount to the deed. She senses that if they were now to make love, it would be no more than a physical act catching up with a notional state of affairs already existing between them. She can't fathom the situation beyond that. No more words or questions issue from her. She has said all she can.

As if that were the moment he has been waiting for, he walks over to where she sits on the edge of the mattress and stands over her. He takes her hands in his. Instead of helping her to stand up, as she expects, he invites her to touch him. Slowly, his penis hardens in her hands. Yet he remains curiously detached from the proceedings. His member comes to life like a third person beholden to neither one of them.

When he is fully aroused, he pulls away from her hands and pushes her back onto the mattress. Now he kneels by her side and caresses her belly with a light brush of his lips in a deliberate, almost ritualistic manner. Then he touches every part of her body, exploring her contours with long sensitive fingers like a blind man reading a statue.

This continues for several excruciatingly long minutes. Just when she can almost take no more, he spreads her legs apart and lays himself upon her. Even now, he remains immobile for several minutes as they lie together, bodies intermingling from toe to fingertip.

Still motionless, he does not kiss her, but rests his cheek gently against hers. Thus they calmly flow into one another through the contact of skin against skin. Finally, he pushes deep inside her. She wraps herself round his firm contours, as if holding on to a missing piece of her own anatomy that has miraculously been restored to her.

Even now he refrains from movement, as if just being inside her is all that he wants. Gradually her eager body begins to seek its own pleasure, moving gently against his. He lets her have her way. With increasing urgency, she arches her back as she draws him in and out. Now, he is ready to respond and helps bring her by exquisite degrees to the very summit of her desires. Ophelia feels a melting sweetness spread through her whole body as finally she erupts like a tender bud that has reached its hour to bloom. Once her battle is won, he plunges still deeper into her soft wetness, reaching further and further towards the very centre of her being.

When he finally explodes inside her, she feels mysteriously liberated, cleansed, purified in her innermost core. It's as if all the ghosts of her painful past have been physically exorcised and laid to rest. Ophelia falls back on the mattress, breathless and tingling from head to foot. Now she wants to kiss him, to caress him. But suddenly he pulls himself free, leaps to his feet and hurries to the window.

'What is it?'

'Out there in the lake. The Scenic Lake. Something is happening. It has to.'

'Has to? What has to?'

He gives no reply but stares intently through the window. She stands up and goes over to him.

'What are you looking for?'

'I don't know exactly. Something. Anything. Some sort of a sign.'

'A sign?'

More silence.

'Yes, a sign. Look, there it is. Out there in the middle. Don't you see the water giving off a strange kind of radiance?'

She looks hard, but is unsure if she has seen anything.

'It's over now.'

Now he turns to face her and scrutinises her intently.

'I knew she must be you the first moment I saw you. You are her.'

What's this? Is she supposed to be someone else? This is not what Ophelia wants to hear after their passionate lovemaking.

'Who must I be? What do you mean?'

The young man suddenly looks lost for words.

'I don't know where to begin.'

She waits for him to speak.

'Three years ago when I first rode by this way, I stopped for no particular reason outside Farthing Abbey. The gates were locked and bolted. But I felt compelled to enter. I had no say in the matter. I broke in where the wall had collapsed. I immediately came alive the moment I set foot in the park. I had entered a totally new dimension. Yet I was in a familiar landscape. One I knew from my dreams. I walked about for hours in this enchanted realm. It belonged to me and I to it. Inexplicable.'

He turns away from her and contemplates the Scenic Lake once again.

'I simply had to stay. No question. Somehow I had found my destination in life but without knowing why. So I installed myself here in the Orangery. Then I wandered about in the park. The lake kept calling to me but for some reason I was wary of it. In the Temple of Venus I felt I was closest to whatever I was looking for. Or perhaps just waiting for.'

She says nothing, curious to hear the rest.

'There seemed to be no one about except for an ancient butler in a long black coat. So I went exploring. The old bit of the house had no interest for me. But the Palladian Villa drew me like a magnet. One day I stole over and went right through the place. In the Rococo Vestibule I felt the strongest pull. The plasterwork exuded a strange magic. I was on my way back to the Orangery when Sir Horace saw me from the window of his chamber. Our eyes met briefly. But he made no gesture, said not a word. He just stared after me. I could feel his eyes follow me as I walked away.'

The young man continues to stare fixedly out of the window at the lake.

'So I had been discovered. Hardly surprising. My curiosity had given me away. I started immediately to pack my things. Better to leave quietly than be thrown out. But then I saw Withers approach. He had come all the way from the house bearing a bottle of claret and a crystal goblet on a silver tray. He tapped on the door for permission to enter. He presented the wine with the compliments of Sir Horace and enquired whether I was quite comfortable and had all that I wanted.'

Ophelia reflects that not all the Lloyd-Beauchamps were like Gervase.

'But this was only a pretext to have a good look at me. I could tell I was being inspected so Withers could report back what sort of person it was who had taken up residence in the Orangery. When he seemed satisfied with his study of my features, he withdrew. That evening I drank the bottle dry while watching the sun go down.'

Now the young man lowers his voice.

'The following day I received a second visit from Withers and a summons to meet Sir Horace. I went at once. He was old and frail. I sat by his bed. He told me I was the living reincarnation of an Italian *stuccadore* by the name of Paolo Francini. Sir Horace was keen to settle a disputed bill for unpaid plasterwork at the Temple of Venus. He trusted I had not been too badly inconvenienced. I thought he was mad. After that there was a heavy silence. But I could feel there was more to come. Then out came the story of Paolo Francini's ill-fated love for a lady companion to the wife of Sir Archibald Lloyd-Beauchamp.'

'We heard the whole sorry tale yesterday evening from Withers.'

'Well, it turned out that Sir Horace wanted to atone before he died for the sins of his ancestor. He said there was nothing he could do to remedy the personal matter as simply as he could with the debt. But he would like to make some gesture however small that might help lay to rest the spirit of the lady in the lake. He said I was welcome to lodge as a guest in his house. I declined, preferring to remain out here in the Orangery. To roam in the park and take my siesta in the Temple of Venus. This seemed to please him greatly. His eyes brightened. He made me promise to stay. For the summer at least, and to be sure to return the next year. Just like the swallows, he said.'

Ophelia smiles at this charming thought of the old squire.

'By now Sir Horace was tired and rang for Withers to show me out. His last words were that I must present the full account for the plasterwork at the Temple of Venus. Sir Horace was adamant it was long overdue for the debt to be settled. I don't know why, but when I walked back to the Orangery tears bubbled up inside me. Like a deep well of sadness belonging to someone else finding a release through me.'

She can see the tears flowing down his cheeks. He makes no effort to remove or conceal them.

'These tears are not mine. They belong to someone else. They must be a sign that everything is resolved at last. The lady in the lake is now at peace. Thanks to you, it's all over. I feel it in my bones.'

'What is all over? And what is it to do with me? '

'Don't you realise it yourself? Didn't you feel something just now when we were making love.'

'Feel something? Of course I felt something. But what has that to do with that unfortunate creature in the lake?'

'Withers once showed me a pen-and-ink drawing of the drowned lady. By the hand of Paolo Francini himself. He keeps it inside an old ledger in the Butler's Pantry. Her face is indelibly engraved in my mind. I am looking at it now. It is your face, Ophelia. I knew you the moment I saw you at the Temple of Venus. You are the image of the lady in the lake. You are as connected to her, as I am to Paolo Francini. Our lovemaking has released her unhappy spirit. That is what she has been waiting for all these years.'

'So we have been lovers in a previous life?'

'Well, I suppose so. In a manner of speaking.'

'But what now? What next?'

'I don't know. The immediate purpose of my being here has been fulfilled. The rest is a mystery.'

'A mystery? Is that all? But surely we are lovers now, aren't we?'

'Lovers? I don't think so. It wasn't our love that was consummated just now. It was theirs.'

'How can you possibly say that? Are we not together in the here and now, and in the flesh?'

'No, Ophelia. Together we are not. Definitely not. You are Mrs Gervase Lloyd-Beauchamp and mistress of Farthing Abbey. I am merely the poor artist squatting in the Orangery.'

He is laughing now. Whether out of happiness or in merriment at his own jest, she cannot tell.

'And what next?'

'Next? I don't know. I suppose you must attend to your husband. And I shall prepare a little surprise to thank him for his visit last night.'

'A little surprise? Please don't do anything to upset him. He'll have you evicted. Then I won't ... I mean we ....'

She runs out of words. It is intolerable he should be so remote and formal so soon after their great intimacy.

'Don't worry yourself about your husband evicting me. I am sure he will be anxious for us to be good neighbours.'

'So you do mean to stay? At least for the time being?'

'You really mustn't concern yourself about the future. Please go to your husband. He might be missing you already. And I don't want him to come here looking for you. That would be most inconvenient.'

Inconvenient? What a cold expression. So business-like. She picks up her crumpled evening dress and steps into it. As he fastens it, he kisses her neck with a tenderness that takes her completely by surprise.

'Now be gone. I have something important to attend to.'

He leads her to the door of the Orangery and sees her off. She walks away daintily, holding the hem of her dress above the long grass with one hand as she carries her shoes in the other. She turns to look back at him once more, but he has vanished from sight.

Who is he? Where is he from? He made no mention of Italy. He sounds quite English. She knows nothing about him, not even his name, yet he knows everything about her. But for all the mysteries and uncertainties of her situation, she tingles with happiness. She is a complete woman at last. No one can take that away. This new sensation reaches right down to the soles of her bare feet as they flit nimbly through the meadow that is just surrendering a soft dew to the rising sun.

Ophelia has gone a short distance when she comes across the camera bag and tripod abandoned by Adrian Lenshood at the spot where Gervase had attacked him the previous night. Seeing no sign of anyone, she picks up the suspiciously marooned equipment. She now continues at a slower pace towards the house with a sense of mounting unease.

BRIEF ENCOUNTERS

The bright light of morning exposes the landscape. It brings into sharp relief the unconscious body, besmirched with weeds and pond slime, of the photographer Adrian Lenshood lying face down in the grass beneath the wall of the ha-ha, over which he tumbled the night before. Sunbeams play on his closed eyelids, invading his sleep with a blood red glare. As physical awareness seeps back into his body, he feels damp and dirty. He rolls over and allows the warming rays of the sun to penetrate his flesh.

His mind is a revolving kaleidoscope turning over fragmented bits of recollections. He can make no sense of the bewildering series of events that propelled him like a pinball on his disaster course from Chinese Boudoir via Cloister Garth and Long Gallery to the Orangery, culminating in his ghastly skirmish with the macabre lady in the lake.

He struggles to his feet and beholds in wonderment the magical view before him bathed in a bronze light. A thin haze of mist rises from the ground and dissolves into the air. The Scenic Lake gleams like a pool of liquid gold. The sun, source of all this beauty, is as yet entangled in the uppermost branches of a tall poplar. But now it gently lifts itself beyond the last of its earthly shackles to float free in the morning sky.

Adrian's soul soars aloft with it. He would not have been surprised had Neptune brandishing his trident emerged from the lake at this precise moment just to delight in the sheer splendour of the sunrise and to laugh uproariously at the stupidity of human beings and their infinite capacity to make themselves thoroughly miserable.

He waves an arm aloft to salute the glory of the hour and sees his right hand still clutching Ophelia's panties. It will be his first act of the day to discard this painful reminder of the past. He sets off towards the lake. When he reaches the shore, he digs out a large stone with his fingers. He wraps the flimsy garment around it. He hesitates just for a moment as he recalls how wonderful it felt to be intimate with Ophelia. Then he casts the memory aside, draws back his arm and hurls the projectile with all his strength towards the middle of the lake.

He follows its progress, watching the stone disentangle itself and fly on alone to sink with a great splash. The piece of silk wafts gently down like a parachute onto the surface of the water. There is something distinctly Arthurian about this act. He half expects to see a lady's arm emerge from the depths of the lake to receive his symbolic token of a lost illusion.

The splash caused by the stone catches Ophelia's attention. As she approaches the shore to investigate, she sees Adrian across the water on the opposite bank. They stare silently at one another. He is some way off, but she notes his bedraggled state and wonders where he has been. He surveys her scantily clad body, knowing exactly where she has been.

Not a word is exchanged. He remembers all too clearly the wonderful sight of her delectable naked body bathed in moonlight. Then he recalls the noble mission he has sworn to warn her of her fatal embrace in the arms of the young man returned from the grave to claim her. The idea now seems preposterous. In any case, it is too late for him to save her. Even at this distance, he can sense her lovemaking, almost smell it in the clear morning air. It is written all over her, the way she stands there radiant, unashamed, blissfully undone. It is more than he can bear.

He reckons himself doubly discharged of any obligation towards her. Why should he make more a fool of himself? He would banish any feelings he may still have for her just as simply as he has cast her knickers into the lake. Adrian returns her gaze, not saying a word, until she relents and goes away, leaving his camera bag lying on the ground for him to collect. As she departs, his brave show of defiance is swiftly punctured by a sharp stab of jealousy. Outcast and rejected, feeling thoroughly contemptible, he walks round the lake to pick up his gear.

As he trudges along, Adrian reflects that his own role in this affair was a complete irrelevance from start to finish. At least to her. For when Ophelia first drifted across his path in the Cloister Garth, she had just come from her encounter with the young man in the Temple of Venus. Already, she was a woman primed to make love. But not to him. He had never been the object of her desire. He was no more than a humble extra who by chance stumbled onto the film set and for a few sweet moments, tasted the elixir of a star's embrace.

As Adrian Lenshood enters the Palladian Villa, George Burp wakes. He is about to break wind, his customary salute to the new day. Then he remembers where he is, and with whom. Turning his head on a stiff neck, he sees Araminta Fettiplace lying next to him, her long, dark hair spread luxuriantly across the white linen pillowcase. He must depart discreetly if he wants to retain the gallant, gentlemanly image he thinks he created last night.

George Burp extricates himself from the sheets and makes his way to the door. But a loose floorboard and a squeaking hinge destroy his stealthy exit. Araminta stirs just as he is poised to leave. He waves breezily to her as he steps onto the landing. He now gives vent to a powerful blast that he can hold back no longer. He bangs the door behind him, hoping she might confuse the two sounds.

Peregrine Gargoyle is awake on the instant. He feels alarmingly unsure of himself. He has slept badly and would dearly have liked another hour's rest in the blessed calm of his north facing room. The slamming door reminds him all too painfully of the rumpus he caused only a few hours earlier and of his ignominious retreat from the Archive Room.

Gargoyle gets out of bed, walks to the washstand and splashes cold water on his face. The absence of his regular matinal infusion of Single Estate Darjeeling is a cursed nuisance. His mood worsens as it dawns on him he has not been initiated into the direct route to the garderobe via the spiral stair. He will have to go exploring. Wearily, he dons his dressing gown and steps out onto the landing. Down below, he spots Withers on the staircase. He can ask the butler for directions.

'I say, Withers. Good morning to you.'

'Good morning, Mr Gargoyle, sir. And a most fortuitous encounter it is indeed. I was just going to unlock the Archive Room in case you wanted to browse before breakfast. You did express such an interest in our humble collection of documents and I know that your time here is limited. If you please, I will open up.'

'Really, Withers, you are too kind. I mean, I wouldn't want to put you to any inconvenience.'

'No inconvenience at all, sir. It is a privilege to be of service to a scholar such as your good self. I shall open the door and you can spend time there on your own while I am preparing breakfast.'

'On my own? Are you sure that is a good idea, Withers? I'm not properly dressed for the occasion.'

Withers supposes Gargoyle's protestations to be a ritual politeness which asks to be overlooked. He draws an iron key from a waistcoat pocket and holds it up for inspection.

'I always keep the key to the Archive Room on my person. You can't be too careful, can you?'

Gargoyle smiles at the childlike innocence of the butler not knowing there is more than one key that fits the lock. Then he winces at the thought he might not have covered his tracks sufficiently well. Perhaps that ghastly skeleton had come crashing down when he slammed the door? He holds his breath as Withers inserts the key and pokes about until the lock turns.

'After you, Mr Gargoyle, sir. If you please.'

'No, Withers, after you. I insist.'

'Very well, sir. As you please.'

Withers enters the Archive Room. Still Gargoyle hangs back.

'Here we are, sir. Do step inside. If I have remembered correctly, this is the one containing Mr Repton's *Red Book*.'

Withers has his hand on one of the chests. His presence is reassuring. Even so, Gargoyle enters with apprehension, a feeling he seeks to disguise by executing an awkward shuffle intended to look casual and nonchalant. No sooner is he inside the Archive Room, hopping nervously from one foot to the other, than Withers walks off purposefully towards the door.

'No. Don't leave me in here, Withers. There's a good man.'

Withers remains inside the room as he closes the door behind him with a great flourish, thus bringing into dramatic view the skeleton suspended from the coat hook. His next words are addressed not to Gargoyle but to the bones dressed in a butler's uniform.

'Father, allow me to introduce you. This is Mr Peregrine Gargoyle, a scholar of repute who has come to inspect your archives. Mr Gargoyle, sir, I present you my father, Mr Augustus Withers. I thought it best you should be acquainted since I now have to leave you together.'

Gargoyle starts with fright. In his present state of jangled nerves, he cannot be certain the skeleton wouldn't open its empty jaw and betray the fact that the two of them are already acquainted, at least in a manner of speaking. He can do no more than stand there, grinning feebly, while he utters the ritual polite remarks when meeting a stranger.

'Mr Augustus Withers. Delighted, I'm sure.'

Withers junior breaks the ice.

'Father was a sick man, when he returned home from the Great War, unable to carry out his duties. I took over his butlering as a young boy. He spent the last years of his life studying all the documents relating to Farthing Abbey. He catalogued every scrap of paper. Then he wrote a full account through the centuries. He passed it to me for verification against the original records. Father was a stickler for accuracy. He told me to take the greatest care of his opus, since it was to be the sum total of my inheritance.'

Gargoyle waits with bated breath for Withers to continue.

'Here is the book, Mr Gargoyle.'

Withers produces from behind his back as if by some act of conjury a thick tome of several hundred hand written pages magnificently bound in rich red leather: *The Complete History of Farthing Abbey by Mr*

Augustus Withers, Manservant & Major-domo to Sir Horace Lloyd-Beauchamp Bt.

'I devised the title myself, sir. I do hope you agree it is appropriately worded. You will be the first person to inspect it. I fervently trust your judgement will be favourable. It has been my life's work too. Although my task has been of a lesser order, looking up references, compiling an index, penning footnotes and so on. I am sure you are familiar with all those humble chores in your line, sir.'

Gargoyle is indeed all too familiar with the drudgery of the editor's task, the dusty graveyard of many an ambitious scholar. He groans in despair that the great book he intended to write has been snatched from him. It has already been written by a dead butler and edited by his son: two lowly domestic servants with absolutely no academic qualifications.

Having heard Withers hold forth *ex tempore* with such authority on the architectural history of Farthing Abbey, Gargoyle has no doubt but that the book will be a model of scholastic thoroughness. He could weep with disappointment. This is a cruel blow of fate, a bitter pill to swallow.

'With your permission, I will leave the book here, sir. It would be an honour, much appreciated by my late father as well, if a man of your erudition were to peruse it. Perhaps you might consider penning a foreword and advising on a suitable publisher?'

So that is to be his contribution. To act as literary agent and add a few words of introduction to the great project.. Gargoyle can barely find the strength to speak.

'Very well, Withers. I will cast an eye over it.'

Still, he can't give up his dream completely.

'But what about the archives? What is to become of them?'

'Sir Horace left an instruction that the complete Farthing Abbey archives are to be consigned to the British Museum.'

For Gargoyle, this is the final straw. The British Museum? He assumes Sir Horace meant by this the British Library. Same difference. It would be open season for all the academics and so-called experts crowding round like vultures. There would nothing in it for him. Nothing at all. Unless he can find some angle that Withers has overlooked.

'What will become of your good father when his precious archives have been delivered over to the scrutiny of strangers?'

Withers has no ready answer to this. Gargoyle senses he might have found some leverage here.

'Permit me also to enquire, Withers. Why do you keep your father hanging on the back of the door like an old coat? He has obviously been dead a long time. That is highly irregular.'

'It was a shameful thing I did, sir, I admit. But the wishes of the dead are sacred, are they not? Well, just before he died, father made me solemnly swear to dig up his body from the churchyard and store it in the

Mausoleum until it was adequately desiccated. Then I was to dress him in his spare uniform and hang him up here on the coat hook. All this I performed to the letter. He had the idea from an engraving of the Capuchin Catacombs. Located in Palermo, Sicily, as I understand.'

'Indeed. Quite so, Withers. I am perfectly familiar with them.'

'Father couldn't bear to be parted from his beloved archives. Even after his death. He still keeps the keys to the various chests in his waistcoat pockets. Now that you are formally acquainted, it will be quite in order for you to take them and replace them afterwards. Mind you make careful note which key belongs in which pocket. Father is still fussy about such things and he doesn't tolerate sloppiness.'

Gargoyle eyes the shiny cranium of Augustus Withers with fear and loathing. Meanwhile, Withers junior continues.

'But there will be no point leaving father here without his archives. I do hope the British Museum can accept him too. As an item of antiquarian interest. I am sure he would like that. Perhaps you could put in a good word for him, Mr Gargoyle, sir?'

Withers now turns to leave.

'Will that be all, sir? I must now see to breakfast.'

'Hold on, Withers. I'll be coming along too. Perhaps you could show me the short cut to the garderobe. I'll be glad to spend some time studying the archives later. But not now. After breakfast will do.'

'Very well, Mr Gargoyle, and thank you, sir.'

'Don't mention it, Withers. Don't mention it.'

Gargoyle feels the full weight of his years. The heady promise of the weekend has vanished. He must content himself with the crumbs of life's feast. He looks with despair and envy at the worthy tome by Withers senior that sits smugly on one of the locked chests.

'If you would care to follow me, sir.'

'Lead on, Withers. Lead on.'

Gargoyle falls in behind Withers junior. They proceed downstairs to the Rococo Vestibule, then along through the Antique Gallery and descend the spiral staircase. The spring has gone out of Gargoyle's step as he follows the butler in glum, abject silence. They part company outside the garderobe just as Ophelia enters the Cloister Garth through the slype. Her evident vivacity causes Gargoyle to feel all the more jaded. He manages to crank out a cheery greeting just the same.

'Good morning, Mrs Lloyd-Beauchamp. I trust you had a pleasant night's rest?'

'A rest, Mr Gargoyle? Oh yes, of course. And yourself?'

'I must not complain, Mrs Lloyd-Beauchamp. Thank you.'

As Gargoyle pulls shut the door of the garderobe behind him, Adrian enters the Cloister Garth. Suddenly he sees Ophelia. Her flame red hair burns bright against her milk white skin. She is standing at the exact spot, magically framed by the fan vaulting, where he saw her on that auspicious sunlit afternoon of only yesterday.

To his dismay, he finds her even more dazzlingly beautiful than before. Barefoot, dishevelled, with crumpled evening dress hanging off one shoulder, she looks magnificent. The knowledge that she comes fresh from a night of passion with the young man in the Orangery only increases his own desire for her.

They stare at one another in silence. Adrian knows whatever he says, he will instantly regret. So he just looks at her, seeking to possess her with his eyes if he cannot do so with his body. He will not suffer any more humiliation on her account. He is all too aware of the awful sight he presents. His ragged clothes cling to him, caked with mud and slime.

'Whatever has happened to you, Mr Lenshood? That's a nasty cut on your forehead. You must let me see to it.'

She comes towards him full of concern. How he wishes for the strength to slap her across the mouth. Trembling, he allows her to approach. She is so close he can breathe in her scent. She strokes back the matted hair stuck to his wound sustained when falling over the ha-ha. Against his will, he dissolves at the merest brush of her fingertips. His flesh is seared by her touch. He can take no more. Adrian wrenches his head away.

'Does it hurt? How did you get into this state? You look as if you've been dragged out of the lake.'

This brings a hollow laugh.

'If only you knew.'

'Knew what?'

'Let us just say that we have both spent an eventful night out there. You and I. In our own separate ways of course. What happened to me need not concern you. But perhaps it does. Since I was on my way to meet you in the Orangery, just as you requested, when I was almost murdered by that demented thug you call a husband.'

Adrian is spitting the words at her.

'But enough of my own troubles. They pale into insignificance beside your own. I understand your situation better than you do yourself. Your liaison with that person in the Orangery. It places you in the gravest danger. I wanted to help you. Now it is probably too late. As for what happened between us in the Chinese Boudoir, I think I can understand that too. At least, I am trying to, but I can't help feeling ...'

His voice falters.

'But I'm not really sure anything much happened between us.'

'How can you say that? I mean after what we ...'

'Look, I really don't think you should make too much of that ..'

'Make too much of it? You can't deny what happened.'

'I know this isn't easy. All I can say, I mean about what did happen and what didn't, is that it was ...'

She hesitates before taking the plunge.

'Look, I'm at a loss to explain things properly. I can't tell you what it was that happened. But I can tell you what it wasn't.'

'Well, what wasn't it?'

'It wasn't personal. At least I don't think it was for me. No, I'm sure it wasn't personal. I'm so sorry. You do understand, don't you?'

Adrian finally loses his patience.

'Oh yes, I understand all right. Nothing personal. No, of course not. How could I possibly imagine that a lady such as your good self would deign to consider someone like me?'

His voice chokes. When it returns, there is a sharp edge of aggrieved petulance to it.

'Well, I am very sorry that I am unable to return your underwear, Mrs Lloyd-Beauchamp. Believe me, I certainly would if it were still in my possession. But you will have to ask the lady in the lake. She also holds the key to most of what is happening in your life. And now, if you will kindly excuse me, I must take a bath.'

Adrian tries to brush past Ophelia, but she blocks his path.

'What did you say about the lady in the lake? Have you seen her? Tell me what happened.'

'Seen her, Ophelia? I almost drowned in her embrace. You may have rejected me but your other self, that wretched woman of two and a half centuries ago, she wasn't so choosy. You know what I mean. Don't pretend you don't know what's going on. There is an evil curse hanging over this wretched Farthing Abbey of yours. This dead creature is reaching out to take your place. And that man you've been making love to is part of the same infernal plot. You must let me take you away from here.'

Adrian stops. He is all too aware he has just spoken the corniest line in the book. But his evident distress and garbled warnings of dire things have alarmed Ophelia. This ties in with what the artist told her. Desperately she tries to make sense of it all. She figures out that Adrian's near fatal encounter with the lady in the lake must have occurred much earlier during the night. For had not the young man in the Orangery assured her most emphatically that the watery ghost had been exorcised by their love making that morning?

Ophelia can hardly tell Adrian that particularly brutal truth. So she just stands there before him, lost for words. He, fearing he will only disgrace himself further in her presence, pushes past her. This time she does not seek to detain him.

As she heads back to the house Ophelia realises that she now faces a tough confrontation with Gervase. Her husband will be awaiting her return. As she climbs the worn stone steps up to the Squire's Bedchamber, she considers her options. Even as she reaches out to open the door, she has still no idea what she can do or say to avoid his imminent and terrible wrath.

PORTRAIT OF A LADY

Ophelia hears Gervase's heavy snoring through the curtains of the four-poster. His feet stick out like those of a corpse despatched in the night. She pulls off his scratched patent leather shoes and removes his torn, muddy trousers. He is likely to be less aggressive without them. She peers into the murky shadows of the four-poster. His collar is loose and his breathing unimpeded. He has not vomited in his sleep. Good old Gervase. He is far too experienced a drinker for that.

Her husband begins to stir. Painfully, he awakes to the knowledge that he is nursing a monstrous hangover. But he has been there many times before. Instinct tells him he will survive this one as he has survived all the others. His mind is as yet a complete blank. Hesitantly, he opens his eyes. The events of the previous night come back to him in reverse order. First thing he remembers is crawling upstairs to the Squire's Bedchamber to find solitary refuge in an empty bed. He sits up and growls reproachfully at Ophelia.

'Where do you think you've been all night? Screwing that damn Eytie in the Orangery? And on our first night in the ancestral home.'

She lets him wind down before landing her blow.

'What about yourself, Gervase? Have you forgotten what you did last night to that defenceless young man? Do you remember the whip? How you left him for dead?'

That is enough. She watches him squirm as the memory of his violent assault swims hazily back into focus. Gervase can't yet recall how it ended. Is it possible he killed the young man?

'You mean I ...? Is the bastard ...? I only meant to scare the blighter. He is all right, isn't he?'

'Gervase, you nearly killed a man! If I hadn't followed you to the Orangery and taken the whip from his throat, he would have choked to death. You would be facing a murder charge. You've always been a drunken oaf with a foul temper, Gervase. But trying to kill someone? How could you?'

'Is that where you've been all night? With him?'

'What do you think? I had to stay with him to make sure he was out of danger. I could hardly call an ambulance and let him tell his story. You would be in a police cell by now.'

'But he was naked. And so were you. Lying there together. With your arms around him. Goddammit woman! Have you no shame?'

'Yes, Gervase, he was practically naked as well as practically dead. Yes, I did spend the night with him. I did take him in my arms. I had to keep him warm. I had to be sure he was going to live.'

'What the hell have you been up to? I want the whole truth.'

The whimpering edge to Gervase's voice tells Ophelia the last thing her husband wants to hear is the whole truth.

'Gervase, let me tell you that your victim was in no position last night to do anything but recover from his injuries. He slept until morning. When I left him just now, he didn't seem as angry as he might have been. Although he did mention he had a little surprise in store for you.'

'A little surprise? What kind of surprise?'

'How should I know? He didn't say. Well, come along now. You look awful. A hot bath and some breakfast. There's a good boy.'

It is amazing how, after years of cowering deference, Ophelia has effortlessly assumed the upper hand. Gervase sees her in a fresh light. For the first time, he is divested of his authority over her as he is of his own trousers and his personal dignity. His world is upside down. Nothing makes sense to his befuddled brain except that all previous certainties are washed away. His unquestioned dominion over her has crumbled. His fury has broken impotently on a beach of the softest sand. His remaining power is draining away back into the sea. All he can do is bide his time and collect his strength for the next onslaught.

Gervase is grappling with this new reality, when he has a vague memory of another act of violence. What on earth did he do to that bloody photographer? He dimly recalls the shocking confession about Ophelia he had squeezed out of Lenshood in the dead of night.

It all seems so improbable, he reckons he must have dreamed it up. He cannot trust his ability to remember anything with certainty.

'God, I feel awful. My head.'

'No wonder. After all that drink. You are lucky to be alive. What you need is a good hot soak to sweat it out.'

His sullen silence signifies he is not going to remonstrate with her. At least not until he is more sure of his ground. He allows himself to be helped into his dressing gown. He has become strangely submissive. His wife is someone to reckon with, after all.

'Things will get better, Ophelia. You'll see. I promise.'

Gervase slinks off to the garderobe, a shadow of his former self.

An hour later, Withers sounds the gong for breakfast. Guests and hosts assemble in the Privy Parlour. Adrian winces like a dog fearful of another flogging as he glances at Gervase. But his blank expression betrays no acknowledgement of their encounter in the dead of night. Both men look suspiciously at their respective injuries. Gervase sports a hideous black eye. Adrian has been unable to conceal a bleeding gash on his forehead.

'Looks like you too have been scrapping. I thought we were all meant to be friends after the wrestling.'

Gervase and Adrian give Burp a sour look.

'Just joking, gentlemen. But hold on. What's that?'

Burp points to the portrait of Sir Owen Lloyd-Beauchamp. A piece of paper has been stuck over the face of Gervase's identical Tudor ancestor. It looks like a drawing of sorts.

'Well, it wasn't there yesterday. Gargoyle, you're the art buff here. Go and take a look. Tell us what it is.'

Pleased to be consulted so early in the day by his prospective patron, Gargoyle goes over to inspect the drawing while the others gather round, waiting for his comments.

'It looks like a pen-and-ink ink drawing of a picturesque landscape. Yes, that's what it is. We have a delightful panorama of rolling hills and a narrow valley with some pretty shrubs around a small opening. A cave or perhaps a hermit's grotto. There's an inscription. It's in Latin. Most impressive handwriting. Let me see. *Mons Veneris* ... That must be somewhere in Italy. Ah, yes. *Mons Veneris della Signora Ophelia Lloyd-Beauchamp*. I say, it bears your name Mrs Lloyd-Beauchamp. May I offer my congratulations. There's a mountain in Italy named after you. It bears today's date. So the ink can scarcely be dry. No signature. Just PTO.'

Gervase's face, grey with hangover, turns purple with rage. He has immediately recognised the drawing for precisely what it is, namely a graphic representation of a woman's breasts, belly, thighs and pudenda, thinly disguised as a landscape. And his wife is cited as the model. He notes that Lenshood seems particularly intrigued by it and that Burp has a broad smirk on his face as he takes a closer look. Gervase pushes them both aside and rips it down.

'Must be someone's idea of a joke. Well, don't just stand there. Help yourselves to breakfast.'

Gervase takes Ophelia aside, pinching her elbow in a vice-like grip as he leads her out of earshot into the Long Gallery.

'How could you do this to me, Ophelia?'

He waves the drawing in her face. His fury is all the more intense since Ophelia seems completely unperturbed by this public display of her private parts. She couldn't have looked more pleased had her most intimate portrait been hung in the Royal Academy.

'Haven't you heard of artistic licence, Gervase? It must be a sketch of his girlfriend. He probably put my name on it just to wind you up. He said he had a little surprise in store for you. Perhaps this is it? As you said, it must be someone's idea of a joke.'

'Quite a little wag, our Michelangelo, isn't he? I'll give him such a thrashing. I'll ...'

'Well, you've already done that.'

'I'll ...'

'Why don't you read the other side? It says PTO.'

Gervase turns over the sketch and sees it has been drawn on the back of some kind of legal document. He scans it once rapidly, then again more slowly. He groans with disbelief.

'Well, what is it?'

His voice is barely audible as he reads it again word for word.

It is a copy of an agreement signed by Sir Horace Lloyd-Beauchamp giving unrestricted use in perpetuity of the Orangery and Temple of Venus to Mr Paul Franklin of 37 Jubilee Terrace, Swindon. The annual rent to be paid with a painting or drawing by the artist. The original document being deposited with a firm of solicitors in Castle Farthing.

'This is outrageous. We've got this sitting tenant hanging round our necks for the rest of our lives. And we have to accept one of his bloody pictures in lieu of rent. I suppose this is his first payment on account. I trust this isn't typical of his style. It doesn't say anything here about you having to strip off for him.'

Ophelia is delighted at the ruse. The young man's little surprise is inspired. But she is taken aback by the ordinariness of his name and the Swindon address. She expected something more exotic.

'You'll have to grin and bear it, Gervase. Dispute this and he might go to the police to lodge a complaint about the assault. Besides, it is good luck to have an artist in residence. You won't have to meet him. I can act as go-between. I think he trusts me after last night.'

'I bet he does. A perishing oik from Swindon with a lifetime lease on my Orangery! Is this what I deserve?'

'Don't fret, Gervase. He might only stay for the summer. The winters will be far too cold. But we must rejoin the others. Why not have a spot of breakfast? Then we can all take a stroll in the park.'

Gervase is led back to the Privy Parlour, docile as a bull with a ring through his nose. He puts a brave face on things, casually dismissing the drawing as an amusing stunt.

'Some people have a wicked sense of humour, what?'

Ophelia looks more radiant by the minute. It is noticed by all and especially by Adrian who suffers yet more keenly the painful darts of unrequited love. Gervase, however, realises the show must go on.

'Well, Lenshood, when you are quite ready let's wander over to that garden seat in the park and you can do a portrait of the squire and his lady with Farthing Abbey in the background.'

Adrian looks at him blankly.

'I want something just like the flaming Gainsborough in the Antique Gallery, Lenshood. Exactly like that, you understand.'

Adrian nods weakly. Will there be no end to his humiliation? To complete his misery Gargoyle is giving him the strangest looks, some curiously friendly, others full of distaste, as if he can't make up his mind. Now for no apparent reason Gargoyle goads him with a remark whispered at uncomfortably close quarters.

'Come along now, Lenshood. It's a simple enough request. So look lively. This is a highly auspicious occasion. You are graciously required to do a portrait of Mr and Mrs Lloyd-Beauchamp in the

Gainsborough mode as they assume ownership of Farthing Abbey. The dawn of a new era. Much more important than that ghastly *chaise longue* you were so taken with yesterday in the Chinese Boudoir.'

Does Gargoyle know? Adrian stares at the ground. He dares not look up to see the expression on Ophelia's or Gervase's face.

Immediately after breakfast, they all gather by the west front of the Palladian Villa and set off for the selected spot in the park. Adrian feels like a prisoner being led to his execution. He reflects ruefully that a condemned man would at least be spared the taunts of Peregrine Gargoyle whose spiked comments unerringly hit their mark.

'How did the moonlight photography go, Lenshood? I trust you have enough film left.'

When they reach the garden bench Ophelia perches herself demurely on it while Gervase takes up his position as master of the house standing at her side. In the Gainsborough portrait Sir Archibald looked the painter straight in the palette. But Gervase, on account of his black eye, is obliged to show his left profile to camera and assume a distant sideways gaze surveying the broad acres of his estate.

While Adrian rummages in his camera bag, he overhears George Burp inviting Araminta Fettiplace to a pub.

'*Ye Jolly Yeomen* isn't really all that far out of your way. So what do you say to a spot of lunch, Araminta?'

George Burp and Araminta Fettiplace have been skirting around one another with extreme circumspection, avoiding direct conversation over breakfast. Neither is completely sure what happened between them. Araminta is fearful to discover how gravely he thinks her modesty has been compromised. Burp, for his part, worries whether she might read too much into their brief moment of intimacy.

'Well, I'm not sure, George. I don't really 'do' lunch. And I have to be back in London fairly early.'

That's fine by him. But for form's sake he has to insist just a bit.

'It'll be nothing much. Just a pie and a pint.'

On the other hand, she reflects, it would be useful to agree with him on a mutually satisfactory version of last night's events.

'Well, all right. But let's make it a quick bite then.'

Gargoyle, meanwhile, has assumed the role of art director. He hovers over Adrian, barking orders for all to hear.

'Do be sure to get the Temple of Venus in the picture, Lenshood. No, the pose isn't quite right. Mr Lloyd-Beauchamp should be facing the camera. Don't forget, we are conveying the eternal values of the national heritage and the responsibility that comes with owning a piece of the most civilised landscape with one of our greatest architectural jewels in this green and pleasant land. of England.'

Gargoyle directs his next remark only to Adrian Lenshood.

'You would think the man had reason enough to smile with such a charming wife to parade before the world, wouldn't you, Lenshood? Do you find her pretty? I'm not surprised she has a secret admirer sending her drawings. What an original idea to dedicate a landscape to a beautiful lady, don't you think? Would you do a thing like that?'

Gargoyle's spirits are lifting. He has spotted a loophole that offers a ray of hope. Something might yet be retrieved from a bleak situation. Withers had mentioned an instruction from Sir Horace for the archives to be consigned to the British Museum. Well, an instruction wasn't the same thing as a bequest. Not at all the same thing. Perhaps an instruction from a dead man has no legal force. In which case, all Gargoyle would have to do is persuade Mr Lloyd-Beauchamp to countermand the instruction. Or, failing that, to delay its execution indefinitely.

In the meantime, Gargoyle can consume every tasty morsel in the Farthing Abbey archives. He will be the lone vulture picking carrion off the juicy carcass. As for the book by Augustus Withers, had it not been offered to him by the owner for his expert opinion? So he was completely free to take it. And supposing he might just hang on to it for a very long time, on the plausible pretext of showing it to one publisher after another, then that would give him ample opportunity to plunder its contents and prepare his own erudite reworking of the material, thereby supplanting and upstaging the original opus.All things considered, it is game, set and match to Gargoyle after all. Buoyed up on the rising swell of this new optimism, he slaps Adrian across the back with such force that he catches the photographer off balance and sends him flying.

'Do get up, Lenshood. There's a good chap.'

Adrian continues to lie there on the ground, wondering what is the point in carrying on with the charade. Through the long blades of grass, he observes some bees taking their pleasure in a handful of poppies. Perhaps that is how it is with humans too. Easy come, easy go. Just help yourself to a bit of what you fancy, then on to the next thing. Nothing personal in it, just as Ophelia had said. No, nothing personal.

Seeing Lenshood knocked over brings a wry smile to Gervase's lips. As he contemplates the figure spread-eagled on the grass, he recalls exactly what it was the photographer confessed to him about his wife in the dead of night. A dark look covers his face while Gargoyle continues to urge Adrian to get up.

'Now come on, Lenshood. On your feet. There's work to be done. Surely, you can't be hurt.'

The merest touch of Gargoyle's hand on his sleeve is enough to make Adrian spring up in alarm.

'Of course I'm not hurt. I'm perfectly all right, thank you very much.'

The photographer makes himself ready.

'Now do get on with it, Lenshood. You can see Mrs Lloyd-Beauchamp has a lovely smile. Just for you, I shouldn't wonder.'

Ophelia does indeed look lovely. She sits there on the bench, as did Sir Archibald's lady for the Gainsborough. But unlike the oil painting, in which the wife's demeanour suggested deferment in all matters to her husband, in the picture Adrian is about to take, Ophelia is the one who shines. Gervase looks positively transient next to her permanence, a peripheral figure of no fixed abode, a person of lesser rank, like a John Brown in attendance on a Queen Victoria.

Ophelia considers the possibilities ahead. After only a day at Farthing Abbey she looks forward eagerly to what the future might hold. There is the likelihood of an intriguing affair with that young artist in the Orangery. Gervase won't like that. But she is no longer in awe of her husband. She senses he is now harmless. She can be free to lead her own life. As for the lady in the lake, her spirit has surely been laid to rest. All in all, an exciting prospect presents itself to the new mistress of Farthing Abbey.

She looks up to see Adrian Lenshood about to take the picture. The poor fellow doesn't look happy. He has been badly treated, though not really by her, more by circumstances beyond her control. He seems a fine person, even if a bit intense and a touch too devotional. But there might yet be a rewarding friendship there in the fullness of time. If only he can rid himself of his silly notions. Perhaps she will persuade Gervase to commission him for the interior photography.

Adrian Lenshood returns Ophelia Lloyd Beauchamp's serene smile with a tortured look that tries to strike a note of professional detachment. Gervase scowls darkly at him. Plans of revenge and punishment began already to form in his addled brain.

'That's very nice, Mrs and Mrs Lloyd-Beauchamp. Hold it. And again. Just one more. That's it. Thank you.'

The moment has been recorded for posterity.

Meanwhile, the young artist in the Orangery has observed the group gather for the formal photo. But he is far too busy for such frivolities. He stands precariously on a plank resting between two urns. At his feet lies the sketchbook in which he drew the image of the naked Ophelia. Having redrawn the original on the back of the copy of the lease and delivered it to the Privy Parlour, he now traces it out once more, but this time on a much grander scale.

Ophelia's body is transferred to the empty space in the middle of the vast panorama stretching along the wall of the Orangery. For weeks he has been trying to complete his mural. Repeatedly, he has whitewashed over his tentative outlines leaving a blank at the heart of his composition. Now at last, he has found the missing element. He works urgently, darting to and fro along the shaking plank, fearful he will lose the idea if he does not seize it immediately by the scruff of the neck.

Once finished, he jumps to the ground to admire the effect. It is perfect. He cannot believe how seamless, how beautifully composed and utterly right is this merging of the natural landscape into Ophelia's womanly form. Or should that be the other way round? There she is, an integral part of mother earth. No paltry symbol of fertility but the quintessence of female fecundity on a universal scale.

He rushes to the window with a notion of hailing her. Then he changes his mind and returns to the mural once more. His limbs shake with pleasure. A work of art has been born. No one can take it away. It is a moment of pure ecstasy. On an impulse, he races out of the Orangery, dashes across the grass, throwing off his clothes like a man possessed. He reaches the Scenic Lake and plunges naked into the water. He strikes out in a crawl towards the middle where he floats on his back, languid as a lotus. He shouts his delight to the heavens as he waves to the assembled company. Alerted by his cries, they turn to look. Gargoyle succumbs to a panic born of a morbid fear of water.

'You don't suppose he's drowning, do you?'

Gervase mutters darkly under his breath.

'No such luck. Looks like our little Leonardo can swim like a damn dolphin.'

Ophelia responds to the swimmer's wave. She does so with a slow, deliberate movement, hand swaying high above her head, clutching a straw hat. It is the sort of lingering wave people use to salute ocean liners. She wonders vaguely whether the figure in the lake is arriving or departing. His sailing schedule has yet to be published. But at this moment, it hardly matters. The joyous June morning overflows with all the promise of high summer. It will be a while yet before this particular swallow migrates.

Adrian covers his eyes. He has a sudden, terrifying premonition as he recalls his ghastly encounter with the lady in the lake. He lowers his head into his hands. He knows it is too late. Ophelia is the only one still watching when the young man utters a chilling scream. Briefly, his arms flail about before he is dragged beneath the surface. He disappears from sight. Within seconds, the troubled water re-assumes its mirror smoothness. An eerie silence now spreads over the Scenic Lake.

TOGETHER AT LAST

Ophelia hopes against hope this is only a young man's foolish prank. Any moment now his head will pop out of the water at a different spot. But her eyes scan the flat surface of the lake with growing despair. She looks away from Adrian Lenshood, fearing she will only read in his eyes what already she knows in her heart. He had tried to warn her of something. But why had neither of them drawn the obvious conclusion, namely that the young artist was the intended victim of the lady in the lake? After all, their unfulfilled vows stretch back two and a half centuries. Now the waiting is finally over.

The others hover timidly at the water's edge. Gervase wades out into the lake. Adrian's blood freezes at the memory of the deathly embrace from which he so narrowly escaped. But he says nothing. Nor does Ophelia intervene. The lady in the lake would have no interest in Gervase now that she holds her beloved in her arms. Then she recalls with horror that her husband's identical ancestor Sir Archibald was the author of all her woes. Surely she would have her revenge on him?

'Gervase! Gervase! Stop! Come back!'

It is too late. Gervase, having taken the plunge, is not minded to return meek as a lamb at the behest of his faithless wife. A blind fury drives him on. He would damn well fish her perishing artist out of the lake and throw him at her feet like a drowned puppy. Then Ophelia will see the error of her ways. The water is now up to his chest. Weeds wrap around his ankles and legs. Gervase kicks free and swims out powerfully to reach the spot where the young man disappeared.

While all eyes follow Gervase, a lone, sombre figure approaches unnoticed from the house. Withers walks with the measured step and unhurried purpose of someone who knows full well his arrival at the appointed spot will be exactly at the appointed hour. Although still wearing the same uniform as before, he now looks more like the undertaker than the butler. He might well be the Grim Reaper in person.

According to Adrian's rapid calculation, Withers must have left the house even before the accident in the lake occurred. Had he received a summons? Or had he known in advance when and where he needed to be in attendance? To add to the aura of mystery, Withers does not join the group of alarmed bystanders, but proceeds directly to the Temple of Venus. Here he stops, turns and looks out over the Scenic Lake.

Withers slowly raises an arm and points to the water close by to where he is standing. They all hurry to the spot. As they approach, two bodies drift up from the murky depths and come to rest in the reeds. It is the artist from the Orangery entwined in the arms of a beautiful young woman attired in a long dress and bodice of 18th century style.

They all gasp as they look on the corpse and then at Ophelia. She has buried her face in her hands, unwilling to gaze on her identical face staring at her in the guise of a drowned lady. At last, she raises her head and confronts the shocking sight of her own dead image, locked in eternal embrace with the handsome young man who just a few hours previously made love to her with such tender passion.

To add to her confusion, she now feels a bitter surge of jealousy on account of this deceased woman who is her and yet is not her. She wishes to be dead herself. Suddenly, she can bear it no longer. She flees towards the Orangery, that sacred place where she enjoyed the warm sensuality of her lover's living flesh. That cold body in the lake is not the image of him she wishes to keep alive in her memory.

Gervase comes wading ashore and sees the two drowned corpses.

'Good God! It's Ophelia!'

It takes all of his mental powers to pull himself together and remind himself that his wife was right next to him when the accident occurred. But where the devil is she now? He is reassured to see her, albeit at some distance, as she runs away from the scene.

'Come on, give me a hand, someone!'

George Burp helps Gervase drag the bodies from the lake and lay them out on the grass.

'Hadn't you better call for a doctor, Withers?'

The butler stands there, unmoved, eyes to the heavens almost as if unaware of the dead couple lying at his feet.

'There will be no need for that, sir.'

There is a finality to his words which silences any protest Gervase may have been about to utter. Then a different voice is heard.

'Good morning everyone. Pray excuse my untimely intrusion, Mr Lloyd-Beauchamp, but I was wondering whether you had forgotten our little service at eleven. We've rustled up quite a congregation to welcome the new occupant of the Squire's Pew.'

Reverend Inigo Parsnip now notices the bodies on the grass.

'How awful! How terrible! What a tragedy! My heartfelt condolences. Is there anything I can do?'

'Just the usual, *padre*. A funeral service. Perhaps we should take the bodies directly to the church?'

Withers steps forward.

'Pardon me, sir. The right and proper thing would be to lay them out in the Temple of Venus. The Reverend Parsnip may perform the appropriate rites for their souls there.'

It is amazing how Withers has grown in stature. There is no doubting the butler's authority. The corpses are duly carried according to his directions into the Temple of Venus and laid on the floor.

Reverend Parsnip begins to intone in a feeble voice.

'The Lord giveth and the Lord taketh away. There is a time for living and a time for dying. A time for laughter and a time for weeping. Man born of woman hath but a short time to live. Though I walk in the valley of the shadow of death, I shall fear no evil. For no one can know the hour and the day of his appointment with ...'

The funerary miscellany tails off into a mumble. Parsnip's lips continue to move, but no discernible sound issues forth. At last, he makes the sign of the cross over them and closes their eyelids.

'And may their souls rest in peace. Amen.'

Withers draws the proceeding to a close.

'So it is done at last. Now, if you will excuse me, sir. I must attend to some necessary arrangements.'

Gervase nods at the departing figure of the butler who has set off back towards the house with the same measured step as before.

'Please do excuse me to the congregation, *padre*. Another time, perhaps.'

'But of course, Mr Lloyd-Beauchamp. Quite understandable. Please accept once again my sincere condolences. An awful tragedy. Awful.'

Ophelia's fleeting steps bring her swiftly to the Orangery. She circles the building twice before going inside. Her downcast eyes register the slashed sleeping bag, leather whip, and old mattress on which she had enjoyed the experience of real love making for the first and only time in her life. Then she looks up and blinks in astonishment. Miraculously, the sketch of the mural has not only been drawn to perfection but coloured in as well. It is a vibrant fresco in which her own anatomy merges triumphantly with the mythical landscape. The young artist has accomplished a resounding masterpiece of which she Ophelia Lloyd-Beauchamp is the heart and soul as well as the flesh and bones.

With a start, she realises it would be utterly impossible even for a team of artists to have painted so much and so well in such a short space of time. Only a few hours have elapsed since she had lain there admiring the as yet unfinished outline. She approaches the mural and touches it with her finger. It is bone dry. Then she sees some writing in the corner. In an elegant, old-fashioned script she reads the signature of one Paolo Francini and the date. It is 8 June 1741. Ophelia screams but no sound comes from her throat. She flees from the Orangery.

Gervase decides to bring to an abrupt close the calamitous weekend party. With the brusque manner of a gamekeeper ordering poachers off the estate, he tells them all to pack their bags and go home. The house guests are left in no doubt that he wishes them all good riddance. They hasten back nervously to the Palladian Villa, hurriedly collect their belongings and immediately take to their cars.

'Well Araminta, I'd love to hear what you make of all that. But first things first. I need a drink.'

Burp's familiarity irks Araminta. The foetid air in the car is ghastly. But the lady novelist has no choice but to accept his offer of a lift. She feels like an elegant butterfly trapped in a smelly old jam jar.

Adrian drives mutely away. He almost wishes he had drowned in the arms of the former Ophelia of two and a half centuries ago. At least, that would be a heroic resolution to an otherwise drab existence. From the passenger seat, Gargoyle observes his companion's distraught expression looking constantly in the mirror for a last glimpse of Ophelia. Then, just as all hope is lost, Adrian sees her running across the lawn, evidently in great agitation. He brings the car to a sudden halt. Gargoyle raps him sharply on the knee.

'None of my business, Lenshood. But permit me to observe you are wasting your time hankering after a woman like that. A bit out of your league, don't you think? And possibly not your line of country? Male company is so much more stimulating for the truly creative temperament, don't you think? How many women architects have there been? How many lady painters? Now, if I were to take you properly under my wing, your photographic work might one day amount to something special.'

Meanwhile, Ophelia has reached the house and vanished inside. Adrian snarls. He slams the car into gear and roars off down the drive in a shower of gravel. He puts his foot to the floor, watching with grim satisfaction Gargoyle's bony knuckles whiten as his hands clutch the dashboard. They are several miles from Farthing Abbey before his alarmed passenger deems it prudent to speak.

'Don't take on so, Lenshood. It was pure melodrama all those goings on back there at Farthing Abbey. The stuff that dreams are made of, I assure you. Insubstantial occurrences of no lasting value. What really matters is what I have hatching in here.'

He taps his head reverentially as if it were a sacred receptacle.

'The complete architectural history of Farthing Abbey. That is the real prize. And there is a treasure trove of documentary evidence to back it up which I happen to have here in my ...'

Gargoyle's voice falters. His face drains of colour. In his hurry to pack he has overlooked to collect the book by Withers senior from the Archive Room. Now he screams at Adrian.

'Stop! Stop! Turn round! Go back! Straight back to Farthing Abbey! As fast as you can, Lenshood! Go like the clappers!'

Adrian immediately complies with Gargoyle's command. He hopes desperately for one last encounter with Ophelia.

MOMENT OF TRUTH

Gervase's Range Rover is the only car on the drive when Ophelia arrives back at the house. She follows a trail of damp footprints through the Cloister Garth and up the stairs to the Squire's Bedchamber. She pushes open the door. Items of wet clothing lie discarded on the floor. She approaches the four-poster and draws back the drapes. There he is. Gervase Lloyd-Beauchamp has fallen asleep in the foetal position.

Her husband is not an impressive sight. He resembles a little boy, with all the bluff and bluster knocked out of him. It startles her to see him so broken and vulnerable. He is loosely wrapped in a dressing gown which hangs open to reveal a podgy body, strangely immature for a man of his strength. His penis cowers timidly like a field mouse in a nest of straw. Gazing at that morsel of soft flesh, she cannot imagine why she was ever so scared by its angry demands. Is this the dagger whose brutal thrust she once feared? Is this the angry beast that terrorised her? In the cool light of day, it looks harmless. Ludicrously so.

Of its own accord, Ophelia's hand reaches out to take hold of her erstwhile tormentor. Perhaps it is not the fault of the instrument but the way Gervase always lunged and stabbed at her with it, leaving her bruised, wounded, unrequited. Gently, she coaxes Gervase's member out of its lair. She wants to confront her demon. She becomes bolder. She touches his testicles with her fingertips and wonders what mysteries of life are contained within them. She senses the brooding presence of countless yet unborn generations of Lloyd-Beauchamps biding their time, waiting their chance to keep the family bloodline stretching out into infinity like a blind, groping tentacle of destiny.

Ophelia feels an uplifting surge of freedom. Gervase's manhood has no more fears for her. The real power now belongs to her. She holds the future of the Lloyd-Beauchamps quite literally in the palm of her hand. It is all hers to dispose of at this moment: this organ, this man, this family, even this house. The portraits on the wall may be clones of Gervase's male ancestors, but women too had also played their part.

She falls to thinking about Hong Kong and all the oriental orifices this innocent looking fellow must have penetrated. Yes, she had guessed what Gervase was up to. So she had aided him by not challenging his flimsy excuses, pretending not to notice his frequent absences. She was only too pleased to let the ladies of Kowloon draw the sting out of her husband's venomous tail. But that was another time, another place. Now they are here in the Squire's Bedchamber of Farthing Abbey. As she muses on all this, she plays distractedly with Gervase's genitals like a housewife trailing her fingers in a basket of soft fruit.

Meanwhile, in the Butler's Pantry directly beneath, Withers sits at a desk in a dark corner. By the light of a flickering candle he thumbs through a fat ledger from which he withdraws a single sheet of paper. It is a pen and ink sketch of a beautiful young lady. Minutes pass as he studies it. Finally, he takes up a goose quill and traces two thick lines diagonally across the page, folds the paper and replaces it. He closes the weighty tome with the solemnity of a priest. Then he rests his head on it and instantly falls asleep.

As he does so, his arm knocks over the candle. The flame flickers uncertainly for a few seconds and is on the point of extinction. Then it regains its hold and stretches out a small fiery tongue. The fringe of the curtain moves towards the sputtering flame. The house itself, as if by a supreme effort of will, seems to be making a final, desperate bid to end it all.

Soon the curtain is alight. Withers does even not awake as a sheet of fire devours the dry material and soon licks greedily at the beams of the ceiling. He has already given up the ghost. The immortal butler has at last taken his leave of Farthing Abbey.

In the Squire's Bedchamber overhead, Ophelia's conscious will fades away as Gervase's penis swells and stiffens in her hand. She watches it with total fascination. Her whole being responds to it like an obedient musician to a conductor's baton. She has no notion what she is doing, and even less of what she is about to do.

Ophelia now climbs on to the bed. Gervase does not wake as she turns him on his back. In one smooth movement, she hitches up her dress over her hips. She is naked underneath. She squats over his sleeping body. Gervase is still snoring loudly as Ophelia once more takes his member in her hand. Her body lowers itself inexorably on to his and draws him swiftly inside her, seemingly of its own volition.

Ophelia moves in a gentle rhythm as effortlessly as if rocked in a cradle by an unseen hand. Some force other than her own is driving her. She feels her husband's passion rise beneath her. Then, to her alarm, his eyelids flutter. Gervase awakes. He thinks he must be dreaming. It is indeed a dreamlike vision. His wife sits astride him and is drawing him deeper and deeper inside her, until he feels he will be swallowed up entirely. A serene smile spreads across his face. Then he explodes in a shattering orgasm. At the instant of release there is a blissful look in his eye. Gervase Lloyd-Beauchamp is finally at peace with himself and the world. His heart's ambition has been achieved.

At this moment, the master of Farthing Abbey is convulsed by a violent shudder shaking him from head to foot. He is a rag doll in the grip of an angry child. Ophelia is flung backwards as Gervase sits bolt upright in bed, clutching his chest. He looks at her, not pleading for help but trying to say a thousand things his voice cannot now convey. His gaze goes blank as another massive convulsion takes hold of him. After that, he falls back and lies still. She watches the hardness of his member melt away. Her heart softens in response.

Ophelia leans forward to plant a kiss on his lips. But before she can do so, she is suddenly choking for breath. Throwing back the curtains of the four-poster, she is instantly engulfed by wreaths of billowing smoke. The Squire's Bedchamber is on fire. She tugs at Gervase's body, but it resists all her efforts. She cannot shift him one inch. There is no time to lose. She must save herself. She rushes across the burning floor. Tiny darts of flame dance up between the boards. She tumbles down the stone stair to the Cloister Garth. The way out through the slype is blocked by a wall of fire leaping at her from the Butler's Pantry. Her only escape is through the Palladian Villa.

Ophelia staggers up the spiral stair, falling several times before reaching the top. Mercifully, the bookcase door is open. As she runs past the marble busts in the Antique Gallery she sees the Gainsborough portrait of Sir Archibald Lloyd-Beauchamp and his lady. Is it her wild imagination or does this look-alike of Gervase make an obscene gesture at her with his tongue as she races along in mounting terror? The burning house seems to have come alive and it's after her blood.

Ophelia rushes on in blind panic through the Arab Room and into the Chinese Boudoir. Her pounding heart almost stops beating as her gaze falls on that monstrous *chaise longue*. She fancies the dragon's mouth spits venomous flames as she flees on towards the Rococo Vestibule. From here she sprints out through the entrance of the Palladian Villa, stumbles down the grand staircase and collapses on the gravel drive. There she lies, gasping for breath, unable to understand why everything around her is in the throes of total destruction.

She passes out. When she awakes, her face and hands are being licked by several warm, wet tongues. She opens her eyes to find herself being attended to by four red setters. Then the formidable figure of Mrs Beatrice Worthington comes hurrying towards her. The lady bends down to help her.

'You can't stay here, my dear. The old house is ablaze. And I fear the Palladian Villa is about to go up too. Do pull yourself together.'

It is an order, not an exhortation. She is lifted to her feet by Mrs Worthington. She seems amazingly strong. Ophelia recalls Gervase's mocking description of her as the dog woman.

'Gervase! Gervase! My husband! He's in there! He's had a heart attack! He needs a doctor! It's urgent! Please help!'

Beatrice Worthington looks detachedly at the blazing inferno and shakes her head.

'It's far too late for doctors, my dear. But don't worry yourself. Your husband is not needed any more. Come along now.'

'But we must try to save him! And Withers too!'

The arm around her shoulders assumes a steely tightness she would not have thought possible.

'Do calm down, my dear. You've had a very nasty shock. You don't want any upsets in your condition, now do you?'

Her condition? What on earth does she mean by that? Her eyes flash a desperate question mark at Mrs Worthington.

'Must take good care of the little squire, now mustn't we?'

Mrs Worthington beams a knowing smile and wraps her tweed jacket around Ophelia's shoulders with maternal solicitude.

Who is this omniscient woman? How can she know what Ophelia herself doesn't yet know? Even if she were pregnant, how can she be sure which of her two lovers that morning is the father? But Ophelia senses something uncannily compelling about Mrs Worthington's certainty. It leaves her in no doubt there is a tiny speck of new life inside her fighting ruthlessly for its place in the world. She fears it can only have sprung from the Lloyd-Beauchamp loins.

Ophelia gasps at the painful truth now etching itself on her mind. She has ended up playing her predestined role in the endless saga of the Lloyd-Beauchamps. That last blissful look on Gervase's face was not the ecstasy of *coitus eternus* but the satisfaction of a man finally planting his seed. At the moment of his death, Gervase knew his life's purpose had been fulfilled. In my end is my beginning. That could be his epitaph. And she had even wanted to seal his triumph with a kiss.

So the genetic code of the Lloyd-Beauchamps is now entrusted to her. It has passed into her safekeeping. The knowledge that clones of Gervase will again walk the earth and thrive until kingdom come makes her feel weak at the knees. But she could break the chain. She could destroy the last link. At least in theory she could. But her creeping sense of the inevitable tells her she will be powerless to do any such thing. She seems to have as little control over her own body as over the clouds in the sky or the water in the river. Was that why the young artist had portrayed her anatomy as part of the landscape? Her womb belonging to her no more than does a cave to its hillside?

Ophelia is now entirely submissive. The supernaturally strong Mrs Beatrice Worthington leads her away from the blazing inferno consuming Farthing Abbey. She wonders what role Mrs Worthington played in a previous life. Perhaps she was some awesome earth mother, the real power behind the high priest Inigo Parsnip? What was it the Reverend said about Farthing Abbey having once been a hotspot of earth magic and of tribal fertility? Is that the explanation for all that has happened to her and is now happening inside her?

As the two women turn their backs on the flames, Adrian Lenshood comes speeding up the drive. The car scrunches to a halt a few yards away. An exceedingly agitated Peregrine Gargoyle tumbles out and rushes towards the main entrance of the Palladian Villa. But the scorching heat forces him back. The house that would have made him famous is going up in smoke. And he doesn't even have the book by Withers senior as a consolation prize. The distraught architectural writer kicks the gravel and gives out a great yell of pain.

Adrian advances towards Ophelia, still held in the iron grip of Mrs Worthington. He stops two paces away. Desperately, he searches for a tiny spark of encouragement in her eyes. They give him no flicker of recognition. Her look is closed, opaque, impenetrable. At last, Adrian rallies himself to say his piece. A piercing glance from Mrs Worthington commands him to hold his tongue. The half-formed words die in his throat. He can only stand there in impotent silence, inanimate as a statue, while this immensely purposeful woman ushers Ophelia away.

When the two ladies have disappeared from view, Adrian is released as from a spell. Only now does he become fully aware of the fire. He sees it has taken a terminal hold on the attic storey of the Palladian Villa. He watches a single flame spew out momentarily, as if from a dragon's mouth, through the circular window of what was his room in the middle of the pediment. So Gargoyle has his beloved roofline full of dramatic incident after all. This time for real.

'Don't just stand there gawping, Lenshood. Let's get going.'

Adrian recalls his moment of passion with Ophelia in the Chinese Boudoir. Instinctively, he feels in his pocket for that sensual piece of silk. He remembers he had thrown it in the Scenic Lake.

'Come along now, Lenshood. There is nothing here any more for either of us. Everything is lost.'

Adrian thinks of his photos. They are the only visual record of Farthing Abbey and its priceless interiors. Now that the house has gone up in flames his images will be unique, worth a fortune. Doubtless the magazine would claim ownership and milk the syndication rights for all they are worth. Well, let them try and take them from him.

But he doesn't really care. The only pictures that matter to Adrian right now are those he hasn't taken, first of Ophelia in the Cloister Garth and then of Ophelia in the Chinese Boudoir. In his mind's eye he can see her even now, laid back so enchantingly on the dragon sofa, one foot trailing, a shoe about to fall on the floor. The other about to be removed. The whole world has stopped dead in the afternoon heat. There's a breathless hush and he is poised to make his move.

Unlike his previous recollections of this erotically charged moment, Adrian doesn't feel he is in any way a cheap *voyeur*. More like an artist who would paint the scene from memory, and he would paint many other canvases of Ophelia so much more poignant in their intimacy than that almost abstract symbolic landscape mural composed by the unfortunate young man who drowned in the lake.

Perhaps it is now Adrian Lenshood's turn to take up residence in the Orangery and become a truly creative spirit at last? He feels a tiny seed of artistic energy sprouting inside him. Something is definitely there. It has taken a tenuous hold among all the ruins and desolation. It's a tender shoot as yet, but one which might come to something. Suddenly, he is certain of it. It's like being on fire. The sacred flame of Art with a capital A burns inside him. He can't wait to get started.

'Come along, Lenshood. Stop daydreaming.'

Adrian watches Gargoyle walking like a zombie towards the car. He feels no more anger, only pity for the dry old pedant. He resolves never to become so deadened and extinguished in this frightening manner. He almost wants to thank Gargoyle for serving as a warning. But above all he looks forward to meeting up with Ophelia at some point in the future when he can show her his creations, the works already conceived within him — all thanks to her somehow — to which he will soon be giving birth. Not that he has any personal expectations of her. Nothing like that. But her approval will mean a lot to him. In fact, everything.

ONE FOR THE ROAD

A thick plume of smoke from Farthing Abbey drifts languidly across the hazy afternoon sky towards Castle Farthing where an ill assorted couple sit awkwardly in the garden of *Ye Jolly Yeomen of Days of Yore*. George Burp pulls noisily on a pint of bitter. Araminta Fettiplace sips silently at a fizzy mineral water. Both are lost in thought as they figure out how best to draw the curtain on their brief encounter. Whatever they had seen in one another when under the spell of Farthing Abbey has now vanished without trace in this seedy public house.

Burp reckons things have run their course. A nice fat fish has fallen into his frying pan. But he isn't hungry any more, thank you very much. His loins have gone cold. Nonetheless, he continues a semblance of courtship while awaiting a suitable opportunity to extricate himself. As far as he is concerned, this is really the sole point to their little drink at the pub. But what is he supposed to say? Why, he wonders, are men such moral cowards when it comes to the crunch?

Araminta's momentary admiration for the manly triumph of George Burp's homespun earthiness over Gervase Lloyd-Beauchamp's upper-class guile has been fatally damaged by the brutish way he manhandled her into bed. There are literary precedents, of course, but Burp is not a worthy Mellors to hold a candle to her

Lady Chatterley. With all her creative powers, Araminta cannot transform this particular specimen of manhood into anything remotely acceptable. It really would be like trying to make the proverbial silk purse out of a sow's ear.

On the other hand, perhaps she hasn't actually done anything? Burp's lightning performance didn't amount to much. In any case, it was definitely not what she intended. She had certainly not given her consent. Not even for a moment. There is consolation of sorts for Araminta in this line of thought. Nonetheless, the whole business is now a ghastly embarrassment to be disposed of as swiftly as possible. There remains merely the matter of how to pronounce the last rites.

George Burp continues to study the smoke drifting across the sky. It can't be burning stubble.

'Wouldn't it be the perfect ending for your story, Araminta, say if Farthing Abbey were to go up in flames? Whoosh! The whole bloody lot. If there is, as you said last night, some sort of curse on the place, then a good old cleansing by fire should do the trick, don't you reckon?'

Last night. Those are the last words she wants to hear from him. She hopes he doesn't remember things as vividly as she does.

'Well, that just goes to show how little you know about the genre of romantic fiction, George. No, it's totally out of the question. Such a melodramatic finale? Good heavens, no! I am not going to write some gloomy Gothic ending because of a few unfortunate incidents. Furthermore, I have decided there is no need to regurgitate allegedly real events. Where is the art in that? I am not a reporter. Fiction is not about relating facts. It is a mysterious metamorphosis, the alchemy of turning the mundane into magic. Besides, my readers will expect a happy outcome, and I don't intend to let them down.'

Now Araminta has an idea to resolve the Burp situation.

'Indeed, some big changes are needed. Gervase will become a reformed character, though still with a twinkle in his eye. Ophelia to provide him a son and heir. She must. For the sake of continuity and tradition, you do understand. Still, she deserves something more rewarding for herself. So perhaps a liaison with that young fellow in the Temple of Venus? There was no need for him to be drowned before we've even had a good look at him. What a waste of a very promising character. No one is going to buy that.'

Araminta takes a deep breath.

'But I'm afraid the drunken groom will have to go. In a fatal accident most probably. Kicked in the head while trying to shoe a mad horse. Or something like that. Terribly unfortunate, of course. But there it is.'

There, she has said it. It has come out a trifle more brutally than she planned. At least that way he should get the message. But George Burp has already concluded from Araminta's clipped, frigid tone that he is off the hook. Kicked in the head while trying to shoe a mad horse? He reckons, all things considered, that isn't such a bad way to go. Short and sharp. He won't feel a thing. He permits himself a tight-lipped smile of dignified resignation.

'Just as you please, Araminta. I'm sure you know your stuff.'

'Indeed I do. But I'll keep Withers. I know it's a bit of a cliché, the faithful old retainer, but what's so wrong with that? He was perfectly splendid in his way. I'll have to cut most of that architectural mumbo-jumbo. I know Peregrine Gargoyle found it fascinating. But I'm not so sure about the rest of us. I'll have Withers dish up more saucy anecdotes laced with *un soupçon de scandale*, that sort of thing.'

Araminta finishes her glass of mineral water.

'Oh my, is that the time? Can you drop me at the station? It has been a real pleasure and all that, but now I really must be getting back to London. I'll put you on the list for a review copy, of course.'

George Burp holds open the car door in his most courteous manner. Araminta Fettiplace draws a deep breath before taking her seat. A few minutes later, the vehicle pulls up in the deserted station forecourt of Castle Farthing Junction.

'Don't bother to wait. I am sure you must have many other things to attend to. Your car could use a good spring clean for a start. Well, thank you and goodbye, Mr Burp.'

She extends her hand far in front of her in order to pre-empt any attempt at a parting kiss.

It is the last thing George Burp has on his mind.

'Don't mention it. My pleasure, Ms Fettiplace.'

They have come full circle at last. They don't even shake hands and part with a shared sigh of relief. He watches her pass through the unmanned ticket barrier. Now that she is just a small solitary figure on an empty platform, Araminta Fettiplace appears very much diminished both in size and significance. He waves lazily, but she is already in a different world, scanning the horizon for the train that will take her away from all this. Why, she wonders, is everyday reality never quite up to the mark?

Free again, Burp punches the air as he drives off. He motors along the country roads in a rare mood of mounting contentment. He has covered several miles when the thought finally crosses his mind that the trains do not stop at Castle Farthing Junction on a Sunday. He slows down and looks for somewhere to turn. There is a roundabout ahead. He makes two slow circuits while figuring out if he should go back for her. On his third time round, he rolls up the window, lets one rip and sniffs the sweet, familiar smell. A good spring clean, indeed! George Burp puts his foot down firmly on the accelerator and heads for home.

www.ingramcontent.com/pod-product-compliance
Lightning Source LLC
Chambersburg PA
CBHW060432030726
47495CB00003B/842